Inconsequential Nothings
By Jon Gillman

Inconsequential Nothings

Part 1

It has been nine days since I received news of Mike's death and I'm still unsure how I feel. Should I accept some responsibility? Certainly it would be truthful to admit that I had been involved, that I had helped set events in motion, but would it be fair to apportion any blame to me? The circumstances leading up to this turn of events are far from straightforward and my emotions have been left confused.

I heard about his passing on the local news, but my mum had also phoned to tell me what happened. That hadn't been easy. That hadn't been easy at all. Conversations with my mum, of late, have been strained to say the least. We don't know where to start the rebuilding process. I don't yet know if I truly want to start the rebuilding process. My wife, Maz, tells me that I can and I must and, as much as I love her, she can't possibly begin to understand how I'm feeling. She hasn't been through what I have.

Right now I'm sitting in the garden at the patio table watching the birds peck at stale bread that lies strewn across our lawn. They jostle for position, fighting over the remaining scraps, like desperate refugees swarming around a Red Cross food lorry. In my hand I've got a nice cold beer and the sun is shining brightly, warmly. I'm dressed in shorts and a t-shirt, and the garden umbrella docilely offers me shade should I care to move my chair a short distance. The garden has potential to be beautiful, but no amount of care and attention is going to disguise the large circular trampoline, sitting there brazenly like a UFO descended from the sky, or the bright orange swing and slide set. With eyesores like that having taken up semi-permanent residence my enthusiasm to spruce up our outdoor space has deserted me.

My wife has taken our son, Zak, to a school friend's party in a local soft-play centre, affording me a rare moment of peace and calm. There are plenty of things that need doing around the house. A door handle needs fixing; a cracked tile in the bathroom needs replacing; the washing-up bowl and dishwasher need emptying. But I need time to think and I do my best thinking when it's quiet. Mike's death, the problems with my mum, and all that has gone on in my past are things that can only be contemplated when I am alone. If Zak were here he would be pestering me to kick a ball or jump on the trampoline. Pestering is not the right word, because it implies that he is a pest. In truth, I suppose he can be at times, but he is a welcome pest and a much loved distraction, yet his presence is not conducive towards time for clear thinking.

Taking a slug of my beer I consider my son for a while. He reminds me of Shane in many ways and doesn't seem to have inherited the shyness that I displayed as a child. He is bolder, braver and more reckless than I ever was. Often this worries me, especially when I think of how Shane used to sometimes behave, but Maz always tells me that I'm stressing unnecessarily. She says that it is supposed to be the mothers that molly-coddle their children and that I should 'man-up'. She always has a wicked little smile when she teases me. That smile drives me wild. I love it.

Mike. My mum. Shane. There's so much to ponder. So much to try and get my head around. I'm in my early thirties, but often I wish I could turn back the clock to my childhood and change the course of events. For Shane's sake more than anybody else, but also for my own.

As I take another gulp from my beer bottle I attempt to recall my earliest ever memory of Shane. I try to relax my mind as I search my brain's back catalogue, but for quite some time it eludes me, and then in a flash I have it, and a chuckle escapes from my lips.

We were only three years old. We were in the garden. We were having a fight...

Chapter 1

Maz always finds it amazing that I can remember so much about my childhood, especially the very early years. For example, I can recount all of my teachers' names going as far back as the start of my school days. I can even remember some of the names of my pre-school carers. Events from my life when I was as young as three are ingrained upon my mind with fine detail. Holidays, arguments, Christmases and birthdays. Day trips out, family gatherings, weddings and parties.

Maz, or Esmeralda to give her full title (hence the nickname), just can't get her head around it.

'Adam,' she'll say to me, 'there is simply no way that you can remember the name of the hamsters that were the class pets when you were five years old. No way! I'm sure that part of you truly believes that they were called Larry and Len, but these names are merely figments of your imagination. This is yet another fabricated memory, something that you have somehow convinced yourself to be true, yet isn't.'

I smile and shrug. 'You're just worried that you're going senile already. You're worried because at the age of thirty-four you can't even remember what we did last weekend. I knew it was a mistake to marry an older woman.'

She'll give me that mock huffy look that she always does, before racking her brain to think back to last Saturday to prove to herself that she hasn't got the memory of a goldfish.

I don't blame Maz, or anyone else for that matter, for being sceptical, but the truth is that I do have this ability to recall events from my own past, even my very early years, in fine, precise detail, even down to particular conversations. This is without question. So when I tell you about my first memory of Shane from when we were both three years old, and everything else that came after, you know that you can trust in what I'm saying. And, let's face it, whilst I do have a remarkable memory, it's not as if that is an unheard of super-power.

The pair of us, Shane and I, were outside in my garden playing in the mud patch. My mum, Samantha, was quite precious when it came to her flower-beds, but a separate section of earth had been set aside where I was allowed to dig with a small plastic spade, or more likely with my hands. Like most little three year old boys I had no qualms about getting dirty, and was seemingly oblivious to the notion of keeping clean. Were I to get my hands caked in mud now, as an adult, then I would feel an urge to wash the grime away as soon as possible, to rinse the mud out from the lines in my palms and to scrub the grit from between my fingernails. But, give two young boys licence to sit and play with mud to their hearts' content, and you won't get too many refusals.

My mum was down the far end of the garden with Shane's mum, Karen, presumably showing her some vibrant display of impressive perennials or burgeoning runner-beans. Or perhaps they were in the greenhouse admiring the splendour of the tomatoes, their full red bodies causing the stems of the plants to rely on sturdy canes for support. Whatever our parents were doing, I know that Shane and I were digging. I don't suppose we were digging with any great ambition, purpose or goal, but I'm sure we were going at it with gusto, even if the earth's core was unlikely to be breached. We didn't have too much to say to each other (not too many three year olds will hold in depth conversations after all) but obviously we were comfortable enough in each others' company to be left alone by our mums for a short time. Shane was using my red plastic spade whilst I employed my hands to scrape out tiny fistfuls of dirt at a time, putting the meagre contents to one side.

Shane's older sister, Caroline, was at school otherwise she would have been digging with us, being something of a tom-boy in her younger years and not averse to getting her hands dirty. Perhaps if she had been there I might have acted less boldly when Shane flicked the mud at me, the first I knew of which was when it hit the back of my head, some landing in my ear and even more finding its way inside my t-shirt, tickling its way down my back like a spider squeezing beneath a bed sheet.

If I had been facing Shane then perhaps our altercation may never have transpired. The dirt would have flown in my mouth and invaded my eyes, causing me to spit and rub at my face. I would have undoubtedly started crying and screaming bringing my mum running to make sure everything was alright, that her precious angel hadn't stumbled and cracked his head open on the unforgiving concrete of the crazy paving.

But fate ordained I was turned away from my friend and my unsighted, less vulnerable rear took the brunt of the assault with greater resilience than my face would have, but with no less indignation. At such a young age one doesn't stop to think that another individual's actions may have been an accident. Most likely the spade got caught on a lodged stone or a compacted clod of dirt, and Shane's efforts to free his tool resulted in the earth being flicked towards me. Yet at three years old such a concept was beyond my consideration, and Shane wasn't exactly mature enough to vocalise his innocence either. *Objection! Your Honour, the flicking of the earth was merely an accident on the part of my client. Over-ruled!*

Screwing my face up into an angry grimace I turned around to face my attacker and buried my hands into the soil, grabbing as much earth as my tiny palms would allow. Shane just sat open mouthed amongst the dirt, his white blonde hair shining brightly in the sun and highlighting his young face as a clear target.

I pulled back both of my hands at the same time and then threw them forward, casting the mud in his general direction, whilst simply voicing the instruction *Don't* as I launched my missiles. Sat only a few feet apart as we were, even a three year old would have struggled to not strike home, especially as the earth sprayed outwards like pellets from a farmer's blunderbuss chasing the tail of a fleeing fox. Hit square in the face with the barrage, Shane toppled over backwards, his feet momentarily pointing skyward as he landed on his back. I looked on, no doubt some small part of me feeling proud of myself that the score had been evened up. Deuce!

Slowly Shane hauled himself back up again. He made a sort of a noise somewhere between blowing a raspberry and spitting as he sought to clear the mud from his mouth. Two pudgy little hands balled into fists and rubbed at his piercing blue eyes to try and clear them. Perhaps already, at such a young age, the differences between us could be clearly seen. Whereas mud in my own face would have undoubtedly elicited a call for the protective hand of mummy, my friend was made of sterner stuff and clearly felt that this was a situation that he could handle on his own, thank-you very much.

Having cleared the dirt from his mouth and eyes he looked up and turned his attention back to me. Picking up the red plastic spade he dug it into the ground once more, with greater enthusiasm than before, until a generous mud projectile sat ominously on its shelf. Almost contemptuously he swung his weapon and threw both the dirt and the actual spade itself in my direction. Fortunately for me he missed my face, if that is where he had even been aiming, and the mud, complete with spade, landed harmlessly on my lap. The clod of dirt he had excavated was a firm solid lump, so whereas my missiles had sprayed in a wide arc guaranteed to hit home, Shane's required greater accuracy. The surprising thing about his attack was that, unfortunately for me, he didn't stop there, and had decided to follow up his initial barrage by launching himself at me.

Before I knew what was happening I was lying on my back in the mud pit and Shane was slapping at my legs time and time again. I kicked out at him and called out, *Mummy*, which immediately prompted him to climb on top of me and clamp his hands over my mouth.

This scramble for superiority must have been a far from impressive spectacle. It was hardly a high-tempo fist-fight in the style of the Wild West with nimble evasive movements and devastatingly rapid counter attacks. Instead we were two young boys, little more than toddlers really, who had inadvertently upset each other and acted purely on our natural instincts. Our movements were clumsy and uncoordinated, but regardless of this Shane easily had the upper hand, and for a short time I struggled, trying to dislodge him from his position atop of me, but to no avail. He was both too heavy and too strong and I soon gave up and started bawling a muffled cry as he looked down upon me with his fair hair hanging across his face, a mask of concentration and determination.

No sooner had I started crying when our mothers appeared on the scene, running up the garden and exclaiming and fussing over us, likely embarrassed at the situation they found themselves in.

'Shane, what are ya playing at? Wadda ya think you're doing? Get off 'im. Look, you've made Adam cry! Wadda ya say to him? Say sorry!' Karen was beside herself, looking frazzled, her green eyes encircled in her customary blue eye shadow. 'I'm so, sorry, Sam, I don't know what to say to ya.'

'It's fine, don't worry. I'm sure it is just six of one and half a dozen of the other,' said my mum, managing to keep her emotions in check. 'Adam, just what has been going on here? You two boys mustn't fight. We should always be nice and kind to each other.' She set me back on my feet and started brushing dirt from my clothes and hair.

I proceeded to try and explain using my limited vocabulary but just ended up getting upset and burying my head in my mother's mustard coloured skirt.

Karen continued to scold Shane and he just sat there, amongst the dirt, taking the lecture with all the calmness of a sulky teenager that had heard it a thousand times before. At no point did he start to cry; at no point did he attempt to protest his innocence; at no point did he even look close to cracking.

Eventually Karen gave in to his reticence, grabbed him by the hand and explained to my mum that it was probably about time she got the two of them off home. Realising that her friend was a little distressed my mum offered some placating words and assured her that no harm had been done. She was sure that I was as much to blame as Shane.

As they headed towards our back gate Shane suddenly pulled away from his mum's hand. She made a grab for him, but was too slow, and he came running towards me. At first I feared another assault and I felt my mum tense as well, but as he neared he slowed his pace until he stood facing me.

'Soorree, Adnam,' he said, looking me squarely in the face, boldly, not hiding from his apology. He stepped forward and gave me a clumsy cuddle. I stood stock still, arms down by my side, unsure how to react. He turned back round once again and, taking his mother's hand, the two of them exited the gate and disappeared from view.

My mum scooped me up into her arms, shaking her head. 'Come on, soldier, let's get you cleaned up. I don't know. Boys!'

At such a young age are the strongest elements of our characters already determined? Are our personalities tentatively moulded as we wallow in the comfort and serenity of our mother's womb, before being firmly established in those first few tender years of infancy? I believe they are, and the differences between Shane and I were already becoming apparent. He was stronger, both mentally and physically, as well as bolder, more determined and more resilient. And yet, despite our differences, we had started out on the path of a friendship that would mean so much and play a large part in defining the person I was to become. This day we had thrown mud at each other and come to blows, but it had ended with a gutsy apology from my friend. It would be the last time either of us ever raised a hand to the other.

Chapter 2

Shane and I lived opposite each other in the last street of the ABC roads in the small town of Brompthurst in Kent. The ABC roads consisted of six different hilly streets that ran parallel to each other starting with Appledore Avenue, followed by Beechcroft Avenue, Castleton Avenue, Downbank Avenue, Edendale Road and Foxhole Avenue. What made Edendale a road and the rest avenues is beyond me. I thought an avenue was a tree-lined street, but no trees graced the houses with their exalted presence.

Most of the properties along all six streets consisted of modest two-or-three-bedroom semi-detached houses or bungalows, built in the 1960s, with comfortably sized rooms sporting generous bay windows to the front. Each residence had either a front driveway or a garden large enough to be converted as such, and were, for the most part, well looked after and maintained. They were the sort of streets where everybody seemed to know each other and where nobody was too shy to extend a warm greeting to an unfamiliar face. It was not a rich community, but not on the breadline either. Typical middle class Britain in all its glory.

Shane's family consisted of his mum, Karen, his older sister, Caroline (both of whom I've previously introduced) and his dad, Mike. Then, when Shane and I were four, almost five, Karen popped out another child, who she named Molly.

My dad always used to say that the only reason Molly was conceived was to bring Shane's parents closer together.

'Shhh,' my mum would hiss. 'We don't want Adam to hear what you're saying and go repeating it.'

'You worry too much. He's not interested in what we gas about.'

Sometimes parents can be stunningly naive. They think that just because a child is in another room, or occupied playing some fantastic game, that they aren't tuned in to what is being said. I remember overhearing countless conversations between my parents, especially just after I had gone up to bed. When you're lying there in silence, the chatter from downstairs travels a considerable distance, and young ears tend to be better suited to successful eavesdropping than those of an adult.

In one respect, though, my dad was right. My mum did worry too much. Even if I didn't always understand the meaning behind some of these adult conversations, I was astute enough to appreciate when something was best not repeated. Children are often surprisingly receptive to things like that. Besides, it would be very rare when something caught my interest enough for me to even consider repeating what I'd heard. After all, I was only a young boy, and the only thing of any great importance to me were what games I was going to be playing the next day. Gossip wasn't high on the agenda.

Looking back now, with the endless wisdom I have acquired as an adult and, more accurately, with my parents' stories of how Mike was, I think it is likely that my dad was probably right. Mike and Karen almost certainly decided to try for another child in order to patch up their relationship.

Mike was a difficult person. No, that's an understatement of unforgivable proportions. He was an *impossible* person, and I don't mean that in a biological, Incredible Hulk sort of impossible (although it would be fair to say he and the Hulk shared certain characteristics). I mean there was no warming to the man, no getting on with him, because that was the way he made things. He seemed to like not being liked. He went out of his way to create ill-feeling. Mostly it would be small inconsiderate actions, but in truth I'm sure his un-neighbourly behaviour was entirely considered, purposefully designed to be antagonistic, to try and draw out an argument from those in the street who simply wanted to live in peace in an otherwise harmonious neighbourhood. He would park his car across peoples' driveways; send that same car shooting down the road at alarmingly dangerous speeds; regularly come home from the pub singing drunkenly to the stars, or even bellowing up and down the street calling for someone, for anyone to come and fight him – an invite that no-one deigned to accept. Bonfires lit as soon as washing lines were dressed; stones aimed at invading cats; provocative glares; intimidating stares. On occasion a fellow neighbour had had enough and risked calling the police to complain of such anti-social behaviour, hoping that Mike wouldn't guess it was them who had dared to spin that number 9 round three times. But resultant visits from the Boys in Blue seemed to accomplish little. Yes, he behaved himself for a couple of weeks following, but it left the street in a state of nervous anticipation, as the man's temper boiled below the surface, fuming at the injustice of the attempt at justice, and held at bay by nothing more than a reprimand from a bored policeman. Did Mike know who had made the call? Standing just shy of six foot tall with powerful, thick-set arms, nobody in the street relished the prospect of the man's retribution following a foolish act of tale-telling.

Poor Karen, who was kind, polite and thoughtful – the very antithesis of her husband – had to live with this man day in and day out. What did she ever see in him, that hulking bully of a man? When they had first dated perhaps he had been so charming that she was mesmerised by his manner, like a cobra dancing to the tune of a wailing pipe. Maybe his cruel side was hidden from view with a wink and a kiss, and he conned her into this life with him. But then again, maybe not. Some women seem to be drawn to bad men, to the way they take control and do things their own way. Is the charm that they see these men as strong guardians who will fight to defend their honour or keep them from danger? Perhaps the lure is the challenge to lead them onto a better path, to save their souls from the clutches of the devil. A loving wife will tease out the good that is hidden behind the scowls and the raised voices. A beautiful, kept house, with comfort and warmth will first reduce the boiling anger to a simmer, and then give it the means to slowly cool. And if all this fails to transform the ogre then the innocence of a son or a daughter will shoot to his heart with an arrow formed of gurgles and a bow carved from cuddles. And if this fails...then what? Then you cut your losses and run, or you stand and fight in the hope that one day there will be light, a change in the brute and you can say to yourself that you held the family together to finally reach this point.

Which makes the decision to try for another child ever more bewildering. The presence of Caroline and Shane had failed to tame their father, so why should one more child make any difference? I just don't understand it.

To me, having a child to save your marriage seems a ploy that is surely doomed to failure, and yet so many couples opt to try this. If anything, such a drastic course of action puts a greater strain on relationships. Admittedly you suddenly have in your midst an adorable bundle of joy that most parents will dote on. I also concede that watching a baby grow up can bring much shared pleasure for a couple, especially when those key markers are reached, such as the first smile or their initial steps. But, make no mistake, that beautiful new baby's middle name is Pressure. The inevitable pressure from lack of sleep; the financial pressure of an extra mouth to feed and body to clothe; the persistent pressure of attempting to agree on what is the best way to bring that child up. If you want to find something else to bicker over then have a kid.

And yet, if any child ever born to this world should have been capable of cementing a relationship it was the glorious Molly. So sweet and so content from the first day that she arrived, I doubt that a more relaxed baby has ever been born. Most babies will start smiling from around the six to eight week mark, but I can almost imagine that Molly slipped from her mother's womb with a huge beaming grin of joy, even if the experts insist this isn't possible.

Regrettably, however, despite the wondrous nature of the world's most chilled-out baby, it wasn't what Karen and Mike needed to haul their relationship out of the depths and, let's face it, Mike being Mike I'm not sure anything would have worked. Instead this extra burden, cute as it was, caused more arguments, more shouting and an eventual trial separation. Mike went to live with his parents for a time, at the age of thirty-five, to give him and Karen time to consider what course of action they should take.

I find this extraordinary, that the controlling, dominating figure of Mike would agree to move out of his own home. Maybe, despite the way he behaved he recognised some things were worth saving. Karen was a terrific mum to her kids and an attentive housewife. The house was always clean, the food tasty and her patience impressive – although not without limits as proved by this separation. Mike, it seemed, did care about some things in life, and whether that was his wife and kids or how easy he had it at home, I don't know. Whatever the full story, he agreed to give the trial separation a go.

As a happy consequence born from this unfortunate news, both Shane and Molly found themselves in our house on a regular basis as my mum helped out with babysitting, whilst Karen took on more hours at the pub where she worked during the day in order to find some extra money for her expanded family. Shane and I were almost five years old at the time and were not due to start school for another couple of months, so the two of us got to spend a lot of time together.

For Shane this must have been a confusing and unsettling period in his young life. The new baby, the arguments between his parents and finally the separation. His dad was now only seen sporadically when Karen allowed him to visit or she dropped the children round her in-laws. Whatever Mike's feelings for his family, and however deep or shallow his feelings ran for his children, it was obvious that Shane missed his dad in some way. Every time Karen appeared to pick him and Molly up following her work shift, Shane would immediately enquire *Is daddy home yet?* The negative response would elicit a disappointed *Oh! When is he coming?* accompanied by an accusing look at poor Karen as if she was solely to blame. Despite the hostile version of Mike that was displayed to the rest of Foxhole Avenue, apparently in private there was a softer, more amiable side that was reserved for his children, on occasion at least, which led to them wanting him back home.

For my own part, and here we witness the all-consuming yet forgivable selfishness of children, I was delighted with the way things had worked out. It meant that I had a regular companion to play with, which, being an only child, was a blessing. Sometimes my days could be lonely and playing by yourself has its limitations, even for the most inventive and imaginative of minds.

Whilst the birth of Molly had only served to push her parents apart, for Shane and I it had a contrasting effect. Previously we had only spent a limited amount of time in each other's company, when our mothers arranged to chat over a cup of tea or to take us to the park together, and aside from the altercation in the mud-pit in my back garden we had always got on famously. Now, a friendship that had already shown early signs of promise, had those foundations solidified. We never argued or bickered. We never had disputes over what to play or who was using a particular toy. We never lost patience with the other if our ideas didn't go to plan. Call it what you like: a meeting of minds, a match of personalities; the fact is we just got on, and we got on with a calmness rarely seen between two young children of that age. There was always a willingness to compromise during our play, a give and take that allowed both of us our turn at getting our own way. We demonstrated all of the qualities needed for a relationship to be a success, and Mike could have learnt a lot from watching us.

Eventually, a couple of months into their separation, Karen and Mike agreed to give things another go. I wonder what promises Mike made to his wife. Did he promise to be more caring? To play a bigger part in helping with the children or the chores around the house? Perhaps he decreed that he would treat Karen with the respect that she deserved, or that he would stop going drinking with his mates after work, or even, God forbid, he would stop being so difficult with the neighbours. For Karen's part did she give in too readily to words that seemed to slip so easily from his tongue? Did she genuinely want him back in her life, not just as a father to their three children, but as a man that she still loved and wanted beside her in their bed? Maybe to take him back was simply the easiest option, as he wore down her resistance with promise after promise and plea after plea, determining that things would be like when they first met.

Whatever the reasons and the truth behind their relationship troubles, Mike's return spelt the end of my mother's regular babysitting of Shane and Molly. Karen dropped her hours again as Mike made a more determined effort to be a good husband and found some building work, leaving her free to look after the children.

I was disappointed that Shane, and indeed Molly, who I had taken a real shine to, were no longer such regular companions. Admittedly I would often be invited to Shane's house and he to mine, but it wasn't as frequent as I would have liked. Nonetheless, the time we had spent together had set our friendship on a solid path and the bond we had formed was tightly bound.

If we had known the path that lay before the two of us, we would have released those knots that bound us together with all the speed of a kidnap victim afforded a rare opportunity to break free.

Chapter 3

School days are, allegedly, the happiest days of your life, and this exact clichéd expression was what my parents decided to churn out when I made my trepidation at starting primary school abundantly clear.

As with most new ventures in life, starting school was something that I went into with my eyes downcast and my head hung low, like a scolded dog sent from the room having displeased its master. Confidence is not my thing, is not an attribute that appears on anyone's list of five words to sum me up. Bold, fearless, courageous, reckless, brave - the opposite of Adam Wickes. Admittedly as I've got older I've become more out-going, but I'll still be the one that stands in the corner at parties. I don't like surprises or change, but prefer life to tick over at a pace chosen by me, with activities chosen by me. Incredibly boring I know.

Aside from trotting out their clichéd piece of wisdom I should be fair to my parents and state, for the record, that this isn't all they did to try and calm my nerves. They told me happy tales from their own Victorian sounding school days and reminded me that many of my friends from Jumping Beans play-group would also be in my class, not to mention Shane, who had attended a different pre-school to me, but was of course a very familiar face. My mum kept regaling me with stories of how I had shown exactly the same symptoms when I started at Jumping Beans, clinging to her with all my strength and begging her not to leave. It had taken me several months to properly settle in, through no fault of my parents or the staff, and even then I would have the occasional set-back and start crying once more as my mother prised me from her leg with strong arms and gentle words. Never let it be said that my mum is not a patient woman.

When the first day of school arrived I tried my best to keep the tears at bay, but it was a battle that I was doomed to lose, and when new students were called forth by the teaching staff my flimsy resilience was washed away in a pouring cascade. My mum did her best to coax me into the school and into the care of the waiting teachers, but her words were about as much use as an umbrella made from tissue paper. Any hope of a photograph to preserve this historic event was out of the question. I wailed and bawled, fiercely gripping her arm and creating such a hullabaloo that the entire playground stopped and stared. It must have been tough for my mum, not to mention embarrassing. Taking your child to school for the first time can be an emotional episode, and if your beloved offspring decide not to go quietly, it must be ten times worse.

And then Shane was there.

We had been waiting together in the playground and when summoned he had bounded forward eagerly, hungry to start upon a new life experience, to devour all it had to offer. But now he had returned, having noticed my distress, and stood at my side. I felt his small hand slip into my smaller one, like that of a protective big brother.

'Come on, Adam. Come in with me. I'll look after ya.'

There was always something about Shane that put me at ease. I find it hard to convey the true sense of just what a calming influence my young friend had on me, but I'll try.

Imagine that you're walking alone down a deserted road on a dark night; the street lights are out and the wind is whistling through gardens, sending dustbin lids clattering and setting neglected gates creaking. Around the corner appear two young men, their faces shrouded in darkness by the gloom of the evening and the shadow from their hoodies. They kick a stray beer can out of their path and it clatters randomly along the pavement like a drunk stumbling home. As the gap between you and them closes a particularly strong gust of wind blows one of their hoods back from their head, revealing a face sporting a jagged scar and a lip curled in contempt. How would this scenario make you feel? The answer is obvious. Now imagine the same scenario except this time you have by your side a fully grown, male Rottweiler. It pads along obediently, its breath frosting in the cold air and its short hair ruffling slightly in the strong wind. It walks in a straight line, looking directly ahead, showing no fear and never straining at the leash - and yet despite this you can feel the undoubted power of the animal coursing through the lead into your hand. A more comforting picture I'm sure you'll agree, and this is how my friend often made me feel. His confidence and strength were at my disposal. He was there for me.

Back in the playground my mother wiped away the tears that had settled upon my cheeks, and gave me a quick kiss. Finally I made my way into school, hand in hand with my best friend. No more words of coercion had been required, simply the hand of friendship.

With this stressful hurdle successfully overcome I settled into my young school life in much the same way as I settled into any new place or situation. Slowly, slowly, one foot forward at a time, feeling my way cautiously towards acceptance and familiarity.

I sat on a group of six desks with three other boys and two girls. Shane sat to my left, either by chance or because Mrs. Archer, our teacher, had noticed my opening day distress and seen how my friend had calmed me. Mrs. Archer, incidentally, was a lovely lady whose charming manner, as much as Shane's friendship, helped to settle me into the first year of school life as quickly as my shy personality would allow. She had a fantastic way of explaining things, both in terms of the curriculum work and life experience, that made everything so clear in my mind. A few years ago I was sad to hear that she had been killed by a drunk driver whilst out walking to the local shops, robbing her family and friends of one of life's great enhancers.

Whilst I took my time to adapt to the changes brought on by being rudely thrust into primary education, Shane appeared completely at ease. Each morning he strode confidently into class without so much as a backward glance to his mother or sister Molly, whom he had doted on since her birth only a few short months ago. He laughed and joked easily with anybody in our class, or more accurately anybody in our school, both children and teachers alike. Nothing and nobody seemed to faze him. He was a bubbling cauldron of charisma crammed into the body of a five year old boy, and the social situation that school forced upon you suited him very well indeed.

I have often wondered why the two of us got on so well, seeing as there didn't appear to be much common ground character wise. Shane quickly became one of the most popular boys in the class and was a natural leader, whilst I was at the other end of the spectrum and, if I'm honest with myself, would hardly have been missed by my peers if I'd moved away and never come back. Shane was confident, I was shy. He was brave, I was nervous. So what was it that drew the two of us together? At five years old all you really want to do is play, so maybe personality differences are less important, but even younger children feel a natural affinity with certain peers, a simple comfort in the presence of the other that ensures they are good company to keep. Some people just get on better with others.

Whatever the reason for our connection, the fact that Shane considered me his best friend was obvious, and if this was in any doubt he proved it the day one of my shoes went missing.

We were about half-way through our first school year and were getting changed as quickly as possible following P.E. in order to get outside for lunch hour. Games such as Tag and Bulldog beckoned and, although I was generally pretty hopeless at anything where speed was a key benefit, I found that I still enjoyed them immensely. A few of my classmates had already started making their way outside when I noticed my left shoe was missing. I got on my hands and knees and peered under the wooden benches in the changing room. It should have been where I'd left it, snuggled neatly next to the right, under my peg where my other clothes had been carefully placed.

'Come on, Adam. Hurry,' said Shane, pulling his jumper over his mop of fair hair.

'OK, I'm nearly ready. Got to get my shoe.'

'See ya inna minute then,' he replied and headed outside, oblivious of my plight.

I looked frantically for my shoe, aware that the changing room was rapidly emptying out, and equally aware that the blue track-suited P.E. teacher would soon notice something was amiss. That wouldn't do. If the teacher realised my shoe was missing then they would undoubtedly take me to task over my inability to take care and responsibility for my own possessions. Even worse, they might tell my parents who would then be mad at me for losing the shoe and I would be in big trouble for the extra cost and inconvenience I had caused. Of course, in truth, both the teacher and my parents would likely have been helpful and understanding rather than critical of my situation, but as a child you are prone to panic and over-react at minor issues, situations that to a young mind are not so inconsequential. If something goes wrong or someone misbehaves there is blame and then punishment, both of which must be avoided.

I had to decide quickly on a course of action, and soon realised that there was only one option open to me to avoid being discovered. Keep quiet. Don't tell a soul. Mum's the word.

Doing my best to appear as nonchalant as possible I simply walked out of the changing room wearing only one shoe, attempting to keep my unfortunate left foot hidden behind the fully clothed right. Had the PE teacher paid any notice to my departure I surely would have been rumbled, walking in lop-sided half-steps as I made my escape like a manacled prisoner with a club-foot, but fortunately he was pre-occupied harassing a tubby lad to hurry along and get changed faster.

Once outside I continued my shuffling progress into the playground where the damp ground instantly left the sole of my sock wet-through. I looked up and saw Shane and some other classmates organising this lunch hour's entertainment. My friend looked my way, saw me coming and waved me over encouragingly. With a cold, wet foot that was rapidly discovering just how many sharp little stones were scattered across the tarmacked playground, I hobbled as quickly as I could towards the group. How I thought I was going to join in whatever games were being planned is beyond me, let alone how I was going to make it to the end of the day without the teachers or my parents noticing that I was bereft of some footwear. What was I planning to do tomorrow? Just pop off to school with my solitary shoe for company without so much as a word to my mum?

As soon as I made it across the playground and joined my friends the game was up, amongst them at least.

'Adam's only got one shoe!' exclaimed a particularly short lad called David Frogatt.

Everybody turned to look and the inevitable cacophony of laughter ensued, which is understandable from a group of children. Come to think of it, most adults would probably be pretty amused as well. A barrage of predictable questions and comments followed.

'Why are you only wearing one shoe?'

'Your sock is wet.'

'Where's your shoe gone?'

Indeed. Where had it gone? I was keener than anybody else to find the answer to that question, but then, when I did, I wished that I had remained ignorant.

'Hey! There it is!' It was David Frogatt that had spoken. 'Those bigger boys have got it.'

We all turned and looked as one in the direction that David was pointing. Sure enough, a group of three lads were openly throwing a black shoe backwards and forwards amongst themselves whilst frequently glancing in our direction. They must have somehow sneaked the shoe from the changing room and then waited, watching, as our class all filed onto the playground, keeping a close eye on us to see what their unfortunate victim would do.

The unfortunate victim did little but stand and gawp. The unfortunate victim's best friend, however, immediately starting striding decisively towards the cackling trio with his head up, chest out and fists clenched firmly together. The boys must have been three or maybe four years older than Shane, but he appeared unfazed. Pathetically I hobbled after him while the rest of the class decided the more sensible course of action was to watch from afar.

Shane stood before the three boys. They stopped throwing the shoe from one to the other, and the tallest boy held it securely behind his back. Smirking, they looked down upon my friend with all the confidence and superiority that their greater age bestowed upon them.

'What do you want, Blondey?' said the tallest boy. A crop of dark hair sat atop an angelic face that was marred by wicked little eyes.

'Give that back! It's not yours.' Shane was direct.

'It's not yours either. Have you got any money? Give me ten pence and you can have it back.'

Shane indicated me. 'It's his. Give it.' At five years old the power to put forward a convincing argument was beyond him, but the spirit wasn't lacking.

'10p I said, otherwise you ain't having it.' Wicked Eyes was revelling in his role.

'I don't have money,' I whined.

'Me neither,' said Shane

'Well,' said Wicked Eyes casually, 'you'd better be good at climbing then.' In one fluid motion he swung his arm and sent the shoe hurtling onto the roof of a nearby building, and then he and his two mates ran off laughing, bumping Shane and I out of the way as they went.

Shane was mad. He was so mad I'm surprised that he didn't go running after those boys, but perhaps he knew it would have been futile. He might have been brave but he wasn't foolish. He couldn't hope to beat them in a fight and fighting wouldn't get my shoe down.

'What am I going to do now? Maybe I should tell a teacher.'

'Don't tell,' replied Shane, looking up at the building where they had thrown my shoe. 'You might get into trouble.'

It seemed that Shane's young mind thought along the same blurred lines as mine: confess to an adult about something that's awry and the blame falls squarely on your shoulders.

The building on top of which my shoe had unceremoniously been deposited was more of a hut than anything else. It was single storey in height with a flat roof and was one of a trio of cabin-type classrooms that had presumably been added to the school at a cheaper cost than bricks and mortar. Leading up to the entrance were three steps, flanked on either side by a wooden handrail dressed in flaking white paint. It was towards this handrail that Shane now approached determinedly and without hesitation.

After a quick glance around to ensure that no teachers or dinner-ladies were watching, he nimbly clambered up onto the narrow handrail where he stood for a moment with one hand resting against the side of the building to aid his balance.

'What you doing, Shane?' I asked.

'Climbing to the top to get ya shoe,' he said, supplying the obvious answer.

'But...' I left the word hanging. But what? I wanted my shoe back and if my friend was willing to get it then I was happy to let him. We were both naive about the inherent dangers of such an undertaking, so there was little discussion to be had in regards to what if.

With a second glance around Shane reached up from his position atop the handrail and grabbed hold of a piece of wood that jutted out slightly from the hut and which encircled the whole of the building like some sort of decorative trim. Then, with his left leg, he stretched out his foot until it was resting on a cross-section of the nearest wooden window frame which effectively divided the window into two sections of glass - a top and bottom half. Shuffling to his left slightly his right foot then followed before it too rested on the centre of the window frame.

For a few seconds he looked like Spider-Man, hanging from the hut with two hands clinging onto the wooden trim and both feet balancing on the slender frame of the window. He was approximately half-way to the roof in his current precarious position.

'Careful, Shane.' He didn't reply, either through fear or concentration, I'm not sure which, but knowing my friend it was likely the latter.

Gripping the wooden ledge tightly Shane then started to haul himself up towards the roof where his next intended handhold, the guttering, glared down at him tantalisingly. He reached forward and stretched his hand out towards the black plastic, but he didn't have quite enough body strength to attain his target. I watched with trepidation as, almost in slow motion, his body slid back down to his previous position. His hands managed to once again firmly grip the wooden ledge, but his feet, flailing wildly and desperately seeking purchase, crashed into the window and sent the thin glass to a grisly end as the pane smashed in a shower of jagged shards and attention-seeking noise.

Shocked into releasing his grip, Shane fell the short distance he had climbed back to the floor, landing in a heap on the concrete, but mercilessly away from any of the broken glass, most of which had been kicked inside the hut. He got up straight away, fortunately unharmed, and as the two of us turned around we saw that virtually the entire playground had stopped what they were doing and were now stood staring at us, like a horde of flesh-eating zombies having spotted their prey. The crash from the glass had cast its spell. My heart sank as I saw two dinner ladies running over towards the pair of us.

Shane looked across at me and shrugged his shoulders. 'Sorry!' he said.

We stood there and waited for the dinner ladies to reach where we stood. One of us with a hole torn in the knee of his trousers following his tumble, and the other wearing only one shoe. Dishevelled, defeated, but standing side by side.

***

My mum was understanding following the missing shoe incident, but then my mum always seemed to be understanding in regards to any bad decisions I made. She dealt with this situation in the same way that she handled any minor crises - with a relaxed voice and a firm grip on perspective.

My dad, Trevor, was incredulous. 'Why didn't you just go and tell a teacher?'

My mum was calm. 'Because he is only five years old and was worried about getting into trouble.'

Incredulous. 'Yes, but even still, Adam, you need to tell the teachers about things like this. What did you think would happen? You can't walk around with one shoe.'

Calm. 'He...is...five...years...old.'

My dad sighed and looked at me as I sat cuddled up on my mum's lap sporting reddened eyes.

'Ah, come here, buddy.' He held his arms out wide, and I slid from the comfort of her embrace and walked over to him, where he smothered me with love. 'I'm not mad with you, boy, but next time you get into trouble then you've just got to tell a grown-up, OK? And certainly don't go trying what Shane did today. Blimey! How does a kid that age even manage to climb half-way up a building anyway?'

'You know Shane - he's one determined little boy,' said my mum with a smile.

'He was trying to help me,' I squeaked.

'Yes,' she said, 'and that's commendable, it's a sign of a good friend, but your dad is right. It is best to tell a grown-up. Shane could have hurt himself badly today. Always try to think things through before you do anything dangerous.'

'What does commeetamble mean?'

My mum stood up and wandered over to where I sat with my dad. Her tall skinny body had been passed down to me in her genes, and as time went on this would become more obvious.

'Commendable,' she said kissing the top of my head. 'It means he tried to do a good thing, but this time he just did it in the wrong way. I'm off to go and start dinner.'

My dad turned on the television and started watching some snooker. I had no interest in seeing different coloured balls pinging backwards and forwards across the green baize, but for a short while I stayed sitting on his lap, enjoying the cuddle and the warmth that emanated from his paunch.

This was the way it was in our house, but I wonder how things were for Shane. Did Mike embrace him in a loving bear-hug and tell him to be more careful in future? Was he sent to his room without anything to eat and a bottom stinging from the slap of his dad's slipper? Did he sit down with both of his parents and discuss the pros and cons of his actions, offering him guidance on his future choices in such scenarios?

Being of such tender years Shane and I were hardly about to discuss how our parents handled the situation, but I doubt that he received the same amount of love and support that I did. In my mind I picture his dad yelling at him, perhaps even questioning why I couldn't get my own bloody shoe back in the first place. I picture Karen doing her best to keep the peace, offering conciliatory words and a hug as well, at least once Mike has calmed himself down or gone out down the pub. Her tired green eyes, seemingly permanently surrounded in pale blue eye-shadow, look lovingly upon her son, forgivingly, but just as she is about to offer advice Molly needs changing, or Caroline starts stropping, or the telephone rings, or she has to prepare dinner, or…

Being an only child could, at times, prove lonely, and I would have loved to have had a sibling. Someone to play with, to compete with, to fight with. Yet a massive bonus of being an only child is that the love and attention from your parents is not diluted by the demands of a competing brother or sister. Shane didn't have this advantage when a situation, such as the shoe incident, raised its ugly head. Instead he had to settle for an often volatile father, a mother that loved him dearly but whose time was thinly stretched, and two demanding siblings, one of whom was merely a baby.

Had I been asked to step into his shoes, and he into mine, I think it is fair to say that only one of us would have coped with the change. Not only did Shane seem stronger, both mentally and physically, always ready to face the world and its varying problems, but in a role reversal situation he would have been warmly welcomed and loved by my parents. The same, sadly, could not be said for Mike and over the ensuing years it would become increasingly obvious that my friend's dad held no such love for my family, and the consequences of his hatred would eventually lead to a tragedy of epic, life changing proportions.

Chapter 4

It was a warm sunny day when Mike started the argument over our neighbour's dog.

Whereas my mum and Karen had built up a strong friendship over the years, brought together initially through their children, my dad and Mike had nothing to do with each other. My mum would regularly pop to Karen's for a cup of tea, and vice-versa, and this was likely fuelled by how well myself and Shane got on. They didn't need to concern themselves with any squabbling and this allowed them to sit and relax for a short time.

My dad and Mike, in contrast, rarely spoke a word to each other. The most they would ever stretch to would be an occasional greeting across the tarmac that separated our houses. This could be by way of a gruff 'morning', or simply a raise of the hand or nod of the head. Sometimes, perhaps if they'd got out of the wrong side of the bed or had a rough day at work, they would simply ignore the presence of the other, and either pretend they hadn't seen their neighbour, or just not care that they had seen them.

This implies that my dad was like this with everyone, which is neither fair nor true. Had he seen Karen, for example, or any number of other neighbours, then he would have quite happily struck up a conversation with them, spending the time to ask after their children or their work. Even those neighbours that he didn't know so well would be hailed with a warm and friendly greeting, followed up with some polite comment on the weather or a throw-away joke about the state of our front garden.

I never saw Mike make this level of effort, not with anyone in our street. He was equally cold and impolite with all of our neighbours. As I've indicated before, there was a warm community feeling in Foxhole Avenue, but Mike only seemed interested in doing his best to rip that apart.

The day of the argument fell on a weekend and my dad and I were out front of the house washing the car. We didn't have a driveway so the car, a blue Ford Escort, was parked in the road. I was somewhere around the age of six and a half or seven.

Washing the car with my dad wasn't a chore, but a pleasure. He would always go out of his way to make things as fun for me as possible, whatever we were doing. It's possible this was partly due to the fact I was an only child and lacked that sibling to fool around with, but I like to think the truth is simply that he enjoyed seeing me laugh. When cleaning the car the two of us would invariably end up as wet as the vehicle. Sometimes a sponge would get thrown at the back of my head when I wasn't looking, or my dad would cause the spray from the hose to pass across my body as he washed away the suds from the windows. Whatever happened, it would invariably escalate into a water-fight.

Like many young boys at that age, I looked to my dad as the one to mess around with. Dad was the one that would swing me around by my arms and legs and then set me down to watch me stumble around the garden putting the safety of mum's plants in jeopardy. In fairness to my mum she would swing me around too, but with my dad it was always that bit faster and that bit more reckless which, as a child, amounts to more fun.

He was the one that would roll around the floor with me in mock battles, whilst my mum looked on, sometimes laughing at our antics and sometimes asking us to be more careful, both of each other and her furniture.

He was the one that would push me harder and faster on the swing or on the roundabout, and then pretend that he was going home, walking away leaving me trapped on the playground equipment, calling him back breathlessly between giggles to come and rescue me.

He was the one that would take me on visits to the bus depot, where he worked as a bus driver. Together we would watch the buses going through the huge industrial cleaning machine, or run up and down inside the empty vehicles in games of tag. He would let me sit in the driver's seat and pretend to be a passenger that urgently needed to be taken home before they wet their pants, or that needed to be taken to the Land of Chocolate Bars, that was in danger of melting from a fiendishly hot sun, and needed eating before it was too late.

At home he made me a wooden model of a bus, large enough and strong enough to sit in. It was similar to those ones you see at fairs on the Merry-go-Round where smaller children can choose to sit upstairs or down. Together with my mum the three of us painted it, and its eye-catching red form took pride of place in the back garden where I rewarded my dad's hard work with hours of use.

I didn't only look to my dad for fooling around, but also saw him as the protector of the family. Calling him 'The Protector' perhaps sounds a little over dramatic, as it's not as if my family was under attack from a gang of thugs or anything like that, but generally most young children probably do see their father in this way. After all, children aren't known for trotting out the phrase *my mum's bigger than your mum,* although perhaps the same can't be said for certain, more notorious parts of the country. My dad would be the one that I would go to in times of trepidation; the one I would want to sit with during a bad thunder-storm; the one I would seek to calm my fears if there was a noise in my bedroom late at night. If I wanted comfort because I had hurt myself in a fall or was feeling unwell then my mum would be the answer, but safety from threatening situations came in the guise of a tall, balding and slightly overweight man called Trevor Wickes. This doting image of my father would be called into question the day that Mike decided to cause trouble over the dog.

The two of us were busy applying the soap suds to the car with our sponges, and our work had not yet descended into the inevitable water-fight. I was keeping a close eye on my dad, determined not to get caught by surprise with a flying sponge and looking for an opportunity where I could strike first. Walking up the hill towards us I noticed Violet Mayton, who lived three doors down from our house at number Twenty-Three.

She was taking her dog, a white and brown King Charles spaniel called Winston, for the first of his two regular daily walks. Violet was in her early seventies, so the pace she was setting wasn't exactly Olympic standard, but for somebody of her age she still seemed to have plenty of energy and was firm and steady on her feet. She was a kindly old lady with a skinny frame and jet black hair that had seen more dark dye than a ninja's clothing factory. I didn't know her that well but she would always ask me and my family how we were if she saw us in the street. My parents always took the time to engage in brief conversation with Violet, being aware that she lived alone and likely got lonely at times. Once upon a time she had been married, but her husband had died before I was born. In the privacy of our own home my dad always used to refer to her as 'The Curtain Twitcher', which he often just shortened to 'CT', as Violet always seemed to be keeping a beady eye on the comings and goings within the street. There was nothing malicious about her behaviour, but was an understandable consequence of somebody living alone with nothing but a dog for company.

At this stage I should also point out that Violet had a daughter, who did pay her mum regular visits, along with her grandchildren. It would be unfair of me not to mention this, as it would imply that the old lady had been abandoned and neglected by her off-spring which isn't true. Nevertheless, one or even two visits a week still leaves a lot of spare time for a retired person, living alone, to fill.

As Violet approached I was able to relax my guard as I knew my dad was unlikely to launch a surprise attack for fear of soaking our neighbour.

'Morning, Violet,' said my dad.

'Hello, boys. You look busy,' she rasped. Her voice sounded like that of a heavy smoker, and yet I had never witnessed her with a cigarette before.

'This is just the start,' said my dad making a fuss of the dog and stroking its head. 'Hello, boy, how you doing? I'm going to get him started on the windows next' I noticed my dad had left a large soap-sud bubble on Winston's head, most likely intentionally, but I somehow managed to stifle my laughter.

'Oh, well, send Adam round to my house when you're finished and he can start on mine.'

'OK, I'll do that. And then he can cut the grass, weed the flower-beds and put the hoover round. That's alright with you isn't it, son?'

I smiled shyly at the two adults, looking down at my feet. 'No,' I mumbled.

'No! No!,' said my dad in a mock-stern voice. 'I don't know, Violet, kids these days are far too lazy.'

Violet cackled her throaty laugh. 'Don't listen to him, Adam. He's just teasing you.'

My dad and Violet continued to exchange pleasantries whilst I stood next to the car waiting. As friendly as the old lady was I wished she would hurry up and carry on with walking her dog. I was keen to continue washing the car and she was getting in the way of our impending water-fight.

Movement from across the road caught my eye and I saw Mike walking down his driveway. The houses on that side of the road were mostly set higher up than on our side, and so the driveway sloped quite steeply from the road up to the house. He was wearing his blue Chelsea t-shirt, and was presumably on his way to watch his favourite football team with his own father, as he did most weekends. On rare occasions Shane would also get dragged along to these matches, but only if it didn't get in the way of any planned post-match drinking sessions that his dad had planned.

Shane was actually a secret Manchester United fan, but he always pretended that he followed Chelsea to please his dad. Supporting 'The Blues' was a major part of Mike's life, and I know that Shane was always concerned about his dad finding out about his true allegiance. I don't believe this is because he was worried about his dad getting mad at him, but more like a genuine desire to please him. His family formed a long line of Chelsea supporters, from his great grandad, to his grandad, to his father, and Shane was conscious of the disappointment he would cause if he admitted his true colours.

Just as Mike was ambling down his driveway, and my dad and Violet were talking, the dog decided to defecate on the pavement. Some of the pavements around our local area were riddled with dog excrement and in particular spots you almost had to tip-toe through them very carefully, like a military patrol navigating a mine-field. For many people this was a real pet-hate and in fact the local council had recently launched a campaign to crack down on the situation. Caught up in the wondrous small-talk that she was sharing with my dad, Violet was oblivious to her dog's action. I'd noticed what the animal had done but, aside from finding it quite amusing, as anything toilet related was at that age, I didn't really care. I just wanted Violet to go away. My dad, who was by now starting to look quite bored of the conversation too, also failed to notice as he sought to maintain an impression of polite interest and remained focused on Violet and her husky voice.

Somebody who most certainly did notice, however, was Mike.

He stood watching from the other side of the road, his broad arms, decorated in tattoos, folded across his chest and his lips pursed. I watched him from the corner of my eye, and the manner in which he was glaring across the road made me instantly uncomfortable. Even at my young age I could tell when somebody was mad.

'What is it with you bloody dog-owners?' His voice sliced through my dad and Violet's conversation, halting their flow instantly.

Violet looked across to him. 'What do you mean?'

'Oh, come on!' he snapped.

'What's the problem, Mike?' My dad kept his voice neutral, unconfrontational.

'The problem? The problem, *Trevor*, is that I'm sick to death of dogs like 'ers shitting all over the place. The owners just let 'em dump their crap wherever they like and then leave it sitting there for some poor bastard to come along and step in.'

'Let's watch the language, Mike, eh.' My dad inclined his head in my direction.

Violet had now seen where the crime had been committed by Winston and was proceeding to clean up the mess with a small plastic bag that she always carried for just such an eventuality.

'I always clean up after my dog,' she said from her position crouched down on the pavement. 'That's why I carry this bag with me.'

'Yeah, well, of course you're going to clean it up now ain't ya, now that I've embarrassed ya. I wonder how many of the turds scattered up and down these pavements are from your mutt's arse.'

'I don't know why you're shouting. Of course I was going to clean it up. I just hadn't noticed. We were talking.'

'Ya know what really gets me,' Mike continued, ignoring Violet's protestations, 'is that young children play outside on these streets, and your bad attitude towards ya dog shitting everywhere don't help make it safe for 'em to enjoy themselves. It ain't exactly a pleasant environment.'

The irony of the unpleasant environment that his demeanour and intimidating nature were creating was seemingly lost on Mike.

'Come on, Mike,' said my dad, attempting to play peace-keeper, 'there's no harm done. Violet's cleared up the mess. She's one of the few conscientious dog-owners that we seem to have round here. It's a shame all owners aren't like her.' He attempted a friendly chuckle but it sounded hollow and out of place.

Mike wasn't about to be so easily pacified. 'I can't believe you,' he raged. 'That old bag lets 'er dog take a dump right outside your 'ouse, and all you can do is stick up for 'er. What kind of a dad are ya? Yer son is standing there watching and yer teaching 'im that it's alright for dogs to shit wherever they like. She should apologise.'

'No-one needs to apologise for anything. There's nothing to apologise for. Violet has cleaned up the mess. She always does. You're not hearing me.' My dad was still keeping his voice calm, but did I detect a slight quiver too, an indication of uncertainty? 'Look, I suggest we just leave this. It's just a misunderstanding that's got blown out of all proportion. I'd sooner not be shouting across the street at each other, especially in front of my son. That's not really the sort of atmosphere I want him subjected to.'

At my dad's last comments Mike suddenly strode across the road, eating up the tarmac in the blink of an eye, and stood facing him, eyeball to eyeball. Violet had shrunk back at his approach, pulling herself and her dog off to one side. She manoeuvred Winston behind her skinny frame as best she could as if fearful that Mike was about to launch a kick at the poor thing that had innocently been the cause of this scene. My dad had inadvertently taken a step back but otherwise stood his ground.

The tension in the air was palpable, particularly so now following Mike's undisguised act of intimidation. He now spoke in a calm and whispered voice, almost like that of a gentle breeze that precedes a devastating hurricane.

'You think yer better than me, don't ya? Think you know it all? Yer nothing. Just some stupid fat git who drives a bus for a living. You criticise me for creating a bad atmosphere for your son, like yer such a better parent than me. Like ya precious wife is any better too. You don't know shit about what goes on around here. Yer fucking clueless. Pathetic! Just make sure you stay out of my way, OK?'

There was an eerie silence as Mike stood glaring at my dad, who either refused, or couldn't summon the courage, to meet the gaze of the other man. It seemed to go on forever until a motorbike passed by, interrupting the quiet of the scene like a mosquito gliding past your ear in the dead of night.

'I said, OK?' Mike punched each word through the air between the two men.

I looked up at my dad as he mumbled his response. 'Okay.'

Mike nodded, seemingly satisfied, before turning on his heel and walking down the road on his way to the football match. He hawked some phlegm onto the pavement, marking his territory like a dog on heat, and seemingly uncaring of how hypocritical this made his criticism of Winston's defecation seem. He didn't look back.

'Trevor, I'm so sorry.' Violet stepped forward, the dog leash held tight in her hand. 'I never wanted to cause any trouble.'

'Don't worry about it, Violet, it's not your fault. Mike's obviously not feeling in the best of moods today. Let's just hope his team wins today eh?'

My dad's cheap attempt at a joke failed to lighten the mood, although Violet was polite enough to offer a smile.

'I'd better let you get on, Trevor. Sorry again for the bother. Truly. That man...' She left the sentence hanging and continued on her walk, being sure to travel in the opposite direction to our unreasonable neighbour. I'm sure if I hadn't been present she would have stuck around and offered some stronger opinions.

My dad looked across at me, and he seemed smaller than before. I remember feeling a confused sense of disappointment that my dad had so clearly come off second best to Mike. As a young child there is always the misplaced belief that your dad is indestructible, that he is this powerful superman immune to pain and fear. Today was the day that this heroic status was given an honest, yet cruel, rebalancing.

'Come on, son, let's finish cleaning this car.'

From his tone and the atmosphere that had descended on the bright, sunny day, I knew there would be no water-fight today.

***

That night I couldn't sleep. I lay awake in bed pondering over the events of the day as shadows danced on my wall against the glare of the moonlight, fidgeting across the wallpaper like the restless thoughts in my head. I was trying to come to terms with the harsh reality that my dad was human after all. He suffered from fears and worries just as I did. He wasn't simply a machine that could crush anything that crossed him.

I suppose, to be brutally honest, I was disappointed. I wanted to believe that my dad was the biggest and toughest dad around, and that nothing could stand against him. Isn't that how heroes are supposed to be? In many ways I idolised him, as many young sons do their father. I had raised him up on a pedestal, a pedestal that had just been detonated by some TNT called Mike.

On reflection I feel ashamed of these thoughts that I had as a child, but I have to remind myself that I was just that: a child. Now I look at my father, both the man that he was then and the man he continued to be, with an immense feeling of pride. How lucky I was to be granted such a parent. How jealous other children would have been if they had known the true extent of what a brilliant dad Trevor Wickes was.

When the two of us continued with the washing of the car after Mike's open aggression he could have easily shut down, but instead he made the decision to confront the situation head-on, rather than to carry-on as if nothing had happened. He had been left embarrassed in front of his own son, and yet he was man enough to apologise to me, although no blame should have been apportioned to him. He took the opportunity to educate me.

'The world is made up of lots of different people, Adam,' he began. 'Some are boring, some are fun; some are fast, some are slow; some will laugh at anything, and some will cry at absolutely nothing; but remember this: whilst most will mean you no harm, sometimes you get those that just seem to be raging at the world, for whatever reason. Those people, those angry people, you've got to keep your eye on. You should still smile at them and be polite, (always be polite), but *never* trust them. You hear me? Never! Because once you drop your guard, then you're bang in trouble.'

He dipped the sponge into the bucket and squeezed out the excess water. 'One more thing. If someone ever gets aggressive with you, like Mike just did with me, then walk away. There is no shame in refusing to fight someone, especially one of those angry people I was talking about. People that angry are unpredictable, like a wild animal they are dangerous, and it is better to back away sometimes, even if that feels humiliating, o.k?

I nodded. I didn't fully understand what he was saying, but I understood the general drift and his words stuck with me.

In bed I was laying on my back staring at the ceiling and was finally starting to drift off to sleep when my parents voices snaked up the stairs to rouse me once more.

'No! I won't accept that, Sam,' my dad said to my mum. His voice was raised slightly, yet controlled, despite the obvious anger that emanated from his tone.

'Listen, let's not go making any rash decisions based on this one incident.' My mum spoke firmly yet placatingly.

'But it's not just one incident though is it? He's always at it.'

'Oh, so what other incidents can you name?'

'Well, OK, maybe not specific incidents as such, but his general behaviour is hardly hospitiable. Reckless driving. Drunken noise. You know, Sam. There's always an underlying current of malice with that bloody man. I always get the feeling that he could blow at any minute. I don't trust him.'

Slowly, I got out of my bed and crept to the top of the stairs, anxious to hear everything that was being said. It was obvious that they were discussing the confrontation with Mike from earlier in the day.

'I don't trust him either,' replied my mum, 'but we can't just stop Adam going to their house. Shane is his best friend, and I get on great with Karen as well.'

'I'm not suggesting that you stop seeing Karen am I? This is about the safety of our son.'

'No, I know that. Mike's not even there most of the time anyway. He's at football or down the pub. And if he is home he's probably sleeping off a hangover or what-have-you.'

I could picture the two of them sitting downstairs and both trying to keep their tempers in check. My mum's thin body with her perfect teeth, sitting across from my dad with his lovable paunch and thinning hair. As a couple they rarely fought, but bring me into the equation and passions ran high. I was their only child.

'I don't mind Shane coming over to our house, I don't have a problem with that at all. He's a nice lad. But I do not want Adam going over to theirs.'

'You're right, Trevor, Shane is a nice boy, and that's my argument. All of their children are lovely. They're polite, always nicely turned out, and a credit to Karen.'

'Ah, exactly. To Karen! A credit to her, but not to him.'

'I don't dispute that, but my point is that despite the way Mike is the kids are no trouble. And to be fair, although Karen does most of the work involved in bringing up those kids, Mike does love them, and they love him. When they separated a couple of years back Shane couldn't wait for him to come back home.'

My dad remained silent, which either meant he was sulking or trying to think of another way to approach the argument to ensure he got the result he wanted. He might have been a great father, but he wasn't entirely without fault, and one of his major flaws was a stubborn attitude King Canute would have been proud of. Generally speaking my dad was the main decision maker in our family, but if my mum felt strongly enough about something then she could be quite persistent in putting her foot firmly down.

'Look, Trev, I know that Mike is far from being a nice person, and what he did today is typical of the man and his attitude to life, but let's not penalise our son for someone else's failings. I think it's so lovely that he's got a play mate that lives right opposite us, and they get on so well together. It would be a shame to ruin that.'

My dad gave an audible sigh that was so heavy it still reached my vantage point at the top of the stairs. 'OK, perhaps I'm just over-reacting because he made me look so small in front of Adam. The last thing I want him to see is two men involved in a punch-up. What would that teach him? I guess you're right. I just don't trust him.'

'Mike's just full of a load of hot air. If I felt that he posed any danger to our son in any way, shape or form then I wouldn't allow him over there. You know that. He might cause trouble with other adults but I hardly think he's going to go out of his way to hurt a child, even less so in front of his own family.'

I sometimes wonder if my mum remembers her words from that long ago night. Do they haunt her on dark evenings? Do they scratch at the inside of her mind, like a caged bird that can never be set free? Does she wish that my father had won the debate and got his way?

If she remembers, then the answer to all three questions can only be *yes*.

Chapter 5

The day that my mum came home and started crying was a Friday. My dad had collected me from school having been on the early shift for his bus round. She walked in the front door and called out a muted *Hello* and then proceeded to remove her coat out in the hall-way. My dad got up from the lounge floor, where the two of us had been working on a jigsaw puzzle of a soldier, and went to greet her. I followed along behind him to go and greet my mum.

'Well?' he asked her softly. Just the one word, nothing more. I kept quiet, sensing something wasn't quite right.

She looked at him and then at me, before bursting into tears right there on the spot. My dad took a few steps forward and enclosed his crying wife in his big comforting arms.

The door-bell has just rung. Not back then whilst my mum was crying, I'm talking about now, in present day. With a tut (after all, it's such an inconvenience to walk the twenty paces or so to the front door) I get up from my place in the garden and go to answer it. My reward for making such a strenuous effort and opening the front door is to be bombarded by an annoying man in a smart grey suit trying to sell me double glazing. After mouthing several *Sorry, not interested* comments and being blatantly ignored I offer a more final *Good-bye* and shut the door in his face as he continues to blabber away. I could hear quite clearly the names he called me once he was faced with a closed door. Perhaps I should look into getting improved double glazing to cut out the sound of such unwelcome abuse. I allow myself a chuckle at my own joke.

As I'm up I decide to treat myself to a second beer and head to the kitchen where I grab a nice cool one from the fridge. It'll help me to think. A quick glance at the digital clock on the oven reveals that I still have plenty of time before Maz and Zak get home. I might as well make the most of the remaining peace and quiet, so I head back outside where I sit once again on the chair in the warmth of the sun and regather my train of thought.

As I observed my parents hugging each other in the hallway of our small house I felt like a nosey passer-by, wanting to join in but not knowing if I should. After a short while my mum pulled away from my dad.

'I'll talk to you later,' she said to him, wiping the tears from her face with her slender fore-fingers.

'Yeah, sure, OK,' said my dad, 'but how long did she get?'

'Twenty-eight days,' she replied. 'Later, o.k? Right now I want to see how my little boy is.'

'What's twenty-eight days?' I asked. 'Why are you crying?'

'I'm alright. I'm not crying anymore. Don't worry. Now, more importantly, tell me what you've been up to. How was school?'

'Fine. Me and dad were just doing a puzzle. Want to help?'

'I'd love to.'

'It's my soldier one though, so a bit of a boy's puzzle.'

'I don't mind,' she said.

How selfish young minds are. So easily distracted and moved along when the subject turns to them.

It was a couple of days later before my parents decided to tell me what had happened to cause my mum to be upset. They must have decided that they had to tell me as, being such close friends with Shane, it was inevitable that I would find out anyway and would then perhaps ask indelicate questions at inopportune moments. At the time I was only seven years old, so still relatively naive and lacking in tact.

That day my mum had been to the local magistrate's court to act as a character witness for Karen. She had been charged with shop-lifting from the local supermarket, having allegedly concealed some skinless chicken breasts about her person. I say allegedly, but there is no allegedly about it - she did it, she was guilty, and she freely admitted to the crime. This was the third time she had been caught in the act of shop-lifting and had been let-off with warnings from the police on the previous occasions. Then, upon being caught for a third time it was decided that she wasn't getting the message and that a harsher punishment was required to show her the error of her ways.

But, let's put this into true context, and here I am likely repeating some of what my mum would have said when she took the stand. Karen was a good person. Her only crime was marrying Mike, and even that perhaps she should be forgiven for, as who knows how charming he came across in their earlier days of courting. She was trying to bring up three children and feed five mouths with a budget consisting of her hours working behind a bar on minimum wage, and the sporadic income that Mike brought in, much of which he squandered at a local boozer on the tempting amber fluid. He didn't even have the good grace to spend his money in the same pub where his wife worked, which would have at least added to the success of his wife's employer and therefore, in turn, aided her bread and butter provider. She stole because she felt that there was no other option open to her. Who knows how many arguments she may have had with Mike over spending all their cash on pints of lager and Chelsea Football Club tickets, or about his inability to hold down a job and bring in a steady income. As far as I know, and this has been passed onto me over the years from my parents, Karen was never frightened to speak her mind to Mike. She never cowered from him for fear of getting a slap, and to my knowledge this wasn't his way, but it also seems that she couldn't get through to him either. The lure of the pub got the better of him. His temper at work got the better of him, resulting in the loss of numerous jobs. Where was the steadying hand that Karen needed to help her put food on the table. No understanding, support or dependability seemed to be forth-coming from her shameful husband. The trial separation the two of them had gone through, back when Molly was first born, seemed a world away. Whatever promises Mike may have made to bring him and Karen back together equally seemed a world away. Did Karen consider separating once more? Perhaps, but perhaps she simply accepted her husband would never change.

Why didn't she seek help from close friends or family if money was so tight? Maybe she had done so before and felt too proud to do so again, or felt that too many favours had been cashed in, after all my mother had once assisted with baby-sitting duties whilst her friend took on extra hours following the afore-mentioned separation. Maybe she didn't want to be a burden, or place people in an uncomfortable position where they felt they couldn't say no. Knowing the good heart that Karen carried with her, this is a likely scenario. Karen was the victim in all of this. A victim of circumstance. Perhaps she could even be viewed, in a round-a-bout way, as Mike's victim. If there was any justice, it would have been him that stood accused.

Whatever my mum said when she took the stand, it fell on deaf ears. A custodial sentence of twenty-eight days was passed. The father wasn't working, having been sacked from his job, so he could look after the children during this time, decreed the Magistrates. As my mother read her kind words from her piece of paper then that piece of paper had been ruthlessly folded closed and cut into the shape of a prison key.

'What Karen did was wrong, Adam, there is no doubt about this,' said my mum, now able to keep the tears firmly in their own prison. 'But, you must understand that she is still a good person. A very good person.'

'So why did she steal then?'

My mum paused, thinking.

'You know when you couldn't find your shoe, because those boys had taken it? You didn't know what to do. You decided not to tell a grown-up because you thought it would lead to more trouble. Well, this is a bit like that. Karen was in trouble, she had no money but she needed food, and she didn't know who to ask for help. So, she made a decision about what to do, but this time she made the wrong decision.'

'She should have asked us then. We've always got food.'

'Yes, I wished she had asked. I would have gladly helped her out. But, listen, the important thing to understand is that Shane, Caroline, and even Molly, are going to be missing their mummy. We have to make sure that we are good friends to them now. You mustn't laugh about this to Shane, OK, because he might be upset. Do you understand?'

'O.k,' I said, although in truth I couldn't imagine that Shane would be upset. He never seemed to cry.

***

Shane had been crying. His eyes were red and puffy and streaks ran down his cheeks. I might have only been a young lad but it didn't take a detective to notice that tears had reared their unwelcome head.

My friend stood at the threshold of his front door. He was wearing some black shorts and his blue Chelsea top. His fair hair was in need of a cut and looked like it was now estranged from the comb. He looked at me and gave a small smile, but it was empty of joy. I assumed that he must have been upset due to his mother being jailed.

Next to him, but standing slightly forward, towered Mike. His expression was grim, unwelcoming, and his thick-set forearms were crossed in front of his chest like two huge railway buffers intent on letting nothing get past.

'Hi, Mike, Shane, how are things?' began my mum, trying to sound upbeat yet sympathetic all at the same time.

'What do you want?' snapped Mike, all pleasantries immediately discarded.

'I just wondered, that is *we* just wondered, if we could help out in any way. I know that it must be tough for all of you right now, what with poor Karen being so harshly treated...'

'Poor Karen!' He spoke the words slowly, drawing out each of the three syllables with deliberate clarity.

'...yes, exactly, so, I just wondered if there was anything that I could do.'

My mum glanced at Mike, clearly nervous, but determined nonetheless. She stood a good couple of inches taller than him, but his menacing presence alone gave the impression that the opposite was true. He said nothing, and an uncomfortable silence crashed down around us. Mike sniffed exaggeratedly and rolled his shoulders as if to loosen tight joints.

My mother could stand it no longer. 'So...is there?'

'Is there what?'

She chuckled anxiously. 'Is there anything we can do to help you out? Look, I've made you a casserole,' she said, holding forward a pot that Mike couldn't have failed to have already seen. 'It's beef braising steak, and there are carrots in there too, but you can fish those out if you're not a fan.'

'So why are you asking me then?'

I glanced at my mum quickly. She looked confused and flashed Mike a smile with those perfect teeth of hers. I wasn't used to seeing her caught off-balance like this. She always seemed unflappable to me.

'Asking you what?' she said.

'Why are ya asking me if I need any help when ya have so clearly already decided that I do? I mean, ya come over 'ere, trying to look like your life is so bloody perfect, with ya home-made beef stew as some pathetic supposed act of generosity, asking if I need help and then trying to offer it anyway without even waiting to see what I think. You presumptuous cow! There's one reason and one reason only that you've come over here and that is to gloat!'

'Now, hold on a minute, that is simply not...'

'Yeah, it bloody-well is. All you're about is trying to look superior to the rest of the people in this street. I've seen ya, always washing ya net curtains, cleaning ya car, chatting to all the neighbours like yer this perfect wife and mother.'

I looked at Shane, and I caught his eye, but he quickly looked away, as if feeling guilty for the way his father was behaving. My mother may have been made to feel uncomfortable by Mike's manner, but she wasn't about to just stand there and take it. The difference was that she remained polite.

'Those are unfair accusations. All I wanted to do was to see if I could help in anyway whilst Karen is...away. That's all! Nothing more! I know that things are likely quite tough for you right now...'

'Karen's not away on some round the world cruise, is she? Let's say it like it is. She's doing time for stealing, the stupid bitch!' Mike suddenly looked over my mum's shoulder and raised his voice significantly. 'I said, ya nosey old bag, that me wife is in jail for stealing, got it?'

I turned to look at where Mike was directing his anger and just caught Violet Mayton's curtain falling guiltily back into position. The curtain twitcher had been caught in the act.

'Now, as fer you two,' he continued, 'why don't ya run along and take yer stew with ya.' He leant in close to my mum then, dropping his voice to little more than a whisper, but loud enough so that I could still hear. 'Perhaps, Samantha, you should think about the mistakes that you've made in your own life before you go round making judgements on other people's. Now piss off!'

The door slammed loudly as it was closed unceremoniously in our faces.

'That man!' my mum muttered, before turning to me. 'Come on, Adam, it looks like our help is not wanted after all.' She grabbed my hand and the two of us made the short walk back to the security of our own home.

That night during dinner, once my dad had come home from his shift, my mum recounted what had happened over at the Metcalfes and how her kind offer of assistance had been rudely rebuffed.

'What do you expect from that caveman?' asked my dad between mouthfuls. 'He wouldn't know good manners if they jumped up and bit him on the bum.'

I sniggered at the use of the word 'bum' by my dad. My parents ignored me.

'I wasn't doing it for him anyway. More for the sake of the kids really, and for Karen's peace of mind of course. I still want to visit her tomorrow, and was hoping that I could say we were helping out. It seems without her here to keep him in line his manners get even worse, although I wouldn't have thought it possible.'

'Well, look, you tried, you can't do anymore than that. The kids'll be alright, they're a hardy bunch, and I doubt they'll keep her inside for the full twenty-eight days. Plus I'm sure that the grandparents will be doing their bit. Besides, their loss is our gain - this stew is magic.'

My mum nodded slowly, but her face looked troubled.

I noticed that when she explained to my dad what had happened on that unwelcoming doorstep, that she forgot to mention Mike's comment about mistakes from her own life. I almost reminded my mum about this part, but didn't bother as I assumed it must have been unimportant. It is only now, years later, that the full story has been revealed to me that I understand exactly what Mike was alluding to.

***

'My dad says that I'm not allowed to play with you anymore.'

I was in the playground with a glum looking Shane at morning break when he dropped his bombshell.

'Why not?' I asked, whilst reminding myself not to call Shane's dad a caveman as my dad had done the night before.

Shane kicked a stone aimlessly across the tarmac. 'Dunno. Just can't.'

'Oh. Do you think it's because my mummy made that stew?'

'Dunno really. Probably. But I don't know why that means we can't still be friends. It was just a stupid stew.'

'But...'

But what? I was only a child and I didn't understand what went on in the minds of grown-ups to make such silly decisions. Shane and I were best friends, so why weren't we allowed to be just that?

'Let's still play.'

'What?'

'Let's still play,' said Shane. 'My dad won't know will he?'

'But...you might get into trouble.'

'Not if we both promise to keep it a secret. He won't find out then will he? I'm sure none of the teachers know.'

So that's what we did. For the next couple of days we carried on as usual, with Shane organising games of Tag and Bulldog, or the two of us would just wander around together, making up whatever nonsensical fun sprang to mind. The only difference was that once outside school we had to maintain a distance. There could be no playing together outside on the pavements of Foxhole Avenue, but then with Mike on hand to restrict Shane's movements this was never even a possibility.

But on the third day everything changed. A snitch had put paid to our plans, and we had both been naive enough not to have considered the spy in our midst. Caroline had obviously clocked the two of us playing together during one fun-packed lunch hour and had then gleefully gone home and told Mike. To say this in such a way perhaps makes Caroline sound like more of a trouble maker than she truly was. To put it in perspective, she was an eleven year old girl in her last year at junior school, who enjoyed (if enjoyed is the right word) a traditional sibling rivalry with her younger brother. Siblings everywhere around the world tell tales on each other to their parents, to experience a feeling of power, to gain favour or simply as an attention seeking exercise. Shane and Caroline were no different.

'Hello, Shane,' I said that morning once I was certain that Mike had dropped his son off and left.

Shane looked around cagily. 'Adam, I can't play with you anymore.'

'Why? I promise I won't tell. It's our secret.'

'Caroline will see. She told dad last night. I got really told off. He smacked me.'

'Oh! Did it hurt?' My parents never smacked me so the concept was a little scary, and I suppose I also felt guilty that Shane had suffered because of our plan.

'Not really. A bit I suppose.' Shane was likely trying to appear tough by not admitting to the pain. 'So, I'll see you later. At least we will still be sitting together during class.' With that he ran off before Caroline saw us and starting kicking a tennis ball around the playground with the other boys from our year.

I stood in the playground, alone, whilst the rest of the boys charged around haphazardly after the ball, like a horde of ants scurrying frantically to and fro from a disturbed nest. It was at that moment that I fully realised how important Shane was to my school life. Without him by my side I was the loner. The kid that always seemed to spend his lunch-times walking with the dinner ladies as they patrolled the playground. The boy that nobody really wanted to be with. Shane's natural charisma meant other children gravitated towards him, and he was always, without fail, one of the first people to be asked to join in with various games. If he was to be the one that the other boys wanted to play with then that meant I would be excluded thanks to Mike's decree and Caroline's prying eyes. The immediate future looked miserable.

Sure enough at morning break the boys from my class continued where they had left off, kicking the tennis ball backwards and forwards and scuffing their shoes on the unforgiving floor. My friend was the type of person who took naturally to any sport he tried his hand at, whereas I most certainly did not. He was recognised as one of the best football players in our class, while I was at the other end of the spectrum, and consequently everyone always wanted Shane to play and to be on their team. Although I was far from the next Pelé, I still enjoyed football and wanted to join in, and yet how could I when I knew that such a selfish action could result in further punishment for Shane. Even at such a tender age I was still smart enough to realise that getting a friend into trouble was not the done thing.

I watched from my position on a bench as the boys rampaged around the playground, laughing and screaming their enjoyment at the freedom of play, innocence in motion. At one point I caught Shane's eye, but then he was quickly distracted again as the ball passed near, causing him to set-off in hot pursuit, like a dog on a walk allowed off the leash. *As long as you're having fun,* I remember thinking to myself sulkily.

My relief as the bell sounded to signify the end of play was palpable, even though morning break was only fifteen minutes long. How would I get through lunch-time today, not to mention the countless breaks and lunch-times that stretched away ahead of me? As an adult this wouldn't be such a big deal. You would go for a walk, read a book, or entertain yourself on a mobile phone. Your greater age has also likely bestowed upon you increased social skills and confidence to make new friends within various circles, but adults are also much more comfortable spending time alone. As a child you just want to be involved, you *need* to be involved, yet the skills to handle such a situation are tantalisingly out of reach.

Thinking about this now I almost feel that I owed my friend an apology. Several times already during our young friendship he had demonstrated a surprisingly mature and sensitive nature. An understanding of how people are feeling, or of my feelings at least. For example, he noticed my distress on my first day of school and he also did his best to help when my shoe was taken. As I enviously watched him playing football that day I both misjudged and underestimated him.

Once we were all settled back in the class-room, and been instructed by the teacher to get on with some task or other, our table of six started chattering away amiably about the latest television programmes, what we'd been up to that weekend or whatever random thoughts popped into our heads. Never one to take the lead in conversations I sat even more quietly than usual as my classmates voices jabbed at my bubble of silence, threatening to pop it with their joviality. All I could think about was how to entertain myself at lunch-time, how was I going to make that lonely hour pass? Walking around by myself kicking a stone? Chatting to the dinner ladies in a desperate quest for companionship?

And then Shane spoke. His words like a knight in shining armour that rode upon the white steed of his voice.

'Adam, at lunch time it's your turn to play.' He spoke loud enough so that all on our table, and perhaps those on the adjacent tables, could hear.

'Pardon?' I had heard him, but didn't quite follow his meaning, or wanted to make sure that I wasn't only hearing what I wanted to hear.

'We can take it in turns. I played this morning, so at lunch-time it's your turn. Tomorrow we can swap round, to be fair.

I will play at lunch time and you play at morning break. What do ya think? Just 'til me dad stops being grumpy.'

Everybody in our class was aware of our situation, perhaps even the teachers, so there were no questioning glances, just curious ones. I wonder if the teachers had approached Mike about his decision, to discuss it with him and perhaps explain how important mine and Shane's relationship was. Most likely they stayed out of it, watching us closely to see if the situation would resolve itself.

'OK, Shane. That's fair. Thank-you.'

'I hope this won't be forever, Adam.'

'Me too.'

My feelings of relief and gratitude were interspersed with guilt. I had watched Shane playing football that morning with anger bred from jealousy, thinking him to be selfish and uncaring. Wrong! Incorrect! Nil point!

Chapter 6

Karen and my mum sat in our small lounge drinking tea and chatting. She had only been released from jail two days before but had eagerly accepted my mum's invite for a drink and a catch-up.

'I'll say something to you once and once only,' my mum began, 'and that is: hold your head up high. I watched you as you crossed the road over to our house just now, and you looked like all you wanted to do was hide.'

'People are bound to be talking though, Sam, ain't they?"

'Well, let them talk. It's none of their business and they'll soon tire of it. You made a mistake, but you felt your back was against the wall. I'm still cross with you for not asking for help, mind, but I understand why you didn't. Next time I won't be so understanding though, you hear?'

'Thanks. Sam. I appreciate that.'

'It's no problem. Just don't go around feeling like you owe people an explanation. You're a good person, it's just that things haven't been going your way of late.'

Sat upon the floor, Shane and I were busy constructing opposing fleets of paper aeroplanes. He was representing the UK and I was Germany. We had each set-up our rows of plastic soldiers which the paper aeroplanes would soon be targeting as they swooped down upon the small figures like hawks bearing down on defenceless voles. Every now and then Molly would toddle over to the pair of us and do her best to join in, which generally meant accidentally knocking over the lines of soldiers or stepping on the planes. At two years old she wanted to get involved in everything and, as frustrating as it was for both of us, we were very patient with her. Her almost permanent sunny disposition made it virtually impossible to get mad with the girl, even if she was inadvertently ruining our game.

'Talking of help,' said Karen, 'I'm hoping there is something ya can do for us.'

'As I said, I'd be cross if you didn't ask.'

'Well, oh, I don't really like to. It's too much.'

'Will you just come out with it? The worst I can say is no.'

'Alright, I was wondering if ya can look after Shane and Molly during the week? It would be from around two o'clock until Mike gets back around six. And only three days a week. Shane will be at school for some of that of course, and I'd pay you.'

'Oh, don't be silly, Karen. I'm not going to take any money from you. I'd love to help out. It'd be my pleasure. Your children are no bother. Have you found more work or something?'

'Yep. It's the same job as before. I went to see me boss yesterday to ask for extra hours, and for once luck was on my side. He had to let one of the other bar-maids go. She'd had her hands in the till you see. I was worried he wouldn't want me back after what had happened, but he wasn't even interested in talking about it once I brought it up. As far as he's concerned my time spent inside never happened. He told me I'd always been a good worker, and that I was popular with the punters.

I listened closely to everything that was being said with one ear, whilst Shane's fighter craft laid waste to my rapidly expiring ground troops.

'What about Mike then? You said he won't be home until six.'

'Well, yeah. I think me fortunes are changing. He's got himself a job as well. It's a three year contract type thing, working on that new estate just round the corner from the playground at Parkside Road. You know it? Orchard Estate or something.' My mum nodded as Karen took another gulp of her tea. 'e got offered it a coupla weeks ago, and should start next Monday. One of his mates from Chelsea put his name forward.'

'That's great news. Really pleased to hear it,' said my mum as she brushed some biscuit crumbs from her lap onto the floor. 'You'll have so much cash you won't know what to spend it on!'

'It'll make a nice blinkin' change. I just need to make sure that useless oaf of mine don't go and blow it this time. 'e gets so impatient sometimes with the managers or foremen or whatever, that 'e just loses his temper and they boot 'im off the job. 'e's promised that 'e's gonna do his bit now though. Apparently me being inside has made him realise he needs to get his act together.'

The two women continued to chat away about how life in prison had been for Karen, whilst Shane and I proceeded to wage war. Shane had discovered that by tearing a small section away from the bottom of the planes you could allow small screwed up pieces of paper, or bombs as we saw them, to fall from the fuselage mid-flight. Now we commenced with propelling them over our mothers' and Molly's heads to see if we could land successful strikes. Molly giggled delightfully as the paper missiles flew over her head and she chased after them gleefully with her clumsy toddle, invariably stepping on them or falling over.

'Mike told me that 'e had stopped Shane playing with Adam whilst I was away. I'm sorry, Sam. The boys can play together again now. I don't know what got into 'im. I tried to talk to him about it, but didn't really get anywhere.'

My mum waved away Karen's embarrassed apology with a slender hand. 'Don't worry about it. It probably did them good to be apart for a while.'

'I don't know what got into 'im. What was 'e thinking about stopping 'em playing. If your Adam was trouble I could understand. I've put 'im straight on that one.'

'Ah, well, Mike was under a lot of pressure. People don't always make sound judgements when they're stressed about things. You hear that, Adam, you and Shane can play together at school again.'

'Really? Hurray!' I tried to sound surprised but Shane had already passed this excellent news onto me the moment he arrived.

'But I just don't understand what 'e was thinking. Why would 'e go and make a stupid rule up like that?' Karen ran her hand wearily through her fair hair. It was scraggly and unkempt and the darker roots of her natural colour smugly revealed the untruth of the bleached locks. 'And then to cap it all off 'e goes and turns down your kind offer of a stew. When 'e told me that I was so cross with 'im. I'm so sorry, Sam. 'e can be so rude sometimes it makes me wanna tear me hair out.'

My mum reached forward and rubbed her friend's arm. 'You've got nothing to apologise for. It's not a problem. Really. I'm just glad to hear things are hopefully looking up for you at last. It's already forgotten about.'

'e's not a bad egg really you know, my Mike. I mean, I know that e's got a bit of a temper about 'im, and 'e's not very patient with people, but his heart is in the right place. 'E adores the kids, that's obvious, and 'e even said how much 'e missed us whilst I was in jail. 'e was very pleased to have me home again.

'I've often wondered though,' continued Karen, 'why 'im and your Trevor have never really gotten on. Why'd you think that is?'

'Oh I don't know. I suppose they just haven't got much in common.'

'Do you think that's it? I dunno. I mean, I know that you and 'im don't have much to do with each other, but you'd think the two blokes would. After all they both like football and sport, they're both into DIY. We get on, the kids get on. I just think it would be nice if all of us could spend a nice evening together. You know, like a social thing.'

'Well, I wouldn't say that they don't get on. It's more a case that they haven't really ever had a chance to get to know each other.'

'Well,' said Karen, 'perhaps us girls should sort something out then.'

'Hmmm.' My mum's response was totally non-committal and I noticed her perfect teeth were clenched together as they would often be whenever I was in trouble. 'Yes, maybe we should sort something out sometime.' The tone of my mum's voice made me look up at her from my position on the floor. Somehow her words sounded strained or like they were being spoken by somebody doing a bad impression of her voice. Then she stood-up and announced she would get some more tea and biscuits, which effectively closed a topic of conversation she blatantly had no desire to entertain. Karen coughed uncomfortably, clearly aware of the change in mood, and then filled the temporary silence by questioning us on our paper aeroplanes.

The arrangement that our parents had agreed upon worked out perfectly for Shane and I in the ensuing months. We had gone from not being allowed to play together to spending more time than ever in each other's company as Karen gratefully accepted her boss's offer of more work. Caring for two extra children was a big deal, especially as one of them, Molly, was still very young. Her chilled out nature obviously made life a lot easier but she still took a lot of looking after, as no two year olds are capable of doing much for themselves. Us two boys were that bit older meaning having Shane at our house was in truth little extra work for my mum. If anything his presence made life easier for her, as I was entertained and therefore never hounded her with whines of *I'm bored* or *what can I do?*

When Karen did her best to insist that my mum take a weekly payment for her child minding duties she refused, vehemently. Our neighbour tried arguing, tactical coercion and finally resorted to posting cash through the letter box, which my mum simply used to purchase Molly some new clothes. There was nothing Karen could do to convince her friend that her generosity warranted some form of reward, so in the end she gave up and instead purchased the odd bunch of flowers here and there to show her gratitude.

'I don't know why you can't just take a bit of money from her each week,' complained my dad one evening over dinner.

'We've been through this, Trevor.'

'God-knows we could use a little extra money ourselves. I'm never going to make my fortune driving that blinkin' bus.'

'They've been through some hard times, and they've got more mouths to feed. They're just starting to get their finances in order.'

'Yeah, but what about our finances? I didn't ask them to have three kids did I? The boy keeps growing into new clothes, and his plate looks fuller each time you plonk it on the table. Can't you stop growing, Adam?'

'No. I want to be big, Dad, like you.'

'I'm not backing down on this one, Trevor. I'm happy to help them out. I want to.'

'Well,' said my dad resignedly, 'I can see I'm wasting my breath on this one, but I don't get why you're always so keen to help Karen out. I mean, I know you're mates and all that, but you seem to go beyond the realms of what any friendship I've got covers. It's not like you're *really* good mates or anything. Yeah, you get on well and share the odd cuppa, but it doesn't go much further than that. Too blinkin' generous for your own good you are.'

Perhaps my dad was right, I thought at the time. My mum was doing a big favour for her friend, so it wouldn't have hurt her to accept a small recompense. But, truthfully, I didn't care. My best mate and I were enjoying the extra time we got to play, and I found that I adored seeing so much of Molly as well. I bonded with Shane's younger sister, and she constantly had me in fits of laughter with her cute attempts at new words or funny facial expressions. Before too long she was just as excited to see me as she was her brother when we returned home from school and she felt almost like a sister to me.

There's one other observation to make from this turn of events in my young life, which is that the women in the two relationships seemed to wear the trousers. Firstly Karen had obviously over-ruled Mike's ban on her son spending time with me, and secondly my mum had won the argument with my dad in regards to offering her free baby-sitting service.

My mum had shown that she was a determined woman. Just how determined she could prove to be I had no idea.

Chapter 7

I was eight years old when I realised that Mike, hadn't exactly taken a shine to me. This realisation dawned on me during the uncomfortable incident with the conkers. Looking back there were other indications before this, other hints of his dislike for me, such as snide remarks when Shane popped to the toilet and we were left alone, or dirty looks whilst I giggled with my friend at some ridiculous game. I had noticed previously that he always seemed to be grumpy around me, I wasn't a total idiot, but I just assumed it was the way he behaved with everybody. But, that time with the conkers was as if he decided to make his ill-feeling clearly obvious.

As far as Shane and I were concerned Foxhole Avenue was a great place to grow up. We spent countless days playing either at each other's houses or outside on the street together. Such was the sense of community that was felt in our neighbourhood, that we were afforded a freedom that would perhaps be considered as reckless by many adults today. I'm sure that our parents kept a closer eye on us than we realised as we gallivanted up and down the street, with frequent glances out of the front windows, but wrapped up in the excitement of our games we were oblivious.

The gentle slope of our road meant it was perfect for performing acts of daring-do on anything with wheels. Bikes; roller skates; scooters; skateboards. You name it, we rode it. Countless hours were spent straining our young leg muscles to propel us up the hill in order to enjoy the speedy trip back down that was our reward. Impromptu ramps, made of old wooden planks and spare bricks, were often introduced, to add extra spice to our downhill dashes. Obstacle courses, time trials, games of tag, cops and robbers - all played out on sets on two or four wheels. Scraped knees and bumped heads were par for the course, without a single safety helmet in sight to protect the precious paving stones from being stained crimson.

As well as Shane and I, there were plenty of other children roughly our age that would frequently join in our games. Sometimes there could be as many as ten of us trundling up and down the pavements outside our houses, like a troop of tireless worker ants plodding back and forth between their nest and some mouth-watering food source.

Shane's natural charisma, that I have previously alluded to, shone through when these larger groups were assembled, and the rest of us naturally looked to him to take the lead in the games we were playing. Even at such a young age he just had a presence about him that emanated confidence to others. His peers felt relaxed in his company, knowing that there was one amongst them who was in control.

Whereas my friend rose to the fore in larger groups I was the opposite and sank backwards into the crowd. I didn't want to be the one who determined the rules of a game or what the sides were going to be. I had no desire to be the one in the spotlight making important decisions such as where the baddies base should be located, or where the start and finish points were for a particular race. No thank-you. That wasn't the way I was then and it isn't the way I am now either.

When playing outside with the other children from the street Shane would always ensure that, if we were playing a team game, we were always on the same side, be it the good guys or the bad. Once one of the other boys remarked on this happy co-incidence and questioned why we always had to be together. *He's my best friend*, Shane had responded with a shrug, *so of course he's going to be on my side.* The boy earnt himself a glare, as if he was some kind of idiot, until he blushed and started self-consciously kicking at the floor with his pair of already badly scuffed trainers. I don't remember anyone else ever questioning this again.

If we weren't playing some sort of game that involved speeding around on wheels then we could still normally be found outside, whatever the season or weather. In the spring we would sometimes just sit on the pavement and simply pick the moss from between the paving slabs in long oblong chunks of dirt, seeing who could free the longest, single, unbroken piece from its concrete sandwich. This would then descend into an inevitable battle, with the moss being pelted back and forth, and a head shot in particular greeted with much laughter. Summer would have us hunting for opposing ant nests - one red and one black - capturing a hero from each side and then placing them inside a clear, perspex pencil sharpener container to battle to the death in the name of the Dark Queen or the Scarlet Empress. Cold winter days were spent splashing in puddles, spinning carefreely in the wind or, if fortune smiled upon us and it snowed, having snowball fights and making ice slides on the pavements.

As for autumn, that brought with it the joy of conkers.

Every year, at least until we were considered old enough to go on our own, my dad would take Shane and I to the local woods which was populated with an abundance of Horse Chestnut trees. Our primary aim: to take home as many conkers as our carrier bags would hold. Our secondary and most important aim: to find the Champion of Conkers; the Destroyer; the Destructor; the Obliterator; to find a conker so tough and so resilient, that all its kin would quiver at the very sight of this hero in their midst. A conker to be worshipped. A conker to be adored. A conker to take over the world.

The process of getting the conkers out of the tree was simple. Find a stick, as big a stick as you can manage, and propel that stick high into the tree canopy. Throw it high enough and hard enough and your reward will be a shower of conkers thumping to the ground around your feet as they get brutally snatched from the branches - or at least the protective spiky outer casing that holds the prize will plummet down. Next simply apply firm yet gentle pressure to the spiky chrysalis with the heel of your trainer and, hey presto, the conkers are yours.

Typically Shane always used to have greater success at this fun challenge than I did. Being bigger and stronger than me he always chose heavier sticks and he always launched them further and harder into the branches than I could. I sometimes wondered if this made me a disappointment in my father's eyes, but knowing him as I do now I find this notion laughable.

Regardless of who managed to secure the most conkers from the trees, at the end of the day we always both took home a full bag each, especially as my dad knocked enough out of the tree to fill a suitcase. Even when we were considered old enough to go to the woods by ourselves the spoils were divided evenly between us.

'You take the most, Shane. You got 'em,' I would sheepishly protest as my friend shared them out.

'No, it's a joint effort. We'll share them evenly. Fifty-fifty. I might have knocked most out of the trees, but you picked the most up.'

Shane had a way of making his decisions sound so final and so definite that it was clear when a topic was closed to further discussion.

I'm getting ahead of myself. The game of 'conkers' is a dying art in this sorry world of playground health and safety overkill, so perhaps I should explain what the whole purpose of this squirreling of the horse chestnut's finest is all about. When I used to go to school it seemed that almost everybody would be busy playing conkers, but since then the game has been banned in schools up and down the length of the United Kingdom. In my opinion, as somebody who has fond memories (mostly) of playing conkers, this is a great shame.

To play you first need a conker, which probably won't come as too much of a shock. Choose carefully now as you want one that is not just hard, but invincible. Do you opt for the biggest, roundest vessel you can find, or instead choose a flatter champion, commonly referred to in conker circles as a 'cheese-cutter'? Take your time now, choose wisely because only the strongest survive. Next you need to ask an adult to push a hot skewer through the centre of the horse chestnut seed until you have a hole large enough to squeeze a piece of string about a foot long. Tie a large knot in the end of the string so that your conker is secured. Hey presto, you've got one new gladiator ready to fight to the death at your command.

Now the all important rules and object of the game. Simply stated two players take turns to swing their conker at their opponent's until one of them breaks apart leaving an empty piece of string swaying in the breeze. Players must also agree on the finer rules prior to the battle. For example, you can have a rule called 'windmills' whereby if you send your opponents conker into a full 360 degree revolution (as in the sails of a windmill) then you get an extra go to smash your warrior into thine enemy's, and to smite him down.

Another rule, and one that most people tended not to use, and that Shane and I *never* used, was 'stampsies'. Stampsies only comes into play if, following a successful strike on your opponent's conker, it is knocked from their hand to the floor. Now it is a race - can the owner of the conker pick it up from the ground before the attacker rushes over and stamps on the fallen combatant, squashing it into the ground with the heel of their shoe in a merciless act that almost certainly ends in destruction? Shane and I always agreed that stampsies simply wasn't allowed. We considered it unsporting. This, after all, was a battle between two brave conkers, and stampsies was akin to a boxer hiding a horseshoe inside his boxing glove.

The day that I realised Mike was far from my biggest fan was a beautifully sunny yet mild autumn afternoon. I had spent the morning with Shane and my dad collecting conkers from the local woods, and we had then returned home to prepare some of the poor little buggers for a fate worse than that imposed on dodgems at a travelling fairground. We had made plans that after lunch I would go over to Shane's house to commence battle and to enjoy a marathon conker session.

Just before I crossed over Foxhole Avenue I recalled that I still had a particularly curious looking conker from last year. When I had freed it from its protective spiky cocoon twelve months ago it had been completely white and soft to the touch, rather than displaying the usual hard brown shell of a fully ripe specimen. At the time my dad had suggested that I leave it on the window ledge in my bedroom to see if it would 'ripen' and change colour. Interested to see what would happen I took his advice and gradually, over the course of a few weeks, the conker turned brown, albeit a much lighter brown than its rivals. Not only this, but the hard outer shell that developed wasn't smooth as with your standard conker, but instead had a shrivelled up appearance as if it had been left lying in the bath for too long. It was a conker that was never going to win any beauty pageants, but, on impulse, I asked my mum to quickly string it and then slipped it into my pocket before trotting over to Shane's.

When I arrived he was in the back garden threading string through the last few of his chosen conkers. His garden was south-facing, benefitting from sunshine for most of the day, and sloped sharply upwards towards the perimeter fence at the rear. A row of grey concrete steps stretched from the bottom to the top, granting easy access to three distinct levelled tiers that had been built into the slope to create a workable garden on an otherwise unusable space. Our battle ground was the patio on the lowest level closest to the house, and before long we were off and running. Conker smashed into conker time and time again with audible crunches that would have made the mother horse chestnut tree raise her branches to the sky in a desperate plea for leniency had she been present. Shane's brilliant blue eyes sparkled whilst his chaotic blonde hair bounced around enthusiastically with every successful strike that he scored. The patio outside the backdoor was littered with the carcasses of the fallen, shards of their broken brown bodies scattered from one corner to the next.

After a while Caroline, appeared. She was now eleven years old and had just started secondary school, and consequently looked down upon the two of us 'little children', who were merely eight years old.

'Who's winning?' she asked, her freckly, yet pretty, face enquired.

Shane looked up. 'Me. Adam's one's got a bad crack.'

'I'll play the winner,' she said with a bossy, assumed dominance.

'You haven't got any conkers,' replied Shane.

'That's where you're wrong, Blondy. I took a handful out of your bag.' I always thought she had some front to laugh at her brother for his hair colour when her own ginger mane was equally as striking.

'Hey, they're mine. I didn't say...'

She held up a hand towards her brother. 'Don't cry about it. Mum said I could take some. Go ask her if you like. Besides, you've got plenty.'

Shane narrowed his eyes at her and took a swing at my conker, with a touch more vehemence previously exhibited I couldn't help noticing.

The battle continued for only a few more rounds when a meaty attack from Shane smashed my conker to pieces. I stood there, defeated, grasping the empty string like a boy holding the cord to a burst balloon which hung uselessly at his side.

'Right, my turn,' chirruped Caroline and she went back into the house, the back door from which led directly into the galley style kitchen. From where we were standing we could see that she was getting something out of the freezer, and when she came back out again the conker that she held was covered in a frosty sheen.

'Hey,' protested Shane, 'you can't do that. That's cheating. You're not allowed to freeze them.'

'Who says it's cheating? I thought the only rule you had was no stampsies.'

'Yeah, but...'

'But nothing, Blondy. Last year you painted some of yours in nail varnish, so what's the difference? Anyway, I'm just doing an experiment. It might not even make them any better.'

'I didn't even say you could play.'

'Oh, stop being a baby! What's the matter? Scared you're going to lose?'

Shane looked at me with a scowl upon his face. 'Come on, Adam, let's smash her conkers to bits.'

Looking carefully at his selection of conkers that were already strung, Shane chose the biggest and meatiest of the bunch, and stepped forward to stand in front of his sister.

'You can go first if you like,' she said, full of confidence.

Shane pulled back his chosen combatant and swung with gusto.

For the next twenty minutes I watched as Caroline's first conker destroyed three of my friend's in quick succession. The frosty jacket from her own was by now long gone, but the conker itself appeared seemingly unblemished, despite some impressive strikes from Shane.

'It's not fair,' moaned Shane. 'You cheated.'

'*It's not fair,*' she mimicked. 'You're just a bad loser, that's all.'

Just then Mike strolled into the garden via the back door. He was wearing some tatty overalls and had white paint over his big hands where he had been decorating the hallway. He took a cigarette from his pocket and lit up.

'What's all the whining?'

'Shane's being a bad loser because my conker has smashed three of his in a row.'

'She put her conkers in the freezer. That's cheating,' complained Shane again.

'No, coz he agreed the only rule was no stampsies.' Mike chuckled to himself. His stocky frame looked like it could shake the conkers out of a tree without the need to throw a stick into the branches. Like his son he also had blonde hair, although his was cropped short, and I don't think I ever heard Caroline call Shane 'Blondy' when her dad was present.

'Sounds to me like you two boys are just being a coupla babies. Just get on and play, or are ya frightened of losing to a girl?' He took a hefty drag on his cigarette and blew the smoke carelessly towards the sun.

Shane looked at me. 'Go on, you have a go.'

'OK.' I rarely had much to say in front of Mike. His appearance invariably brought with it a change of atmosphere and previous confrontations over Violet's dog fouling the pavement and when Karen was in jail, had left me uneasy in his presence.

Sifting through my conkers I couldn't decide which one was best to use, when my hand rested on the side of my leg and I felt a small bulge in my pocket. Reaching in I pulled out the wrinkled up conker that I had kept from last year. *Why not,* I thought to myself as I looked at the pathetic specimen. *What is there to lose?*

'What's that?' laughed Caroline as soon as she saw it. 'Is it a grandad conker or something? I'd like to see you use that shrivelled up thing.'

'Maybe you should choose another one, Adam.' Shane was looking at my conker with ill-disguised dismay.

'I think I'm going to stick with this one. It's from last autumn. Maybe they were made stronger last year or something.'

'Pah! Idiot,' laughed Caroline. 'How dumb!'

I moved to stand opposite her and she sneered at me meanly, a half smile upon her face. 'I'm gonna smash that ugly little bugger to smithereens,' she said, clearly unconcerned about using such language in front of her dad.

I remember thinking that I didn't know what 'smithereens' meant, but it certainly didn't sound very nice.

'The champion gets to go first,' she declared. 'Hold your pathetic excuse for a conker up.'

I raised my conker and held it at arm's length away from my face. Caroline stood poised with her undefeated warrior held back between the first two fingers of her left hand, whilst her right pulled the string taut. In a flash she swung it forwards and down in a wide arc, like the arm of a siege catapult releasing its load. There was a sickening *thwack* as the two came together, and my conker flew up and over in a complete circle.

'Windmill,' she claimed. 'I get another go.'

Again, Caroline attacked, but this time with less accuracy and she inflicted only a glancing blow.

My turn. I pulled my conker back, its wrinkled body nestled between my small fingers, and let fly. My aim was true and I scored a direct hit. Smack!

Shane's sister peered at her conker and a stunned look appeared on her face.

'You've cracked it,' she said looking at the large crevasse that had appeared on her previously indestructible champion. 'With your first hit! Lemme see yours!'

Reaching forward she grabbed my conker and turned it over in her hand, hoping to find some weakness or sign of deterioration. There were none.

'Right. Hold it up again,' she demanded. 'Keep your arm still.'

I did as instructed and she swung once more, but missed, her dismay having affected her concentration.

Pulling my conker back I could see Mike looking on with interest from the corner of my eye. I did my best to ignore him and focused on my intended target as I released my missile.

Another direct hit and Caroline's conker shattered, pieces flying everywhere like a detonated frag bomb.

'Yes,' I said quietly, but Shane was much more enthusiastic at this act of retribution. He clapped me heartily on the back and whooped his congratulations with undisguised joy.

Caroline, on the other hand, had a look of darkening rage on her face, and the more her brother hollered, the angrier she became which, on reflection, was likely Shane's intention.

Glancing round my eyes locked briefly with Mike's. I pulled away quickly, reluctant to interact with him in any way unless absolutely necessary, but that split second was enough to register that the look on his face mirrored his daughter's.

It was Mike that spoke next, and there was an icy edge to his voice that cut through Shane's excessive adulation.

'Caroline, quit moping girl and get another one outta the freezer. That one was already weakened.'

Doing as instructed, and with no little enthusiasm for anticipated revenge, she ducked back into the kitchen and reappeared with another conker, complete with frost jacket.

'Come on then, Adam, let's see ya smash this one,' she said, her confidence restored and her freckles almost twinkling.

Again we faced each other, although this time, as reigning champion I went first.

I swung and missed by a mile, this time my own concentration affected by the sudden confrontational atmosphere.

Caroline swung. She struck home, hard.

My turn. A firm strike.

Caroline. A pile driver to the centre of my conker.

A hit. A miss. A glancing blow.

I swung again and my heart leapt as Caroline's conker disappeared in an explosion of brown shell. The string hung limply from her hand, forlornly, and she stared at it with disbelief.

'That's one hard nut you've got there, Adam,' said Shane squeezing my conker. 'It might be ugly but it's like a rock.'

His celebrations were more muted than before. Was it because he was feeling a little bit sorry for his sister, who had been so full of confidence, or because he too had detected the tone in his father's voice?

'I'm not playing this anymore,' said Caroline.

Mike cut in again. 'What are ya talking about, girl? Go get another conker from the freezer! Ya get beat, ya dust yourself down and go again. Come out fighting!'

The atmosphere, already uncomfortable thanks to Caroline's disappointment and Mike's unnerving presence, was hardly aided by his latest comment. Was it simply a case of his oldest child being his favourite and his hatred of seeing her lose, be it to his own son or his son's friend? Or was this a more personal vendetta against me? Did he have some issue with me? Could he not stand to see the tall and gangly kid from across the street triumph against his daughter in a harmless game of conkers?

'But, Dad, I don't want...'

'Just...get...the...conker.'

In a moment of rare boldness, I spoke up. 'I think I need to go home now anyway. This seemed the easy way to diffuse the situation.

Mike turned and stared at me, and he took a long drag on his cigarette. The lion from the Chelsea tattoo on his forearm seemed to be glaring at me too, as if it was itching to flare into life, leap from his flesh and tear my throat out.

'This won't take long,' he said. There was no argument, no question of me leaving at that moment. 'Stay put!'

Caroline retrieved a third conker from the freezer and stood opposite me once more. I could already picture how this was going to finish. I was feeling surer and surer that this conker of mine, as ugly as it was, just wasn't going to lose. Whether last year's conkers were harder, or whether it was simply that over the course of the past year it had hardened more than the new season's brood had yet had time to do, I wasn't sure. But I did know that it had obliterated two of Caroline's frozen conkers, and that my mum had also had a real struggle to skewer a hole in the damn thing in the first place.

With Mike looking on I prayed that Caroline would win, but knew that my hopes would be in vain.

I swung and hit. A windmill. A free shot. A miss.

Caroline half-heartedly attacked. She connected weakly.

My turn again. Another hit.

Caroline. A miss.

A miss.

A hit.

Another hit, a loud crunch, and yet again a large crack had appeared in Caroline's conker whilst mine remained unharmed.

With one last throw of the dice she pulled back her conker and let fly with more enthusiasm than she had so far mustered for this third match. Her aim was true and her conker smacked into mine with all the force of a plummeting wooden mallet swung in an attempt to ring a bell at a fair ground stall.

As before her conker shattered into pieces, but this time the force of her blow had ripped the undefeated conker from my hand and it went flying across the garden, with the string still attached, where it landed helplessly at Mike's feet.

Mike looked down at the conker. He looked up and me, sneered and very quickly made a decision. Lifting his booted foot he simply said 'stampsies,' drawing each syllable out slowly and pausing momentarily for added malice, before bringing his heel down hard onto my vulnerable champion. He twisted his boot on top of the nut as if he was grinding out a cigarette, before lifting it once more to reveal the shattered shell and carcass of my previously indestructible talisman.

With a satisfied grunt he headed back in doors leaving the three of us to stand there dumb-founded and not knowing what to say to each other.

'Now you can go home,' he called as he disappeared back into the house.

Chapter 8

Life in Foxhole Avenue and at s<del>ome</del> relaxed weekly routine for a time. Since <del>...</del> her prison spell Mike was holding onto his job an<del>d</del> be trying harder to be a good husband and father and a <del>le</del> problematic neighbour, even if those efforts didn't extend towards me. For her own part, Karen found that taking on the extra hours at the pub gave a welcome boost to the family coffers and the pressure on her to feed five hungry mouths was relieved considerably.

My own family seemed happier than ever. My parents had always been blessed with a relationship fed by contentment and this filtered down to me in the way that they behaved towards each other, along with their obvious willingness to fool around with their only child simply to elicit a beaming smile from my young face. My mum was clearly enjoying her role as babysitter for Molly and the arrangement with Shane stopping by after school for a couple of hours was also working out well. In between her babysitting duties, and looking after our family, she had taken on the role of a local dog-walker, getting paid to entertain man's best friend whilst the best friend's man was stuck in some office, factory or building site. This was an ideal arrangement for her, as it fitted easily around her other tasks, whilst she effectively got paid to exercise and spend time with a variety of lovable hounds, and some not so lovable.

'If ya love dogs so much then why don't ya get one of your own?' Shane asked my mum one day.

'Dogs are a tie, Shane. You've always got to make sure you get home to let them out to do their business.'

'So hire a dog-walker then.'

'But I'm the dog-walker round here! I don't want people stealing my business.'

'My dad doesn't want one anyway,' I chimed in. 'He it would chew everything and piss everywhere.'

Shane sniggered at my rude comment.

'Adam! I've told you I don't want to hear you using that word, especially in front of Molly.'

'But dad says it,' I protested.

'Yes, I know he does, but that doesn't mean that you can too. I'll have a word with him about it later.'

My mum started to walk away with a basket of wet washing cradled under her arm, but Shane's next question brought her back.

'Why don't ya have a baby instead?'

'A baby!' she laughed, surprised. 'Where did that question come from? Looking after Molly is plenty enough for me thank-you very much.'

'But if ya have a baby then Adam could have a brother or sister to play with,' continued my friend.

My mum turned to face me. 'Do you wish you had a brother or sister of your own, darling?'

'I dunno,' I said shrugging my shoulders helpfully.

She turned to Shane. 'Has he told you he would like one, Shane?'

'No.' It was true. I hadn't. 'I just thought if you couldn't have a dog perhaps you could have a baby instead.'

My mum laughed, but it sounded forced somehow, unnatural. 'And what would I call it? Rover? Snoopy? No, I can't be having another baby. I'm getting too old for all that now.' She had a point. My mum was approaching her mid-forties.

'I don't think I need one anyway,' I said. 'I mean, Shane is almost always here and if he isn't then he's only across the road.'

'And me, Adnam' said Molly, grabbing me around the neck with two chubby arms as I sat on the floor looking at my Panini football stickers with Shane.

'Yes, we can't forget about you, Molly-darling,' said my mum. 'Anyway, you boys carry on with your game and stop all this gassing. I need to hang this washing up if Trevor's to have a dry shirt for tomorrow.'

My mum disappeared into the garden with her washing whilst Molly skipped happily after her. Shane and I returned to the serious business of swapping football stickers. The two of us were at an age where we were starting to grow up. Shane and I were ten years old, and Molly was four going-on five. Our parents were starting to allow us a little more freedom - we were allowed to walk home from school together and to ride our bikes as far as the adjacent street, provided that we weren't gone for too long. They were obviously well aware that soon it was time for us to attend secondary school, and that greater independence would go hand in hand with such a stage in our lives, so perhaps had decided to gradually slacken the reins of parent-hood before they were brutally ripped free.

School days were flashing past in a blur. Myself and Shane, as well as our extended group of class-mates lived for break-times where we had struck up a friendly rivalry with the other class in our year, games of football between the two groups taking centre stage. Although I had not been blessed with feet that could mesmerise a football, I had nevertheless discovered that I was a half decent goal-keeper, and as nobody else ever wanted to go in goal I was always encouraged in this role by my peers, and even praised at times, most likely in order to keep me taking on this unpopular position. Whatever the reasoning, I felt that I was valued amongst my friends, and not just by Shane, that I belonged, which is surely all that any young child ever wants in their life.

Whilst break-times were obviously the pinnacle of the school day, I was not adverse to the day-to-day curriculum work either. Occasionally it would prove to be boring, but for the most part I found the lessons enjoyable and stimulating.

Shane didn't share my feelings, and he laboured through many of the imposed tasks with a grumble and a scowl, that is at least once our teacher had told him to stop constantly distracting the rest of our table with his persistent chatter. Yet, despite having to actually do some work at school, Shane seemed content with life in the classroom, and our friendship continued to weave a rich strand of satisfaction through our lives.

Then, one day, that happiness was again interrupted, although this time Mike was not to blame. A new boy called Robert Wall had started earlier that school year, and was placed into the same class as his twin cousins, the Jones boys, who were already pupils. The Jones Boys were a year older, but they had both been held back a year due to reasons unknown to the rest of the school, but immediately assumed by the school rumour mill to be because they were stupid. The reality is more likely they had ADHD or a similar condition, or perhaps problems at home had caused disruption to their school life. Either way, this combination of Robert Wall joining and the twins repeating their final year was to spell bad news for me, and consequently Shane.

My troubles started one lunch-time when in the boy's toilets, that most notorious of teacher blind-spots in the school community. I was about to commence washing my hands when Wall and the Jones Boys sauntered in carrying their malevolent attitudes before them like proud Olympic torch-bearers. The tap I was attempting to turn-on was stuck where somebody had closed it shut too tightly, most likely on purpose, and so I was forced to apply pressure with both hands to get the water flowing. The obvious thing to do here would be to simply move to the next sink along, but then Wall and his cousins may have noticed that my skinny little body didn't even have enough muscle to turn-on a tap, which would have undoubtedly led to unwanted embarrassment. Yet my perseverance proved to be my undoing as, at the very moment the three boys passed behind me, I freed the tap from its temporary restraint but in doing so the handle spun suddenly much further and quicker than I intended, causing water to gush from its funnel as if desperate to savour such new found freedom. The speeding water rebounded off the sides of the porcelain and breached the sink's flood defences where it then proceeded to splash all over not just me, but the passing Robert Wall and Jones Boys.

'What the...' exclaimed one of the trio.

'Whoops. I'm sorry. The tap was stuck.' My apology felt inadequate, bearing in mind who the water had attacked. I didn't know any of the boys on a personal level, but I knew who they were. Everybody did. Their notoriety proceeded them, as did tales of their bullying antics and the 'don't give a toss' attitude that both them and their parents constantly wore in their scowls.

'Wat do yer fink yer doing? I'm bloody soaking.' It was Robert Wall that had spoken.

'I'm sorry. It was an accident.' Another apology that I knew wouldn't achieve what it was intended to. The colour from my face must have drained away like a discharged cistern.

'Sorry? Yeah, you will be, Bean-Pole. Come on lads!'

The next thing I knew was that a fist had slammed into my stomach causing me to instantly double over. There was no hesitation, or chance to discuss the finer points of my transgression. I felt my head forced down towards the sink where I bashed one of my cheekbones on the same troublesome tap that seemed to have started waging some personal vendetta against me, which is rude when you consider I was the one that had freed it from its chains. Finally I felt water pouring over my head and face as the three boys held me in position, one of my eyes staring dismally down the gurgling plug-hole. They hauled me up and pushed me to one side where I fell to the floor in a sodden heap. Then, in a flash, with laughter thrown my way, they were gone again, wisely deciding not to stick around should they be caught at the scene of the crime, and presumably finding another toilet in which to empty their bladders.

The toilets seemed suddenly very quiet following the boys' rapid withdrawal. Alone again I just held back the tears and quickly pulled myself together before somebody came. A look in the mirror revealed a red mark and a lump on my cheek where the tap had assaulted me, whilst my hair was dripping wet. I dried my hair as best I could on the towel dispenser, which was one of those old fashioned linen-roller models, and straightened my uniform up, which thankfully remained fairly dry, aside from a couple of minor wet spots. There was little I could do about my impending bruise, and the area was already starting to swell up.

Once outside I took my usual place in goal for the regular lunchtime match that had already begun, but my heart wasn't in it. I kept scouring the playground for my three assailants but they were no-where to be seen. Most likely they were serving a previously organised detention or playing truant, but I couldn't shake the feeling that they were watching me. I'm sure this was simply pure paranoia brought on by the distressing experience that I had just gone through, but I was too young to appreciate this. Eyes that wander from the task at hand are not a good attribute for a goalkeeper, and when I let in a couple of weak shots my team-mates let me know their displeasure.

Amazingly it was only during the first lesson after lunch that the lump on the side of my face was noticed. During the football match all of my friends, Shane included, had been too absorbed in the game to notice and, combined with my attempts at hiding that side of my face by scratching my eye or turning my head, I had somehow kept it a secret. A girl on our bank of desks called Abby, who had gorgeous straight auburn hair and the sweetest voice, was the first one to notice.

'Adam, what happened to your face? It's all red.'

The rest of the table turned to look at me.

'Oh, yeah, look. How did you do that?' It was Shane. 'You've got a lump.'

I still hadn't decided if I was going to tell the truth or not, when my mouth made my mind up for me. 'It was Rob Wall and his two cousins. I splashed them by accident, so they hit me and pushed my head into the sink.'

'Oh my god! Does it hurt? You should tell,' said Abby, her eyes full of genuine concern. 'Those boys are horrible bullies.'

'Nah, don't tell anyone,' said Shane. 'If those three find out you've grassed them up they'll be after ya.'

The table launched into a passionate, yet whispered debate, everyone giving their opinions on the best course of action until, in the end, the general consensus was that it was best not to tell. So, that night when I got home, I lied to my mum and told her that I had bumped into another boy when diving to make a save. It was one of the days when she was also looking after Shane, so it helped to have him there to back-up my story.

'It was a good save as well, Sam. We won thanks to Adam.'

'Well, winning counts for nothing if your head gets stomped on. Just try and be more careful in future. You've already gone through the knee on one pair of trousers this term, so I could do without having to buy anymore. I don't know. You boys!'

But if I thought that was the end of the matter I was very much mistaken. Robert Wall and his hoodlum cousins, for some reason, decided that picking on me was fun, and the simple retribution that they meted out to me that day in the toilet didn't satiate their need to punish me for a perceived wrong-doing. Obviously they were three boys that thrived on violence, that enjoyed exerting some form of control over others weaker than themselves. I had simply been in the wrong place at the wrong time and if it wasn't me that had proved to be the outlet for whatever rage boiled below the surface of their skin, then it would have been some other poor soul.

The next encounter occurred at the start of the following week. For once we were playing British Bulldog rather than football, as our classmate who usually provided the ball had selfishly taken a day off sick. As I ran back and forth across the playground, like a tennis ball rejoicing in a long rally at Wimbledon, I was unaware of the six beady eyes that followed my progress. We were deep into the game and for once I was doing well. I was never the fastest of sprinters at that age, un-like the naturally athletic Shane, so to reach the latter stages and still be a runner rather than a tagger was a rarity to be savoured. Yet my joy was soon brought crashing down, as was I, when I tumbled over a maliciously placed foot and landed on the hard floor of the playground. My hands took the brunt of the sudden fall, skidding across the floor, and I howled with pain as minute stones from the floor mingled with my ripped skin.

From my position on the floor I peered up at a cloudless sky and, forced to shield my eyes from the sun with a battered hand, saw Wall and the Jones boys grinning down at me.

'Enjoy ya trip, Bean-Pole? Send us a post-card', laughed Wall. It would seem that Bean-Pole was to be my new nick-name, on account of my bourgeoning height yet lack of girth, which possibly would have given me greater presence and made me less of a target if I had been so blessed. Instead I was a lanky, scrawny, bag of bones.

'What was that for?' I whined.

'Coz I felt like it,' came the remorseless reply.

And then Shane was there, full of rage and indignation. 'What do ya think you're doing?'

'What's it got to do with you?' said Wall, the three boys now facing my friend, and seeming to revel in the crowd that had rapidly gathered around us.

'This is what it's got to do with me,' he said, and before I knew what was happening he had planted a punch squarely into the face of Robert Wall. There was no drawn out tense stand-off but an immediate decisive response from my friend. Wall, staggered back and fell onto his backside with a surprised look on his face. He clearly couldn't believe that someone had actually had the front to attack him first! The only person that ever dared lay a finger on him was most likely his own dad. Didn't this upstart realise who they were dealing with and the storm that would now result? I think the answer is that Shane certainly did know, but that he firstly wasn't afraid, and secondly would always be the type of person to stand up for himself and those closest to him.

Wall's cousins looked down at him, uncertainty evident on their faces, their hands opening and shutting nervously. This was an unexpected scenario, a previously untrodden path. No-one attacked them! Their fallen comrade had a nose-bleed but the blood was trickling rather than pouring. His screwed up face along with his closely cropped dark hair contributed towards a very intimidating appearance.

'Well,' he yelled, 'what are ya waiting for? Get 'im!'

The Jones twins, Colin and David to give them their full names, turned to face Shane and prepared to pounce, whilst Wall hauled himself up from the ground. In a cautious pincer movement the two of them began to circle my friend, but just as they were about to grab him he launched himself at their younger yet more domineering cousin and planted a second punch on the left side of his face, all be it only a glancing blow. His momentum carried him forward and in a tangle of limbs the two boys fell to the floor.

The customary playground chant from the gathered crowd immediately rose up as the fight moved to the point of no return.

'A G...A G R...A G R O: AGRO.'

Two things always amazed me in regards to this chant. Firstly, that nobody at any point seemed to work out how to spell aggro, and secondly that it always brought teachers and dinner ladies running, so if everybody wanted to see a good fight why do it?

As Shane and Wall commenced a scrappy wrestling match on the hard floor the Jones boys finally lent their strength to the battle, raining punches down on my outnumbered friend.

This level of fear was a new experience for me. Of course I'd had plenty of occasions at that stage in my life when I had felt scared, but nothing compared to this. Normally any feelings of trepidation were the result of an impending scolding from my parents, or when I had to face up to something new and unknown, such as starting school, or even on occasion down to Mike's behaviour. But seeing my oldest and best friend being set upon by three other boys was like an earthquake in my soul. I desperately tried to will myself to get involved, throw some punches and to even up the unfair odds a little. Shane had come to my rescue after all, so I owed it to him to try and return the favour. Yet no matter what my mind told my body to do I stood rooted to the spot, reduced to the role of spectator, as everyone around me cheered along.

'A G...A G R...A G R O: AGRO.'

As the Jones boys had lent their strength to the battle I now lent my vocals to Shane's cause, but not by way of the blood-thirsty chant from the watching spectators, instead by pleas and shouts for leniency and for the fighting to stop. It would seem that I was a born pacifist.

'Get off him! Please stop! Please!'

I even tried to separate the boys, like a referee between two hugging boxers, but was shoved out of the ring as if I was nothing more than an annoying fly.

And then the dinner ladies were there to split up the ugly fracas, hauling the boys away from each other and quieting the noise with their own shouting. Probably little more than two minutes had elapsed since the start of the entire incident, yet it felt much longer. I tried to follow Shane and the other boys as they were dragged away but I was ordered to make myself scarce as my pleas for Shane's innocence were ignored.

I now found myself standing alone at the edge of the playground and realised that I was sobbing gently, not just in pain or at the injustice of the situation, but also at my own failure to help my friend, at my inability to gather enough courage to throw even one little punch or kick.

I was scared. I was scared of what would happen to Shane. I was scared of what further repercussions to expect from Robert Wall and his two lackeys.

But more than anything else I was terrified that my failure to act in my friend's hour of need would spell the end of our friendship. He had sprung to my aid whilst I had stood and watched when my predicament became his. I prayed that my cowardice hadn't taken away from me the very best friend that any young boy could ever have hoped for.

***

About an hour after lunch break had finished Shane reappeared in our classroom. Our teacher gave him what I perceived to be a disapproving look and then told him to hurry along and sit down, before quickly bringing him up to date on what we were working on. She was obviously well aware of what had happened as there were no questions forth-coming, which implied she knew the situation was already being handled. She then barked at us all to settle down, a loud and excited murmur having enveloped the classroom upon Shane's return.

A quick look at his face revealed some blotchy red and swollen skin around his right eye that would mutate into a repentant shiner by the following day. He also had a minor scratch further down his cheek, but appeared otherwise unharmed, at least as far as any visible body parts were concerned. Nevertheless he was aloof and quiet for the rest of the time we were at school, saying little to anyone and answering any questions with non-committal grunts or simple one word replies. This was not the Shane I knew, but he could hardly be expected to be life of the party after what had happened.

As the afternoon dragged on I became more and more concerned that our friendship had run its course, that my inaction had cost me dearly. I ventured a few questions around what had happened when he was escorted from the playground but received only minimal responses. I even tried a couple of jokes that would normally have hit home but were instead left floating lamely in a ruinous silence.

The last bell of the day that signalled home time would normally have been greeted with excitement, but I felt none of that. Ahead of me lay a walk home with Shane, where my mum would be waiting with questions for the both of us on exactly how he came to be sporting a black eye. My true colours would be exposed and the way that my parents saw their son would ultimately be changed forever, and not for the better. I would be seen as the coward I truly was, a cowdy-custard who slunk away from friends in need like a dog with a tail between its legs.

The two of us left the classroom and crossed the playground that had doubled as a prize-fighter's arena only a couple of hours before. We headed for the alley-way which led from the school directly onto Foxhole Avenue, and the frosty silence that enclosed the two of us sent a chill to my heart.

We started walking down the hill towards my house and the very minute that we were away from the other pupils I blurted out a garbled apology that had been hiding shame-faced inside my mind since the events of that lunchtime.

'Shane, I'm sorry. I'm really sorry. I know I should have helped you, especially when all three of them ganged up on you, but I just couldn't. I'm...I'm...I'm just sorry that's all. I was too scared to do anything, and I really wanted to help. I know that I'm not tough like you but I still should have done something. I know that you probably don't want to be my friend anymore but if I can...'

And then Shane was grinning at me with genuine amusement and shaking his head from side to side. 'Adam, will ya please shut up!' he laughed.

'What?' I didn't understand what was so funny.

'Just shut up a minute. You don't need to be sorry.'

'But I let you down. I did nothing to help.'

'You did what ya could. I heard ya shouting at Wall and his idiot cousins to stop it. You were trying to split it up and were probably the only one from our whole class that *did* try to do something to help. Everyone else was just chanting along to that stupid aggro song like a bunch of morons. You must have been shouting loud for me to hear ya past that racket, especially whilst taking a beating, but I know yer voice.'

'So why were you so quiet when you came back to class? I thought it was because I didn't start throwing punches.'

'I was angry with the rest of that lot, my so called friends,' said Shane inclining his head back up the hill towards our school. 'You might not have thrown punches but ya didn't just stand and watch either, like they all did. You're not a fighter, Adam, that's why I hit him for ya, but ya did more than anyone else.'

I looked up and saw that we had reached my house. The two of us crossed the road and then paused momentarily.

'What shall we say to my mum?'

'Got no choice but to tell the truth. Sometimes you've just gotta face the music. The school's gonna be in touch anyway. Come on, Beanpole.'

'Hey,' I called after Shane as he ran laughing to the front door.

***

Mike was fuming. As Shane had relayed the events of the day's story he had listened quietly from where he stood on our front door step (my mum never invited him in when he came to collect his son and youngest daughter) and I watched as his face grew redder by the second.

'I just wanna make sure I'm understanding this right,' began Mike looking at Shane. 'You hit this Wall kid because 'e tripped up Adam, right?

Shane nodded mutely.

'And then ya took a pasting,' continued Mike, 'as a result. Three against one?'

My friend nodded again.

'Shane gave as good as he got,' I said, not wanting it to sound like he had rolled over and taken it. Mike glared at me, a withering look which demanded silence, but said nothing and returned his attention to his son.

'I don't understand why ya were getting involved? Why are you the one that has taken a pasting and Adam don't have a scratch on him. Can't he fight his own battles?'

'No, he can't.' Shane's reply was frank and, if I'm honest, a little upsetting. 'Not against those idiots.' Whilst I'm sure he didn't mean any harm, the words that he spoke did hurt, but only because they were true.

'Look, Mike,' said my mum, stepping in to try and calm things down, 'neither Adam nor Shane are the guilty-parties here. They're the victims in all of this. It's that Wall kid and those Jones brats that started it all.'

'Yeah, but they started on Adam and he's standing there without a mark on him, whilst Shane's the one that got battered. Why is that? I'll tell ya why. Because ya son's got no bottle. He couldn't punch his way out of a wet paper bag.'

'And why should he want to,' said my mum, her voice rising now, 'violence doesn't solve anything.'

'Rubbish! You've gotta stick up for yerself in this world, otherwise people will walk all over ya. Perhaps that's what your son lacks in his life - someone to show him some guts.'

The next voice to speak was Shane's and I think his words surprised us all, spoken as they were with such passion. 'Shut up, dad, just shut up! Why are you saying all this? Adam's my best friend. Why can't ya ever say anything nice about 'im. I don't get a hard time from 'is dad.'

With that he turned on his heel abruptly and headed off home at a pace.

'Wait for me, Shaney', called Molly and she ran after him with her pony-tail bouncing as she went. I watched as the two of them crossed the road, hand in hand. It was the one and only time I ever heard Shane stand-up to his dad.

'Proud of yourself are you?' My mum couldn't help gloating whilst Mike stood there with a surprised look on his face, but he soon recovered.

'Yeah, actually I am. I'm proud that my son has grown up with some balls, instead of being a chicken-shit.'

'Do you know what, Mike, you can say what you like in your own house, but whilst you're standing at my door you can bloody well show some respect. Now piss off.' With that she shoved him in the chest forcing him to move backwards off our step, and then slammed the door in his face.

'Bitch!' he called from the other side before thumping the door angrily and walking away.

My mum and I stood alone in the hallway as we listened to the heavy sound of Mike's footsteps quickly fading. She looked at me and I wondered what she must be thinking of her only son. Was I a disappointment to her? Did she wish that she could snatch some of the courage from Shane and pass it to me?

And then she started laughing, slowly at first and then harder and harder. I didn't understand what was so funny, but it was infectious nonetheless and before long the two of us had to sit on the floor because our sides were aching so much.

'Oh,' she gasped, 'that felt so good to give that horrible man a piece of my mind.'

When we had calmed down my mum placed a hand on my shoulder from our position slumped on the floor, and looked me intently in the eye.

'Brave or not, my boy, I don't care, just be yourself, because I love you no matter what,' and she enfolded me in her arms.

That was all I needed to hear.

***

I stood in the school playground looking at Shane with my mouth hanging open. He had a plan but it meant that I would have to play a large part in order for it to succeed. I didn't know if I was ready to fulfil the role he had in store for me.

'Adam, we need to do this, otherwise those three bullies ain't gonna stop. Everytime they see ya they're going to pick on ya.'

'But now that the Headmaster has dealt with them, and you, for fighting, they'll stop won't they?'

Shane shook his head. 'No way. Bastards like that don't take any notice of what they are told to do. They just do what they feel like. They don't care if they get into trouble.'

'I don't think I can do it. I've never hit anyone in my life.'

'You have to. If I do this on my own then he's going to think that you're still an easy target, or he'll come looking for ya when I'm not around.'

And so I found myself agreeing to Shane's crazy plan. His idea was for us both to catch Robert Wall when he was on his own without the additional Jones-boys' muscle, and to then conduct a pre-emptive strike against our shared adversary. Shane argued that I had to show to Wall that I wasn't frightened to stand-up to him, and in doing so he echoed his dad's words. It took him sometime to persuade me to collaborate with him in this regard, but his usual brand of charisma and his staunch belief in his plan forced my hand. Did I want to be running from Wall for the rest of my school days, constantly looking behind me to check if I was being followed or peering around corners to check the path was clear? Or would I prefer to deal with the threat once and for all? Yet, although I had acceded to the proposed course of action I wasn't convinced that I would actually be capable of going through with it.

That afternoon, when the final bell of the day sounded, Shane and I made sure that we were first out of the class. We left the main building and hurried across the generous school playing field which took us in the opposite direction to Foxhole Avenue. This was the way that Wall and his cousins would make their way home, but once across the field they would separate and head off in different directions. It was after they had separated that Shane wanted to strike, and so we followed the path that the solitary Wall would take and waited for him in a cut-through alley-way that led to the street where he lived.

The short time that the two of us spent waiting for our enemy was only a few minutes, but they were long, painful, drawn-out minutes that dragged agonisingly slowly, the anticipated ruckus leaving me feeling like an in-mate stuck on death-row awaiting my doom.

The alley-way carried a strong stench of urine that assaulted the nostrils and contributed to a thumping headache that was most likely a result of my fear. 'FOR SEX CALL 0800 YOUR MUM' read some graffiti that had been sprayed onto a rickety looking fence that led onto an overgrown back garden. Pockets of weeds were dotted randomly along each side of the pathway, life finding a way to sprout amongst the smallest of cracks in the concrete.

A couple of false alarms set my pulse racing ever faster as other children from our school ambled casually past where we stood, giving us curious glances as they made their way home.

And then the lone form of Robert Wall appeared, his thick-set silhouette bearing down on us like shrouded Death. When he saw the two of us he slowed his pace and then stopped short, around five metres distant. At first his face showed unmistakable surprise, and did I also detect an almost imperceptible hint of fear in those eyes that vanished as quickly as it had reared its beautiful head? Whatever I saw was but a flash in time as he quickly regained his composure and a confident look assumed control - this was, after all, a situation in which he felt right at home.

'What 'ave we 'ere?' he began. 'Two little wimps looking for trouble.'

'We just want to give you a warning, Wall.' Shane's voice was steady, unfaltering. 'You and your cousins leave us alone and we'll leave you alone. Right, Adam?' Shane looked at me and encouraged me to respond with a meaningful stare, but the best I could manage was a weak nod of my head.

'Looks like ya girlfriend ain't so sure,' laughed Wall, stepping closer until the gap between us was only about a metre. 'I've got a better idea. How about you two gays piss off before ya get hurt and me and me cousins do whatever we like, whenever we like?'

My dad's words from several years previous, when Mike had caused a scene over Violet Mayton's dog dumping a turd, reverberated in my head: *If someone ever gets aggressive with you... then walk away. There is no shame in refusing to fight someone...people that angry are unpredictable...they are dangerous, and it is better to back away sometimes, even if that feels humiliating.*

'Come on, Shane, let's just go,' I muttered as those words performed a mocking dance in my mind. Now that

Wall had overcome his initial surprise I also felt like he had gained the upper hand.

'No, come on, Adam, you promised.'

At that Wall starting laughing even harder. 'Oh, did you make a promise to ya little girlfriend?' he said in a whiney voice. 'Pathetic. What a pair of little poofs you two are. One of ya is such a gutless coward that 'e just stands there shitting in his pants, whilst the other thinks he's some sort of tough-guy just because his slag mother went to jail for being too pikey to pay for...'

Before I knew what I was doing my fist exploded into the sneering face of Robert Wall. It was the first and only time in my life, to date, that I have ever punched anyone in anger. My badly disguised fear had suddenly and unexpectedly been pushed aside by a boiling rage whose strength, with a mind of its own, overcame that of my trepidation. My ire was, I believe, built from a compound of a number of things: my initial humiliation in the toilets; Shane getting hurt and into trouble for fighting my fight in the playground; Mike's mocking words of disapproval and Shane's subsequent reaction; my own feeling of worthless inadequacy; and finally Wall showing the belligerence and audacity to pour scorn on not just me but on Shane's mum.

My punch had been true, but lacked the power that it might have possessed had it come from Shane or from a more experienced brawler. Nevertheless, Wall stumbled backwards into one of the fence panels that skirted the alleyway, yet remained on his feet. A sudden silence descended and the scene has been forever imprinted on my memory. Wall's shocked look that rapidly turned to one of rage; Shane looking at me with open-mouthed surprise; the dog that barked from the other side of the fence where Wall had staggered; the watching school-boy that had just appeared at the start of the alley-way; my throbbing fist that I still held clenched and ready.

Then, with a roar, Wall charged at me and, as Shane stepped forward to intervene, all three of us tumbled to the floor in a tangle of limbs, grunts and groans. We rolled around the floor amongst heaven knows what filth had accumulated in that alley-way, as both sides sought to gain the upper-hand. Any feelings of fear that I had previously held were pushed to one-side as adrenaline and a natural instinct to fight back kicked in. The speed with which events had progressed allowed no time to ponder, which in turn left no time to be frightened.

Wall was strong for his age, there was no doubt about that, and he likely carried with him a wealth of experience in regards to scrapping, but Shane was equal to him in terms of brute force if not experience. Which way a fight between the two of them alone would have gone is anybody's guess, and this is where my involvement proved decisive.

Between the two of us we quickly overpowered Wall, and for once he tasted what it was like to be on the wrong side of some uneven odds. Whilst I pinned him to the floor Shane rained punches down on our adversary stopping only when Wall started crying and begging him to stop.

'Leave it now, Shane,' I said, believing that my friend would possibly carry on judging by the crazed look in his eyes. 'He's had enough.'

He looked at me and his tensed up body relaxed as my words sank in and he realised it was over. But there was one more thing that Shane needed to do and I continued to hold Wall down as my friend grabbed him by his shirt collar and held a fist in his weeping face.

'Listen to me, Wall. If you or either of ya cousins cause any trouble for me or Adam then we're going to keep coming after you, understand?'

'Yes,' came the whimpered reply.

'It's always going to be you that gets it. Even if one of ya cousins starts, you'll be the one that suffers. Always you.

So make sure you all stay away from us and we'll stay away from you. Alright?' Silence. 'I said, alright?'

'OK, I heard ya.'

'Just make sure ya stick to yer word, because if ya cause trouble I won't stop coming after ya. Ever.' He let Wall go and the two of us stood up. 'Come on, Adam, let's go.'

We turned, picked up our bags and walked out of the alley-way, past the solitary school kid who stood watching us with awe as if we were Wyatt Earp and Doc Holliday following victory at the OK Corrall.

'I can't believe what just happened,' I said as soon as we were out of earshot. 'I didn't think I could do it.'

'I knew ya would.'

'How did you know?'

'My dad always says that people can only take so much before they crack, that everybody had got something that makes them angry enough to snap. He reckons that's why I got cross with him at your house the other day.'

'Yeah, maybe, but that doesn't prove you knew I would snap,' I said.

'Adam, you're my best friend. I just *knew* you wouldn't stand back. Come on, we're already late we'd better hurry, but see if you can think up a decent lie to tell our parents about the state of our clothes before we get home.'

Despite what Shane said I couldn't buy into the idea that he knew I would stand side-by-side with him in a fight with Wall, especially as I had never imagined myself doing the same and nor had I helped him during the playground scrap. On reflection I think this marked the point in Shane's life where his actions became more reckless, where he started doing what I believed to be stupid things, chancy things, things that made me scared for his well-being, but that seemed to fill him with life.

Chapter 9

Shane was refusing to see sense. It didn't matter what I said to him, he had made up his mind, set himself on a course of action and that was that. I pointed out the obvious dangers to him, the risks, but that only seemed to heighten his sense of excitement and determination.

'You're crazy, Shane. Just think about it for a minute.'

'I 'ave thought about it. I'm finished thinking now. I'm doing it.'

There it was again. That decisive finality from my friend that made it quite clear that nothing could move him from his intended course.

His fair hair had darkened to a light brown over recent years, and he now had his locks cropped short and gelled up into spikes. At twelve years old his voice was starting to deepen, whilst my own remained frustratingly squeaky and child-like. His piercing blue eyes looked beyond me to the railway line that lay on the other side of the inadequate wire fence, its tracks stretching away interminably from left to right like a ladder leading far up into the heavens. Shane intended to cross that track.

When I reflect upon how my friend was at that age, how he sometimes decided to do reckless things, I can't help wondering if some inner part of his soul sensed that he would die young. Was there part of his sub- consciousness that realised his life would be cut short, and thereby determined to cram as much excitement as possible into the brief space of time that remained to him? Perhaps an unknown force was running loose in his mind, taking control of his basic faculties and determined to squeeze as much adrenaline fuelled antics in as humanly possible.

Our days of child-like innocence had been left behind at primary school, days that had been full of exuberance and laughter. Now that we were both at secondary school our eyes were opening upon a world that liked to think it was grown up, yet was a world that often behaved childishly and complained about the adult's ways that it sought to adopt.

Once the time for secondary schools was upon us, mine and Shane's education took separate paths. Academically the brighter of the two I had passed what was known as the 11-plus exam, which granted me the chance to apply to the local Grammar Schools which boasted a generally considered superior education. Regrettably my friend had failed the exam and, as much as I wanted to go to the same school as my best pal, I was intellectually mature enough to recognise the importance of my own education, and consequently agreed with my parents' wishes to put down the stronger schools which were denied to Shane.

'My dad's pleased anyway,' he had commented once we had been notified of our allocated schools.

'Yeah, well, you got your first choice didn't you?'

'Nah, I mean he's pleased that we won't be going to school together anymore.'

'Why, what did he say?'

'I dunno, just something about me making some new mates and ditching the old ones. I don't remember exactly.'

I sensed Shane was being cagey over exactly what his dad had said, perhaps realising he shouldn't have mentioned it in the first place.

'I wish I knew why he didn't like me.'

'I'm sorry, mate,' said Shane. 'I don't think he really means to be so nasty. My mum just says that it's his way, that he's just a grouch. She also told me not to say anything to you, so you'd better keep your mouth shut about it.'

Mike may well have hoped that our attendance at different schools would lead to our association waning, but he was to be disappointed. Perversely our friendship went from strength to strength as we both made a special effort to catch up with each other at weekends and after school and this was obviously aided by the close proximity that we lived to each other. There was so much gossip that we had to share, such as the differences between the two schools and its teachers, what the other children were like, and how mutual friends were faring in the new environment. We were also entering an age where, as a child, you need a confidant to discuss important rumours or concerns, stuff that you want to keep secret from your parents for fear of both embarrassment or from getting into trouble. Parents are fine for sharing problems with when you're younger, or even as an adult, but once you hit secondary school there is no point because they simply won't understand, or so you believe at that age.

Starting secondary school was a daunting experience, not helped by the fact that I would be without my fearless buddy by my side for the first time in years. Yet, whilst I was (and still am) quite shy and reserved, I found that I wasn't overcome with worry as the first day approached. Since starting at primary school, when I had bawled like an abandoned puppy, I had come a long way. Some of the experiences that I had been through with Shane had started to mould my character into a more determined individual, someone who was more likely to fight their own corner in life's every day challenges. The struggle against Robert Wall and his sidekicks, the time that my shoe went holidaying on the roof of a classroom, even the uncomfortable confrontations with Mike - all situations that were character forming, that exposed me to nervy circumstances, and that lent me experience in coping with the more unpleasant side to life.

'Why do you even want to cross it anyway?' I asked of Shane as he gazed almost longingly at the railway line. 'What's the big deal? What's the point?'

Shane threw me a quick glance and returned to peering through the fence. 'I just think it will be exciting. It's the danger I suppose. You know like when you see a car chase on the telly, and you know it's dangerous, but at the same time you think it would be pretty cool to be the driver of one of those cars?'

'Yeah, I suppose so...'

'Well, this is the same...a little bit at least. The danger kind of adds to the buzz.'

'But what if you get caught?'

'I won't get caught,' he grinned. 'Besides, the chance of getting caught adds to the danger-thing.'

I pulled my coat tighter around me. It was mid spring and not particularly cold, but a chill was running through my skinny body nonetheless. Looking around me I couldn't see anybody else in the vicinity. We were stood in a large playing field flanked by trees on one side and Shane's goal of the railway track on the other. Several football pitches were stretched out over the expanse of grass, whose goal posts would soon be taken down and stored away ready for next season. Between Shane and the tracks a flimsy metal chain-linked fence stood guard, its inadequate barrier about as useful as the walls of sand I used to construct on the beach to keep the sea at bay during family holidays. At the bottom of the fence a section had been pulled away from the ground just enough to allow bodies to crawl through the gap. Judging by the lack of grass at this point and the collection of cigarette butts littered on the floor, this breach in the fencing was well used, perhaps by vandals armed with cans of spray paint, or by slobs too lazy to walk one hundred metres to the crossing bridge and who took a short-cut across the track instead.

'Right, let's go,' said Shane. He paused and looked at me knowingly. 'Are you coming?'

'What do you think?' I replied.

Shane laughed. 'I think you're staying put, and looking at yer face I also reckon ya think I'm being stupid.'

'Right and right.'

'Come on, mate,' said Shane getting down onto the floor. 'Don't be moody about it. Sometimes there are things that you just want to do. Like when you hit Robert Wall that time.'

'That's different,' I protested. 'That was a natural reaction. I didn't *want* to do it, it was just something I had to do.'

'Yeah, and so is this. Something I have to do I mean. And want to do.' Shane slithered under the fence, lying on his back and using the heels of his feet and his elbows to propel himself along like a burglar avoiding the laser beam of an alarm. He turned his head to one side to avoid the sharp metal at the bottom of the fence and, with a grunt, he was through. Releasing the fence that he had been holding up with his hands, it dropped marginally back into place, but still too short from its rightful position where it should have married with the ground.

My friend stood up on the other side of the fence and faced me, a foolish yet excited grin clearly evident. The weak rays of the sun shone down and highlighted his face and those startling blue eyes. Behind him the sun reflected brightly from the metal of the rails, the sharp light flashing a warning from the crisp lines of the tracks.

'Wait,' I said as he started to turn.

'What now, mum?' asked Shane smiling amiably. He didn't seem hurried or at all concerned that somebody might come along and find him where he shouldn't be.

'Which rail is the live one? You know, the one that carries the electricity?'

'I dunno,' he replied. 'It's those two isn't it.' Shane indicated the two rails that carried the wheels of the train.

'No, I thought it was that other one. The third one.'

'Who knows? Maybe it's all three of them. It don't matter.'

'Of course it matters.' I almost screamed at him. 'Maybe you should just forget this idea.'

'I mean it don't matter, coz I just won't step on any of them. Now, stop nagging me,' and he turned around and started heading towards the tracks.

As I indicated earlier, this venture wasn't the first time my friend had behaved so recklessly. Aside from the incidents during our primary school years that I've already covered, since we started senior school the episodes of sheer stupidity (in my opinion, not Shane's) increased noticeably, and with an increased element of risk. Perhaps part of this was driven by the group of friends he had made at his new school and their influence on him, but seeing as he behaved this way whilst in my company makes me think it was more a case of growing up, testosterone and his nature.

There was the episode when we went sledging, to give one example. Tiring quickly of going up and down the same hill we had traversed in previous winters, Shane now decided to up the ante and go off-piste. The snow had fallen so thickly this year that there was a good covering in amongst the copse that ran alongside the steep hill where everyone else was content to slide. Shane determined that we should instead sledge amongst the trees, at great speed, and see who possessed the greatest skill at guiding their flimsy plastic toboggan amongst the unyielding wooden sentinels. Perhaps predictably, I refused, too nervous by half to try anything so risky, but undeterred my friend launched himself enthusiastically down the hill and successfully negotiated the first few obstacles, before the inevitable happened and his ride was dealt a glancing blow by an indignant oak tree. He flew through the air like a clown shot from a circus cannon, arms flailing, and landed in a sprawling heap at the foot of another oak, a mere two feet away from a potentially fatal collision. Before I could dash down the hill to his aid he was up on his feet, whooping with the thrill of it all and determined to attempt a second assault, but thankfully the tree had put his sledge out of action, ripping a large chunk from its under-carriage and side. Shane's desperate pleas to borrow my sledge for even *just one more go* fell on death ears. I was alive to the danger even if he wasn't, and my argument that I didn't want my sledge to end up like his was a convincing one.

Another occasion involved a big, dead, old oak tree in a different park, just outside of Barnehurst. The theme of Shane versus Oak Trees is purely coincidental, but perhaps fitting as he was proving as thick and stubborn as one in some of his actions. My friend decided that he was going to climb as high as he could into the twisted branches – maybe not an altogether new idea for young boys, but there is climbing for fun and there is climbing from the Shane School for Adrenaline Junkies. It was an imposing view, a lone tree sited in the middle of a wide expanse of field as if standing guard over the parkland like some huge deformed demon, its scraggly, leafless limbs gnarled and knotty like the arthritic hands of an aging old man. Local kids referred to it as the Dragon Tree, although it held no resemblance to such a mythical beast as far as I could tell. In places the dead old tree was rotting away, and a graveyard of once proud twigs and branches were scattered around its base like the bones of a fallen skeleton army. Most kids that Shane and I knew had at one point or another played at climbing on this once majestic, now permanently leafless, tree. The way its branches were spread out it was almost as if it had been nurtured to such a purpose, and the subsequent lure for children was irresistible. Now-a-days, in this safety obsessed world, such trees would be promptly cut down or have their lower branches removed to prevent any such hazardous fun. Sometimes I pour scorn on such actions from the Health and Safety Police, but then when I think of Shane and how he was confusing the boundaries between fun and danger I can understand how such things have come to pass. Whilst most children were content with adventuring to the lower branches, my friend was at a stage in his life where he *needed* more. So he challenged himself to reach the very top, where he intended to tie a Manchester United scarf that he had found in the street that same day.

'I can't keep the damn scarf, Adam,' he had said as he stood at the base of the tree. 'My dad still thinks I support Chelsea. They might not be my favourite team, but as long as my dad thinks they are then that's cool. I guess it's a father and son bonding kind of thing. It makes him happy to think I support Chelsea, so I don't want to ruin that. But, if I tie it to the very top of the branches he still won't know and it can at least live where Man Utd belong - at the top of the tree.' He chuckled at his own joke.

'You'll never reach the top,' I said, immediately realising that issuing such a challenge was the wrong thing to say.

'Wanna bet,' he laughed, and then promptly set-off on his planned expedition to the summit of the Dragon Tree.

I watched, mesmerised, from the ground, part of me wishing that I had the bravery of my mate, and part of me glad that I didn't. He rose steadily higher, pulling himself up a handhold at a time and almost falling at one point when a tired branch murderously gave way under the weight of his body, the cracking of the wood like a wicked cackle from a witch with evil intent. But, eventually, Shane reached his goal and somehow managed to tie his standard to the highest point that any human could surely reach on this tree, if climbing unaided.

'I'm glad I didn't bet,' I said once he returned to solid ground, my hammering heart slowly returning to normal as relief took control from my unease.

And now his latest challenge stood before him. Six lines of solid metal, four to carry the trains in either direction and two to power them on their merry way. He approached slowly until he was no more than a couple of metres from the first track, at which point he peered left and right, checking for approaching locomotives. From his vantage point the tracks ran straight and true as far as the eye could see, and the nearby vegetation was adequately set-back to prevent any obstructions blocking his view.

'All clear,' he called over his shoulder to me, yet not tearing his eyes from his goal. 'Here it goes.'

My fingers curled tightly around the metal that made up the wire fencing that had failed in its singular duty to keep trespassers out. The knuckles on my hand turned white as my fool-hardy friend stepped across the first of the tracks. My finger nails dug into the palms of my hand as he calmly cleared the second track and the first of the power lines that sat so closely together. My feet tingled with fearful anticipation as he cleared the next power line and first of the second set of tracks, before finally stretching his feet nonchalantly across the last obstacle to leave himself standing victorious on the far side from where I stood.

Grinning from ear to ear he waved at me and I watched as he placed his hands on his sides and lifted his face towards the sky, clearly drinking in the moment as the sun shone down upon his beaming smile.

'Will you get a move-on,' I hissed across at him. 'Quickly before someone comes, or even a train.'

'Well the train's not going to get me unless I stand in its way, is it, Dummy?'

'Shane, just come on, quickly. Stop messing about.'

'Quickly?' he asked, and my heart sank. 'Alright then.'

I watched, horrified, as he launched himself from where he stood over the first of the tracks and then skipped, leapt and bounded over the remaining hurdles as if they were nothing more threatening than a set of stairs in your average family home. His impetus carried him forward and he slammed into the fence opposite me, prompting me to step backwards.

'You idiot!' I shouted, my shock at this sudden additional risk taking quickly turning to anger. 'What do you think you're doing? You could have tripped or fallen or anything.'

Shane looked at me through the holes in the criss-cross of wires. His erratic behaviour made him suddenly seem like a wild beast that I was watching through the fence of its enclosure, and yet the manner in which he peered out made me feel like the one that was being observed from the wrong side of a cage.

'You're cross,' he stated. It wasn't a question. 'Weird.'

'Weird?' I asked. 'Weird? How is that weird? Of course I'm cross. You could have been killed. That was really dumb.'

'It's just that, well, you're normally always pretty chilled. You don't get mad.'

Was I always calm? That's wasn't how I saw myself. Shane was the calm one out of the pair of us, the way he tackled these ridiculous challenges he had started setting himself.

'I mean,' he continued, 'ya never shout at me, not in anger like you did just then. You do try and persuade me not to do some of the stuff ya consider stupid or dangerous or whatever, but ya never sound pissed-off with me like just then.'

'Well, I don't want you to go and die do I? You're my best mate, after all. Plus I wouldn't want to be the one that had to tell your dad. No-way. Now get back through the fence.'

Shane laughed and the momentary tension between us evaporated like an ice cream dropped in the sun by a clumsy child. He crawled back through the chain-link fence just as a train finally thundered past only metres away. The vibrations from its passing reverberated along the length of the fencing into my hands as I raised it up for Shane to crawl beneath, and the sheer power of the speeding hunk of melded metal was undeniable.

My friend stood up once he was clear of the fence and we faced each other. His blue eyes twinkled, they danced, with the thrill of the experience. If ever there was an adrenaline junkie in the making, here he was.

'Sorry, Adam. I never meant to scare you.'

I could tell from his voice that he meant every word, but at the same time it was so obvious that he had got a real kick out of the experience and wouldn't have changed a thing.

'Don't worry. Anyway, what was it like? How do you feel?'

He looked me straight in the eyes, and his majestic blue orbs continued to sparkle.

'It was amazing. I know it was wrong and my mum would go mental if she found out, but I just feel so alive.'

We turned and headed for home, with Shane's words echoing in my head.

So alive.

So.

A.

Live.

Chapter 10

The day that would haunt me for the rest of my life started out as a hot Sunday in late-June. The sun had decided to kick-start the summer in style with a showy display designed to remind people just what it was capable of. In less than a month's time I would have completed my first year at secondary school and, whilst it had been a good experience for the most part, the summer holidays beckoned. I was already looking forward to my family's planned week in Devon, not to mention countless days spent with Shane as well as some new friends that I had made from school. We would doubtless be out roaming the local streets on our bikes or playing football down the park, and generally revelling in the extended freedom that our advancing years were bestowing upon us.

The storm clouds that gathered that day whilst Shane and I were out were completely unexpected. One moment the sky was clear, the endless blue expanse stretching as far as the eye could see, and the next there was a distant rumble of thunder as some intruding grey clouds poked their unwelcome noses into view.

'Did you hear that?' I asked.

'Ssssh, keep quiet, and keep yer head down,' hissed Shane.

We were at the local golf course, watching some golfers on green number 7 that were concentrating on putting their balls before their mates did. I sank back down into the sand that formed the old disused bunker where we were hiding, oblivious to the fact it was probably used as a litter tray by cats, dogs and foxes. Once-upon-a-time it must have formed part of the golf course, but now it sat divided from the green and the fairway by a scraggly group of bushes. As to why this particular bunker had been disowned by the rest of the course I have no idea, but we didn't care as to the reason - it suited our purpose, which was to spy on the golfers and do our best to distract them without getting caught.

'Golfers are grumpy bastards,' whispered Shane, peering at me with a wise look. 'They don't like kids, and therefore they are the enemy.'

'They don't like *some* kids, such as us, because all we do is annoy them by trying to put them off.'

'Well, it serves them right for being so grumpy then, don't it? If they just laughed at our tricks instead of getting annoyed, if they just showed a sense of humour, then maybe we would leave them alone.'

'But probably not,' I offered.

'No,' he agreed with a grin, 'but again, it serves them right.'

Shane always seemed to find some argument to lend justification to his actions, nonsensical or otherwise.

Our methods for distracting the golfers ranged from throwing sand over the bushes and onto the green, forcing out loud burps, and generally making a variety of silly noises, based on whatever came into our heads at the time. On a couple of occasions the pair of us had been forced to make a run for it when highly peeved men, having missed their putt and armed with golf-clubs, had charged around the side of the bushes and invaded our base-camp. We were forced to tear off down the grassy hill on our bikes at a pace, our initial panic turning to uncontrollable hilarity as we realised we had escaped from our pursuers, our sides hurting so much from laughing that we had no choice but to dismount and roll on the ground with our hands clutching at our ribs, whilst praying that the disgruntled men had given up the chase and wouldn't suddenly appear around the corner.

If our mothers had known what we were getting up to then we would almost certainly have been in trouble, but it was hardly the crime of the century, and was purely a bit of mischievous fun.

'Watch out, here come some more,' I said, as a group of four men in garishly coloured golfing attire sauntered over to the green, their clubs dragged behind them on those silly little trolleys in the same manner that their wives were likely dragging their children around the shops.

Another rumble of thunder greeted the men's arrival, slightly louder this time, but distant and drawn out, like a hungry stomach grumbling for food. I looked up at the sky. There had been no noticeable accompanying flash of lightening, but the menacing clouds seemed closer than only a moment before.

'I think it's going to rain,' I whispered. 'Maybe we should get going.'

'Just a minute. Let's have some fun with this lot first.'

One tall man, wearing red and black chequered trousers, had removed his putter from his bag and was lining up his shot by crouching to the ground and checking the lay of the green. He gave a nod of the head and exchanged some banter with his friends before preparing himself to take the shot. As he swung his putter Shane let out what can only be described as a high-pitched mewling noise, but the loud clap of thunder that sounded at the same time snatched it from the ears of anyone but the two of us. The man missed his shot by a mile and his friends burst into uncontrollable laughter. I doubt they would have found his miss so funny had some random squeaky cat noise been the cause rather than the thunder.

'OK, Adam, maybe you're right. That was loud. It's going to chuck it down. Let's go.'

'Agreed,' I said and the two of us climbed onto our bikes.

'Wanna come back to mine for a bit? I've got that new footie game for me PlayStation.'

Going to my friend's house was never my preference, especially if I thought that Mike might be there, but saying *no* constantly would seem rude, so sometimes I just had to go with it.

As we cycled the short journey back to Foxhole Avenue the approaching thunder storm continued to make its presence known. The blue sky was now rapidly being eradicated by the grey clouds, like the green of a rainforest being swallowed by the levelled red earth, but the downpour was still being held at bay by some unseen plug. Another boom of thunder, louder still this time and preceded only marginally by a flash of lightening, spurred us into greater efforts to reach home, our legs pounding at the pedals.

Amazingly we reached Shane's house just before the rain attacked, pushing our bikes up the short yet steep driveway where we promptly abandoned them outside the back gate which led into his garden. We passed through the gate and that was the signal for the storm to start good and proper. The slow and steady build up was replaced by a sudden onslaught as the rain began to lash down.

'Shane! Come here quickly and help me with this washing!' called Karen. She was stood over by the clothes-line frantically unpegging a pair of jeans.

'Oh, mum, why didn't you get it in earlier. Blimey. We're gonna get soaked.' He ran to help her but called over his shoulder to me, 'Go in, Adam.'

I didn't need a second invitation and quickly ducked inside the kitchen via the back door. The rain battered against the windows sounding like a troop of Doc Martin wearing ant-sized drummers in a marching band. Just as I was removing my shoes where I stood on the kitchen mat, Mike strolled in with a beer can in hand. Momentarily he seemed surprised to see me standing there alone, but that look was soon replaced with a scowl.

'Hello,' I ventured rather meekly, my manners ingrained in me, no matter who I was talking to.

'What are you doing here?' His voice was cold, unwelcoming, and more than likely intended to intimidate.

'I'm waiting for Shane. He's getting the washing.'

Mike scrunched up the can that was in his hand and tossed it on the nearest kitchen work-top, making no effort to tidy it away in the bin.

'When are ya going to realise that Shane wants nothing to do with ya?' he said slowly as he opened the fridge and retrieved a fresh can of lager. The smell of alcohol poured from his mouth like water from a breached dam and I nearly gagged. 'He's got new mates now, better mates, from his new school. I hate to be the bearer of bad news, but he's pretty fed-up with having to hang around with you all the time. He just thinks yer a bit too babyish.'

'I don't believe you,' I said, whilst also finding it hard to comprehend that I had actually spoken-up in my own defence.

'Your choice,' he said as he cracked open his can. 'My boy confided in me last night.' Mike tapped a thick index finger against his nose as he said this, a wicked smile perched on his lips. 'His problem is that he's too bloody polite to say anything to ya. His mother's influence. Fortunately for him, I ain't, so problem solved.'

Mike took a long swig of his lager just as the door opened inwards behind me, pushing into my back.

'Shift, Adam, quick, we're getting soaked,' called Shane. 'Hello, dad.'

I jumped out of the way so that my friend could open the door fully and then he and Karen bundled into the room with armfuls of half dry washing.

'Blinkin' 'ell,' said Karen, dumping the washing into the empty laundry basket which sat on the floor next to the washing machine. 'Where did that come from? It's pouring out there. Hi, Adam.'

'Hello.'

Shane dumped his own bundle of clothes in the basket. 'Come on, mate, let's go on the PlayStation.'

The pair of us left the kitchen and headed for Shane's room but, convinced that Mike's eyes were boring into my back, I couldn't resist a quick glance in his direction as we reached the bottom of the stairs. Sure enough he was stood staring after us, and I watched as he moved that index finger to his nose once again and tapped it twice.

***

Shane's room was small yet comfortable, the walls splattered with posters from football magazines of some of his favourite players. We were sat on his bed and I was taking a thorough thrashing on the new football game that he had bought for his console. Effort after effort rained down on my goal, my keeper pulling off numerous stunning saves, and only because he was automatically controlled by the computer rather than me. Nevertheless, even he couldn't manage to stop everything and the score currently stood at 6-1. It was our third match so far, and I had already lost the other two games by equally convincing score-lines.

As hard as I tried to focus on what I was doing my mind simply wasn't in the room with me. It was downstairs in the kitchen with Mike, going over what he had said again and again.

He's got new mates now, better mates...

This was partly true at least. Of course Shane had made some new friends since starting a new school, as had I. For somebody as charismatic as him it would have been impossible not to. If I'm honest part of me might have even been a little bit jealous, even threatened by this fact, but I could hardly expect, or even want, him to wander around his new school all alone.

As to them being 'better mates', was that true? Quite possibly. I myself had started to make some pretty solid friendships in my own school, both with boys and even girls, who were starting to grab my attention more and more with every passing day. But *better mates*? No. Not yet at least, and at that time in my life I couldn't imagine that anybody would ever be a better friend to me than Shane. Yet maybe Shane didn't feel the same way. What if his new school had opened his eyes to a plethora of really fun people, whose company was so enticing it was like a drug that lifted you high and spun you around? And, let's face it, I wasn't cool. Hanging around with Adam Wickes was not about to raise your street cred – I was too much of a geek for that. But then, if these 'better mates' did exist then where were they now? Where were they ever? They weren't sat on the bed getting humiliated by the dancing feet of Shane's strikers. Nor did I ever see them in our street, knocking at my friend's door and welcomed in by Mike with an approving high five.

...he's pretty fed-up with having to hang around with you...

This was the one that was really making me think. Was I just an annoyance to Shane, a clinger-on, like an unwelcome grass-dart thrown into somebody's hair by the playground clown? Did he see me wandering across the road from my house to his and groan with audible displeasure, wondering how he could escape the grasp of such a tedious inconvenience, pleading with his parents to *hide me, hide me* before it was too late? Did my failures to climb trees and cross railway tracks make him realise that our friendship had run its course, that I was simply too boring to provide him with any kind of entertainment. Even now, getting so easily crushed at this infuriatingly addictive football game, was I failing to provide enough of a challenge to stimulate our friendship.

These are the thoughts that spun around and around my head. Bear in mind that I was only twelve years old. Impressionable, self-conscious and lacking in self-confidence. I knew that Mike was far from a fan of mine, and that he wasn't a nice man like my own dad was, yet the secretive way he had shared this news with me, especially when combined with the insecurities of my youth, just made it seem so believable. I was naïve to the meanness in people, a gullible child and an easy target.

Karen's voice called up the stairs. A welcome intrusion to my thoughts. 'Boys, I'm just popping out down the shops. Molly's coming with me. Do you want anything?'

'No thanks,' called Shane, followed by a hearty cheer as another goal thumped into the back of my net. 'Adam, you aren't very good at this are you?'

'No, I s'pose not'

'What's up? You're pretty quiet.'

'Nothing. I'm fine.'

'It's not because I'm giving you such a thrashing is it?' Shane laughed. 'You're not being a bad loser?'

'No, I'm fine.'

I didn't want to tell Shane what his dad had said. I wouldn't know how to broach the subject in the first place plus I already felt like I moaned about his dad too often to him, and even if Shane himself got annoyed with the way Mike behaved, it was his dad so that was his prerogative.

And then all of a sudden my worries and concerns were laid to rest by an innocent comment from the very person that they were centred around.

'Well, seeing as how you're so rubbish at this game you'd better come back tomorrow for some more practice. Or we can go out on our bikes or something if ya can't stand any more thrashings.'

'It's Monday tomorrow, stupid,' I said, my mood instantly brightening at Shane's offer. 'We've got school.'

'Oh, yeah. Damn it! Bloody weekends always go so quick! Perhaps after school then, or next weekend. I wish we still went to the same school. It's not the same now we're split up.

Friendship confirmed. All doubts blown away with a few simple words, like the seeds of a dandelion set free by the gentle puff of a child.

I felt my cheeks redden slightly and Shane appeared uncharacteristically uncomfortable, most likely believing that his complimentary words had led to my embarrassment, although the true cause was my own feelings of guilt for momentarily doubting his friendship. I should have known better than to have listened to Mike.

'Do you fancy one more tonking at this and then we could go out on our bikes again. It's stopped raining now,' he said, peering out the small bedroom window which looked onto his back garden.

'OK,' I said, 'but you'd better be ready for a tougher match this time.'

***

We stood astride our bikes at the top of Shane's driveway, which sloped sharply downwards towards the pavement and road beyond. The storm clouds had emptied their disruptive load and the sun was breaking through once more, accompanied by ever increasing patches of blue sky.

'Where shall we go then?' I asked.

'We could go back to the golf course, but the bunker will probably be soaking now.'

'True. Let's just go over to Shenstone Park and have a go on the BMX track.'

A local bike shop owner had badgered the council into building a BMX race course, and in return he took care of the site's upkeep. Presumably the deal was good business for him and resulted in improved trade, or at least I imagine that is what he would have hoped to achieve. Whatever the state of his sales, the track was well used by many local children and we went there often, although predictably Shane was always much bolder than me when riding the various jumps and berms that decorated the course. His bike would experience some serious air as he tore around the track, whilst my wheels preferred to hold hands with the dirt, like a loved-up couple strolling through Paris.

'Yeah, alright,' he agreed. 'Skids bet?'

'If you don't mind losing.'

A 'skids bet' was a game that the two of us regularly played, and Shane's driveway was the perfect set-up. Simply stated it involved pedalling down a hill and seeing who could perform the longest skid when pulling on the brakes. My mum didn't like me doing it, complaining that skidding wore my tyres out, but my dad always just chuckled and said *He's a boy – what do you expect?* This was generally a pretty even contest between us, but following my numerous trouncings on the PlayStation that same day I was out to recover a little lost pride, and prove that I was still a force to be reckoned with.

'After you, Loser,' I offered, and my friend set-off down the short slope at a pace, giving it all he had. I watched from the summit as he performed an impressive skid, perhaps measuring around three foot distance.

'Ha, beat that sucker!' he called up to me. It would be tough to match let alone better.

'No sweat.'

With a shove as mighty as my skinny legs would allow I propelled myself down the slope, several quick rotations on the pedals thrown in for good measure in the name of greater velocity. The slope was no more than about fifty feet in length, so it was key to reach a good speed quickly to leave enough time and room for a decent skid. I was flying, the air rushing through my hair, my face undoubtedly a contorted mask of concentration as I leant over the handlebars. Shane stood astride his bike at the bottom, pulling faces at me and trying to put me off, but I wasn't going to be denied victory. There's only so many beatings a twelve year old boy can take in one afternoon - it was my turn to win.

As I approached the bottom my hands squeezed hard on both brake levers, yanking them back for all I was worth, determined to turn my speed into the winning skid, the skid to end all skids.

But there was to be no skid.

Instead, in a moment of stunned horror the front wheel locked up and the back of the bike kicked upwards like a wild bucking bronco. I found myself flying over the top of my handlebars and through the air, my arms freewheeling like two great propellers. If I thought the air had been rushing past on my initial descent, now it was tearing past at a frightening pace, and yet everything seemed to be in slow motion. Directly ahead of me, the silly face he had been pulling starting to drop away, was Shane. I watched as he started to try and move out of the way, but standing astride a bike is not a conducive position to enable fast evasive action and there was little he could do. Impact was an unavoidable certainty.

Like a bull charging a matador I plunged into the best childhood friend anyone could have ever wished for, and the two of us, along with Shane's bike, clattered to the floor in a tangled, broken heap, where we then lay still.

From my prostrate position I tried to open my eyes, and achieved only partial success as a narrow chink of daylight shone back at me. Through the feathered blur of my eyelashes I could just make out Shane's form lying next to his bike, only a short distance from where I lay. There was no movement.

Weakly I attempted to rise but gave up as a dark cloud descended across my vision. My eyes began to close, and the last thing I remember seeing before I passed out was the shadowy form of somebody squatting over Shane before moving away once more.

Chapter 11

What do parents wish for their children over everything else, as young boys and girls or adults? Surely the answer to this must be happiness closely followed by good health, or perhaps the latter over the former. A certain degree of wealth is also probably high on the list of many parents, although experience has shown me that there are plenty of rich people whose shoulders strain with the weight of their misery, as their bank accounts strain with their inflated balances. Money can't buy you happiness as the old saying goes.

What about friendship? That too must surely be high on the wish-list for most, for without friendship happiness will prove an elusive fish that refuses to get hooked.

So I wonder, at what stage in our lives do we make the best friendships? When do we form relationships that are so valuable, so satisfyingly elating, that their existence leaves an indelible mark on our very soul? I'm sure different people will again have varying opinions based on their own journeys through life, but the answer from my point of view is quite simple.

As a child.

Teenage friendships and those of young adults are a quagmire of tantrums, testosterone and tits, doomed to be driven by the weight of peer pressure and desire to belong. Adult friendships are a mixed bag, interrupted by the strains of family life, mortgages and idiotic work bosses, which all stand in the way of enjoying such camaraderie which would now benefit from freedom of the encumbrance of the previously mentioned confusion of youth. As for friendships during our twilight years, I can't speak from personal experience just yet, but it seems to me that they are blighted by illness, immobility and the love for cute grandchildren which so far outweighs anything that a friendship could possibly bestow in one's latter years. In short, friendships take a back seat for the older generation. Childhood friendships reign supreme. The relationship between two true friends at such an age is the undisputed champion of uncomplicated enjoyment. Life is for playing, life is for fun, life is for living. Arguments are sparse, meaningless and soon forgotten, centring largely around what to play next or whose turn it is to go in goal. Money holds no sway in a child-hood friendship. Sexual attraction does not interfere. The only thing that matters is to have a blast, and having a good friend to share that with is a prize that money can't buy.

Children that are fortunate enough to share in such a special relationship are completely oblivious to the true value of what they have. As a twelve year old boy on the cusp of adolescence I was no exception to this rule, not appreciating the value of what I held until it was no longer mine to possess.

Shane died that day. A blow to the head, received either from our direct collision or when he fell to the unforgiving pavement, resulted in bleeding on the brain. My friend fell unconscious and by the time they got him to the hospital the battle was already lost.

I myself escaped with cuts, bruises and mild concussion. I had been temporarily knocked out, waking to find myself lying outside of Shane's house with a paramedic leaning over my body and my mother at his side, her face frantic, scared. I too was taken to the hospital where tests revealed no further, more serious consequences.

But, of course, those tests were purely based on my physical health. They showed nothing of the mental anguish that was to be my new permanent companion. Guilt, the terrible guilt, the numbness, the ache that hurt so much yet wouldn't hurt as much as I sometimes willed it to do, desperate as I was for some form of penance. All of these feelings were horrible to bear, but the worst thing about them was what they represented.

Life.

I was very much alive and the pain was a constant reminder that blood still beat strongly through my veins, whilst my friend lay cold.

To refer to Shane simply as a 'friend' seems inadequate. The word doesn't convey enough about the person that he was, about what he represented to me.

And yet, it was me that had killed him. My body was the ammunition, fired from the speeding carcass of my once loved bike, that had slammed into him with murderous devastation.

I asked, what do parents wish for their children, but I think that I have left out two key desires. They are: to be safe and to enjoy a long life.

Shane, these were taken away from you.

I am sorry, my friend, from the deepest depths of my heart.

Chapter 12

The days immediately following Shane's death passed in a blur of numbness. Our street, normally a hive of childhood activity at weekends and following school, fell eerily silent. No children played up and down the pavements that ran past our houses, no boys and girls ran screaming their laughter, expressing their joy to be alive. Certainly no-one was seen riding a bike in Foxhole Avenue, their parents having undoubtedly put a stop to any shows of disrespectful exuberance.

I know this because for the first few days after the tragedy I took up almost permanent residence at the lounge window that looked out over the street and across the road. I sat staring at the three bed semi-detached opposite, its curtains kept closed both day and night, desperately hoping that the front door would open and there he would stand. Shane, alive and in the flesh. A smile dancing on his face beneath his spiky crown of fair hair. His blue eyes smirking with mischievousness as he considered telling me of his latest silly idea. But of course he didn't appear. He would never appear again.

A few scattered visitors showed up at random intervals. Shane's grandparents; Aunties and close family friends; a policeman and policewoman; a man dressed in a neat pin-striped suit carrying a brief-case. All were admitted through a front door that barely seemed to open wide enough to permit entry. At one point Caroline appeared with Molly in tow, the two sisters walking hand in hand down the street, their strides seeming to lack any bounce, any enthusiasm. Caroline glanced my way and I ducked down quickly below the window, despite the protection afforded to me by the net curtains. Where were they going I wondered? To the park perhaps to allow Molly to play? To the shops to get some essentials?

What must it have been like inside that house? How unforgiving was the atmosphere? I imagined almost total silence. A silence that clung to your clothes wherever you went, like a poisonous sludge from a marshy swamp. Did the entire family live in dread of making any sort of a noise, a noise that indicated life? Flushing a toilet, running a tap, closing a door with anything greater than minimal force. Did they sit down at meal-times together? Did they even bother eating to begin with, to feed their empty appetites? Did they sleep in their beds as normal, or did they crash on the sofas in the lounge from where they barely moved one hour to the next? Were uttered words all in hushed tones, anything spoken above a whisper like a foreign language lost amongst the pain? How was it in that house that had so suddenly been cut off from the rest of the world like a colony teeming with lepers? How, after all, does such a household behave when a child is taken from them in such a way, especially when one of the people present is Mike, unpredictable and full of spite, who always seemed to have a boiling rage just below the surface, even on the calmest of days.

My parents allowed me to sit by the window for a time, permitted me to grieve in my own way. As long as I was somewhere where they could keep an eye on me I suppose they knew that I wasn't doing anything stupid, driven by my grief.

Our household received visitors as well. A policeman came to ask painful questions, questions that he put as gently as he possibly could. He needed to know the facts about what had happened. I told him it was just an accident. I didn't mean it. I was going so fast. All I wanted to do was pull off the longest skid. He had laid a hand on my arm at that point and told me that it wasn't my fault. Nobody was blaming me. Another man came to talk to me. Smartly dressed with a grey suit and shiny turquoise tie. I suppose he was a counsellor of some description because I remember him talking to me about my feelings and encouraging me to open up about what had happened. He asked me how I felt right then, at that moment. Empty, I told him. And lonely. Guilty too. Most of all guilty. He smiled wisely and told me that nobody was blaming me.

The family doctor paid a home visit as well. He checked on my cuts and bruises in between sips of the tea that my mother had brought him. He listened to my heart and asked me if I felt pain in any other parts of my body. As he was leaving he rested a big hand on my shoulder and looked down at me until his eyes found mine. Nobody is blaming you, young man.

My parents did what they could. They showered me with love and understanding, and I have no doubt that is what kept me afloat. They talked to me when they felt it was needed and left me alone when they sensed it was right, but there is only so much you can really do to help somebody who has suffered a loss in such a fashion, especially if you too are feeling the hurt. It shouldn't be forgotten that my mum and dad were also deeply upset. They adored Shane, they knew him almost as well as they knew me, such a regular visitor to our house had my friend been. And, of course, they knew how much he meant to me, which in turn made him a greatly valued commodity.

After a couple of days my dad had to go back to work at the bus depot, and in truth I can imagine that he was relieved to get out and be doing something. My school had said that I could take as much time off as I needed, so my mother and I were left at home. Part of me wanted to go back to school, to try and take my mind off things, but I just couldn't face the questions and the looks. Looks of curious people itching to check how I was bearing up, wanting to know exactly what had transpired. No, I wasn't ready.

I was at my spot by the lounge window, gazing across at Shane's house and doing my best to come to terms with what had happened, when the visit I had feared reared its unwanted head. The door to the Metcalfe house opened and Mike appeared at the top of his murderous driveway wearing a grubby looking white t-shirt and jeans. He started heading down the slope, staring resolutely straight ahead, refusing to glance at the spot where his son fell. Karen appeared suddenly, closely followed by Caroline, both of them running after him and grabbing at his arms, which he ripped free as if their hands were nothing more than gossamer thread from a spider's web.

'Mike, wait, don't do this! Please!' Karen entreated her husband desperately.

'Dad, wait! Stop! Please, dad!' Caroline was screaming, almost hysterical. She was fifteen then, almost a woman, but next to her father she still appeared very much a child.

Transfixed I watched as the stocky form that was Mike marched down towards the street, crossed the road and headed directly for our house. As before, I instinctively ducked down below the window as he approached, my heart hammering out a tune that I didn't like the sound of.

'Don't worry, Adam. I'll talk to him.' It was my mum. She was stood in the lounge, drawn there by the noise of the commotion from outside, and had seen him approaching. 'I've been expecting this.' She sounded calm, in control, but her manner was not, unfortunately, contagious.

The force with which Mike banged on our front door sounded like it could shake the whole house from its very foundations. I felt like one of the three little pigs cowering from the might of the big bad wolf.

'Where is he? Bring him out 'ere right now!' The man could shout, that was certain, his voice full of anger, the power unmistakable. 'Samantha, I'm not playing games 'ere. Get that little bastard out 'ere!'

'Mike, this ain't going to help anything. Come back 'ome. Come on.' It was Karen, trying her best to pacify her husband.

'It'll help me,' he bellowed. 'Sam, open up,' and he banged on the door once more.

'I'll talk to you,' replied my mum through the still closed door, 'but I'm not opening this door until I know that you've calmed down.'

I should point out that both of my parents had made several tentative attempts to contact Shane's family. Understandably they felt a pressing need to pass on their condolences and deep regret at what had happened, driven not just by their own love for the deceased, but also by, undoubtedly, their own feelings of guilt at the tragic part in which I played. But everytime they knocked on the door it was not opened to them, rather because our neighbours knew who was standing there or because whoever it was would have been ignored regardless. Now it seemed that a meeting was deemed appropriate, all be it at our door step.

'I don't want to talk, Sam, I just want you to open this fucking door!'

'And what are you going to do then? Take your rage out on my son? Beat him to a pulp because of what has happened to Shane?'

'You're damn right that's what I'm going to do. He killed my boy!'

From my position on the lounge floor, where I had ducked beneath the window ledge, I hugged myself tightly into a protective ball, tears stinging my eyes as Mike's words stung my soul. From my perspective he was telling the truth, and the truth hurt. Shane had suffered the worst possible fate, why should I be spared?

'Listen, Mike, I understand how you're feeling, God knows it's painful for us as well, but taking this out on Adam isn't going to bring Shane back.' My mum's tone was soft, placating, but at the same time there was a steely undercurrent as she sought to protect her own offspring. 'That could have been either one of our boys that died out there, it could have even been both of them, but Adam is not to blame for this. It was a tragic accident, there is no doubt about that. We've all seen our boys pulling skids down that driveway before, but not once did we imagine that something like this might happen, not once did we tell them to stop. And why would we? They were just boys doing what boys do.

'I am so sorry about Shane. Truly I am. I know that words are only a small comfort, but we loved him dearly and I would do anything if it meant that we could turn back the clock. Our two lads were friends, best friends, and the last thing that Shane would have wanted would have been for you to take this out on Adam. They meant the world to each other.'

A silence followed my mum's words as she stood one side of our front door with her head resting against the frame, a silence that seemed to last forever until it was broken by a muffled noise from the other side. Mike was crying, gently at first, but then gradually harder and harder until great heaving sobs tore through the glass. My mum, for her own part, was dabbing at her eyes with a worn tissue, and I joined the party too, tears far from a stranger to me since Shane's passing.

I stood up from my place below the window in the lounge and joined my mum at her side, wrapping my arms around her waist and burying my head into her chest. She pulled me close, hugging me tight and kissing the top of my head, whilst the agonising sound of Mike's sobbing continued unabated.

Slowly, unexpectedly, my mum reached forward and pulled the door open before I had time to realise what she was doing. Was she crazy? What was she thinking? Only minutes ago that door was all that stood between me and the worst beating of my life. There was no way she could know how Mike would react. On our front step sat his hunched form in a grubby white t-shirt with his back to us, shoulders heaving up and down in such a fashion that if we hadn't known better he could have been laughing. Standing facing us and him were Karen and Caroline, whilst Molly was presumably temporarily at home alone, wondering where the hell everyone had got to. His wife and daughter looked lost and uncomfortable, stood as they were with their hands down at their sides whilst Mike let it all out. They hadn't moved towards him to place an arm around his shoulders, nor to sit next to him in sympathetic solidarity. Instead they appeared as if they didn't quite know what to do. Was it a case of numbness caused by too much recent upset, or simply a complete lack of closeness in their relationships meaning they didn't know how to react to the man? Perhaps his general gruffness and aloof attitude had created a gulf that even a bridge of united grief could not span. Maybe they couldn't face the hurt should their consoling gestures be rebuffed.

I pulled away from my mum, ready to bolt, but remained at her side as she offered a sort of half smile to Karen and Caroline that somehow encompassed everything she wanted to say to them had Mike not been present.

'Mike,' my mum began, 'ladies, why don't you all come in for a while. I'll put the kettle on. We can talk.'

Slowly Mike stood up and turned round, stepping back so he was next to his family. He was battling to control his emotions, and finally seemed to be calming down a little, but any thoughts of sympathetic mutterings over a cup of tea were rapidly banished by his next words.

'You really are something else,' he snarled at my mum. 'What planet are you on? Do you actually think that we would want to sit around your lounge having a cosy fucking chat, knowing that your son is sitting there with us? The dirty little murderer!'

'Mike, come on, don't say that, Love,' said Karen, placing her hands on his arm.

'Let go of me woman,' he screamed at her, yanking his arm away violently from her soft touch. Both Karen and Caroline flinched visibly at his reaction, and they both took a step backwards, drawing away from him like two puppies threatened with a stick. 'That boy is a murderer, plain and simple,' he screamed, jabbing a finger in my direction. 'I know it, you know it, the whole god-dammed street knows it. The only person who refuses to open their eyes to the truth is that slag right there. I'm telling you, that boy should never have been born. He should have been killed in the womb when he was nothing more than a blood-sucking foetus.'

Grief does funny things to people. It can leave them unpredictable and out of control. It makes them say things they perhaps wouldn't have normally said, but there is only so far my mother's understanding could be pushed. Once you get personal with her family, she bites back, whatever the circumstances.

'You stupid, stupid man.' Her words were almost whispered and yet they somehow cut through the air as clearly as Mike's hollering. 'People like you bring nothing to this world but poison and hate. My son meant more to Shane than you could ever have done, and yet all you can do is try and lay the blame solely at his feet. Are you jealous of the friendship that they shared? Is that what drives such bile to spout from your stinking mouth? Now get off my property! You're not welcome here!'

'Don't worry, bitch, we're going,' Mike snapped. 'We've got no intention of hanging round with murderers and whores.'

He started to walk away, but then turned back to offer a final nugget of advice.

'Oh, one more thing. Stay away on Friday! Your presence ain't welcome,' and the three of them disappeared away up our drive, Mike in the lead and the two women trailing in the wake of his fury.

I looked up at my mum. She was shaking, her face was red, and tears now spilled down her cheeks, forced out by both the intensity of the encounter and the reasons that had brought it to be.

'What's happening on Friday, mum?' I asked.

She took a short step towards me, closing the distance, and squeezed me with arms that had always seemed just slightly too skinny. Her hug was a little too tight for comfort, but at that moment in time it was what we both needed.

'Mum,' I prompted, 'what's on Friday?'

'Shane's funeral, my darling,' and the crack of her voice mirrored my shattered life.

***

'I'm going out,' I said to my mum. It was the day following the visit from Mike and the day before the funeral.

'Oh, alright, dear. Where are you going?'

'I'm just going for a walk.'

My mum looked at me with concern written all over her face. 'Do you want me to come with you?'

'I'm fine, mum. I just need to get out. You're always telling me to get some fresh air, so I'm just going to go to the park or something. I won't be long.'

Ordinarily I would have taken my bike if I was going out somewhere that didn't involve my parents, but the thought of sitting astride that two wheeled monstrosity again filled me with horror. I think my dad must have put it away out of sight, because I hadn't noticed it in the garden or propped against the side of the house since the accident.

It only took me about fifteen minutes to make it to the railway lines that Shane had foolishly crossed not so long ago. I stood in the same spot where I had before, the chain-link fence in front of me and the wide expanse of field and tree-line at my back. The fence that Shane had crawled beneath was still damaged, and this somehow surprised me, almost as if I expected my friends recent unseen trespass to have alerted the authorities to the danger.

A gentle breeze blew through the trees behind me, the leaves rustling in a soothing orchestra of sound.

I feel so alive.

The words that Shane had uttered that day seemed to be carried on the breeze, perhaps even given voice by the swaying boughs of the trees. How cruel those words seemed now. How they taunted me, the very anti-thesis of the truth that had come to pass. I shuddered, and a coldness seeped down through my spine and settled in my toes.

Another breeze, another stir in the branches. Those words came to me again, reverberating in my mind, humming like a child's spinning top that mesmerises and captivates.

I feel so alive.

And then I was down on the floor, amongst the dust of the earth and the cigarette butts, yanking at the bottom of the fence and shuffling my way through to the other side. A rogue piece of wire snagged on my blue t-shirt and ripped a hole in the fabric of the sleeve, but I didn't care. It was just a t-shirt. Eventually, after a lot of shuffling, huffing and puffing, and with a lot more effort and a lot less grace than Shane had shown, I made it through to the other side so that my skinny 'Bean-Pole' frame stood before the railway track.

I was going to do this, I was really going to do it. I wanted to share with my friend, share in his experience and the buzz that it had given him. Perhaps this would somehow bring him back to me, if I could recreate a magical moment from his life. Maybe my actions would set in motion a burst of electricity that would fly through a conduit in time, to startle life back into Shane's still form, wherever it now lay. Were they the thoughts of a crazy man, or just those of a desperate child confused at the injustice of life?

I walked closer to the tracks and stood there looking at the shiny metal rails which now lay only an arms distance away. I raised a foot. I put it down again. I breathed in and out, gathering my courage, setting my mind on the course of action. I pictured Shane's face once he had crossed back over the tracks, his eyes all aglow, his mouth beaming a smile. I raised my foot once again...

...and then the train was there, thundering past where I stood, appearing as if from nowhere, like a locomotive sprung from hell. So absorbed had I been by my own thoughts, so focused on the sound of the wind tickling the trees, that the train had slowly crept up on me at eighty-odd miles an hour.

I stumbled back as the carriages tore past, the air around me violently disturbed, and fell onto the floor in a shocked heap. What had I been thinking? My mind was a jumbled mosh pit of memories, madness and mourning. Grief had temporarily taken control of this vehicle, and the ride was proving erratic at best.

I had been the one trying to make Shane see how foolish such an idea was, and normally I was pretty sensible for a young boy of twelve, but now I was attempting to tread the same path that my friend had taken, and for what reason? The truth is that I don't rightly know. Maybe part of me truly did believe that such a powerful action would allow me some form of connection with him in the afterlife. By treading the same path I would be at his side once more and could pretend he was still alive and ready for high jinks. Or perhaps I even had something of a temporary death-wish, a desire to have my own pain whisked away.

Whatever the reason, the near miss with the train gave me something of a wake-up call and blew some sense into my head. Shane was gone, no matter what I did, and one way or another I was going to have to come to terms with what had happened.

As I crawled back underneath the worthless chain-link fence, being careful not to damage my clothing any further, I heard somebody call out to me.

'Hey, boy, what do you think you're doing. Get away from there.'

I turned my head and saw an old man wearing a cap and walking his rat-sized dog, perhaps only fifty metres away.

'Get away,' he repeated. 'Stupid boy! Do you want to end up dead or something?'

I quickly got to my feet and ran away from the scene as fast as I was able, the ache in my chest accompanying my rapid footfalls all the way home.

Chapter 13

Courage has never been one of my strong points. I'm not the sort of person, for example, that would perform particularly well if a masked raider broke into my house, or if a mugger assaulted me in the street, pinning me up against a wall. *Take whatever you want* are the words most likely to spill forth from my gibbering lips. The time that I landed a punch on Robert Wall was a complete one-off, an act mostly driven by Shane and Shane's presence at my side, and any form of violence generally fills me pretty much with dread. No, bravery is not my thing. It doesn't flow through my veins as electricity through cable, lighting every corner of my body with plucky resolve.

Yet, it does occasionally spark. Flickering and fidgeting like a candle by a window to remind me that it is actually there, that I do have guts within my grasp. I think that the way it works for me is not like a spontaneous kind of bravery, but more of a considered courage. Somebody attacks me or catches me unawares then the adrenaline that this provokes causes me to take flight rather than to stand my ground, fists raised. But if I know with enough advance warning there is something heading my way, something potentially unsavoury or difficult that requires me to stand tall, then I tend to prove much more impressive in my act of daring-do. I suppose I just need time to think over my options, to get my head around what needs to be done so that I can mentally prepare myself.

But I believe there is one other vital factor that determines how driven I am in regards to bravery, and that is the strength of my belief that the road I'm treading is the right path. Experience has shown that if I don't feel strongly enough about something then generally my courage will desert me, running away hand in hand with my balls and my bottle, to leave me wobbling like a jelly on a plate. I suppose you could say a deserted dessert.

On the other hand, if my belief in the righteousness of something is deep-seated enough, and I have had enough time to pull myself together, then even I can face up to my fears. Impressive I know.

It was the day before Shane's funeral, and I had decided that I was going, no matter what anyone said. That night as I sat with my mum and dad in the safety of our lounge blankly watching the blur of pictures on our television screen, I announced my decision.

'I'm going.'

'OK mate. Good night.' My dad! Seriously!

'No, dad, not to bed. I'm going to the funeral tomorrow.'

My parents looked at each other, trying to communicate how they should react to this news through the power of their eyes alone.

'Adam, darling, listen I understand how you feel, really I do" offered my mum, 'but I don't know if that is such a good idea. You heard what Mike said...'

'Stuff him,' I said.

'Adam, don't talk that way. We need to try to understand it from his point of...'

'I don't care what he says. Shane was my best mate. I want to say good-bye. If I go to his funeral maybe Shane will see how sorry I am and forgive me for what I did. You said it yourself, I probably meant more to Shane than his dad did anyway.'

'Oh, darling, there is nothing for Shane to forgive you for, truly there isn't, but, listen, this is their son we're talking about. We have to respect their wishes.'

'Whose wishes are they though?' My dad's rumbling voice sounded calm and considered. 'Are they Karen's wishes, or those of the two girls? Are they Shane's wishes, are they what he would have wanted? I think we all know whose wishes we're talking about here, and they come from the most unreasonable man I've ever known. Sam, I think going to the funeral will help Adam find some peace over this whole tragic affair. He's got as much right to try and find that as anybody else. He needs closure.'

Voices from the television filled the ensuing silence, the canned laughter almost mocking my dad's thoughts.

'Sam?' he prompted.

'Ah, it's so hard, but OK, I agree. Our son has to come first. We'll go together.'

'No!' I almost shouted. My voice had a decisive finality to it that would have made Shane proud. 'There's no point in making Mike any angrier that he will be already. I'll go on my own.'

I had given this a lot of thought. My main reason for attending the funeral was so that I could offer a good-bye to my friend and because I felt so unbearably guilty. I also wanted to hear what the vicar would say, and hoped that his words would help to bring me some peace and understanding. If my parents were there trying to console me then I would be distracted by their kindness, and possibly even worried about an argument starting with Mike. On the other hand, if I attended on my own then I could give the ceremony my complete attention, and if Mike or anyone else was going to cause trouble then I could decide to leave quickly and quietly before things turned ugly. It would be in my own hands.

'Oh, Adam, I don't know...' began my mum.

'That's a very mature attitude, son.' For once it sounded like my dad was going to over-rule my mum as he cut in and interrupted her. 'Going to a funeral can be a daunting prospect, especially under these circumstances. If you decide to change your mind then let us know, but if not then I'll give you a lift and be waiting right outside for you, close by if you need me. How does that sound?'

'OK,' I said. 'Thank-you.'

***

The day of the funeral was fittingly an overcast affair, the sky blanketed with a carpet of light grey clouds rather than the dirty black thunderheads that had preceded Shane's tragic accident. I didn't have a suit to wear, so just opted for my white school shirt, tie and grey trousers. It was a fairly cold afternoon but I could hardly wear my school blazer as well – I felt I would look silly - so I just had to grit my teeth and bear it. Besides my dad was driving me, so I would either be in the car or the church during the service, and not exposed to the elements for too long.

We were running late, but that was intentional as we had all decided that it wouldn't be a good idea for me to arrive on time, hanging around and chatting to the other mourners – *Oh yes, hello, my name's Adam. You may have heard all about me. Yes, yes, that's right, spot on* – that *Adam! The one with the bike.* That would be really pushing our luck with Mike. The less time I spent there the better.

My mum had given me a solemn goodbye, hugging me fiercely and kissing my forehead numerous times, and now I was alone in the car with my dad. He seemed to be on edge, his fingers fidgeting over the steering wheel as if it was too hot to hold, whilst the paunch of his stomach sat underneath it like a big squashy bean bag. I wondered briefly if my beanpole frame would transform into that of my dad's in latter years, or if I would always be thin and bony like my mum.

'Are you worried, dad?' I asked him.

He chuckled half-heartedly. 'Is it that obvious?'

'A little bit, yeah. What are you thinking about?'

'Just you, boy. This is a brave thing you're doing, you know. Incredibly brave. Aren't you nervous?'

'Yeah, of course.'

'Listen to me, would you! I'm a lot of help aren't I? If you're already feeling nervous the last thing you need is me carrying on. Sorry'

I looked out of the window as we passed a row of shops. Two boys were standing outside of a newsagents, their bikes dumped haphazardly on the ground, sharing out some sweets between them that they had just purchased. I swallowed hard.

'I'm not worried about the actual funeral. Well, I am a little bit I suppose, but I want to go whatever. I'm just worried about what Mike might do.'

'Yeah, I know.'

'Does he make you nervous too, dad?'

He glanced across at me quickly before returning his attention to the road. 'I wish I could tell you he didn't, but I'd be lying. He's a nasty piece of work. I don't trust him. He's too unpredictable.'

'What do you mean?'

'Just that you don't always know how he is going to behave, or what he is going to do. But you don't need to worry about him. You're going into a church packed full of people, and I'll be right outside. If you start feeling unsure about him or anything you just come right out and we'll drive back home again. I'll only be a matter of seconds away.

'I suggest that when you go in you sit right at the back, closest to the doors. That way you can make a sharp exit if you want to, and you're not getting right in his face. Do you know what I mean?'

I sucked in a big breath and let it out loudly. 'Yeah. Got it.'

Shortly after we pulled up outside the church. An old stone Gothic archway stood at the entrance to the church grounds, and a path led from it up to a pair of chunky wooden doors which gave entrance to the church itself. All of the mourners had already gone in and the doors were closed.

'Right, I'll be waiting just here, OK? Are you sure you don't want me to come in with you? Last chance.'

'No, thanks, dad. Just knowing you're here is enough. We don't want to annoy Mike any more than needs be.' I glanced at the church and then back at my dad, a fearful look surely evident in my eyes.

'Come here, boy,' he said, and we reached across to each other over the gear stick and hand brake, which were surely designed by car manufacturers to make any form of hugging feel awkward. 'I love you, boy. You make me so proud. Send Shane best wishes from me and your mum.'

I climbed out of the car and started heading down the narrow gravel path towards the doors. The impressive church spire stretched up to the grey clouds overhead, like an accusing finger raised in defiance against the injustices of life. Graves flanked the path on either side, some headstones standing straight and true and some older ones bent at haphazard angles, as if the weight of the epitaphs written thereon was too great to bear.

With a final look back at my dad, and several more deep breaths I reached forward for the door handle and slipped quietly into the church.

To say I was nervous at this point would be an epic understatement. The last funeral I had attended had been my grandmothers, and that had been five years previous where I had been surrounded by loving family members. What was I thinking coming to this funeral on my own and where my presence was expressly unwanted? Was I showing that considered courage that I told you about, or just plain idiotic stupidity?

I stepped into the church proper, beyond the small entrance foyer, and was handed a booklet of the service by an old lady wearing a dark blue suit. On the front of the booklet was a picture of Shane smiling back at me, all of the confidence he showed in life beaming forth from those piercing blue eyes of his. Seeing the image of my friend steadied my resolve and reminded me why I had determined to come, no matter what anyone said. There was no turning back now.

Moving a few paces on from the lady in the blue suit, I looked up from the photo of Shane that had held my gaze and took in the scene before me. The church was of an average size with traditional wooden pews lined up like soldiers, and stunning stained glass windows that undoubtedly would have shed beautiful coloured pools of light onto the stone floor had the day been brighter. At the front of the church was a stone altar presided over by a large wooden cross suspended from the ceiling by sleek steel cables. Aside from the last few pews at the back of the church, close to where I was stood, all of them were virtually full-up with people that had known Shane either as friends or family. The vicar was stood at the front next to the altar and was conversing in hushed tones with Karen, who was dressed head to toe in deep black. Amongst the mourners there were a few that I recognised, although for the most part I could only see the back of people's heads. I saw some family friends and a couple of neighbours from our street, although I doubted that Violet Mayton, the curtain-twitcher from number 23, was amongst them. Her relationship with Mike was little better than my family's.

A number of people looked round and saw me standing there as I dallied over where to sit, my inexperience of life driving my indecision. Then, before I knew what was happening, the unmistakable hum of a crowd of people whispering to each other filled the church like a throng of cicadas, rapidly growing in intensity and accompanied by numerous looks back to where I stood as if I was a suspect in a police station posing for a mug-shot.

Suddenly I felt dizzy and my legs seemed to be losing their ability to support me. The sea of faces momentarily blurred into one, as they bobbed and weaved from where they sat, desperately vying for a look at the boy-killer who had shown the audacity to attend his victim's funeral.

I shot out a hand and grabbed hold of one of the pews, biting hard on the inside of my cheeks at the same time until, mercilessly, my head began to clear and my vision re-focused. People were still looking back at me, stealing glances here and there, and generally making a terrible collective effort at subtlety. I'm sure that one or two people even stared at me with their mouths hanging open in outright surprise, any attempt at a clandestine operation ignored.

Karen and the Vicar were also looking at me, their conversation interrupted by the whispered commotion. Karen looked deathly pale against the black of her outfit, her ever present pale blue eye-shadow an intrusion of colour on her face. The vicar said something to her and she nodded in response.

What did he ask her?

Is this the boy who killed your son? The one you warned me about. Shall I have the organist remove him from the church?

Or perhaps he had no idea who I was and his question to Karen was entirely unrelated.

Whatever he said, any thoughts I had on the matter, and indeed my decision on where to sit, were further delayed when the sight I had been most dreading loomed into view.

Mike rose up from the position where he had been sitting at the front of the church, his presence previously obscured by the rows of mourners between us, and slowly turned to look at me, his head seeming to rotate as gradually as that of a possessed doll in a classic horror movie. The scowl he wore on his face conveyed hatred, pure hatred, and his eyes practically bubbled with rage.

Having already hesitated where I was stood for an attention grabbing length of time, now I was frozen to the spot for longer still as Mike fixed me in his glare. The malevolence in that look was unmistakable, and if loathing itself could kill then I would already have been dead. Purposefully he stepped away from his pew and headed towards the central aisle that split the church in two and ended at my position in front of the main entrance. What was he going to do? Pick me up and physically eject me from the church? I shouldn't have come I thought, it was the wrong decision. What right did I have to intrude on this family's moment of grief, to add to the heart-break they were already suffering by showing my unwelcome face.

Mike turned the corner into the aisle and started heading towards me. His fists were clenched and his cheeks were flushed red, and not for once as a result of drinking too much alcohol. I was no longer left with any choice but to turn and bolt, to run out of the church and its murmuring mourners to the safety of my dad's car, where he could whisk me off home once again to the relieved arms of my mum.

But then something totally unexpected and amazing happened, as a blur of purple movement caught my eye. Molly ran from her position in the front pew and headed my way, breezing past Mike with the fluid grace of a seven year old, her shoes clattering out a staccato on the stone flags of the floor, as numerous heads turned to follow her progress. She almost knocked me over as she slammed into me in her eagerness to share an embrace, but I kept my footing and gladly returned the cuddle to Shane's younger sister. A quick look over the top of her shoulder revealed that Mike had stopped dead in his tracks.

'Hello, Adam,' said Molly. 'I'm happy you have come.'

'Me too, Molls.'

I realised that a hush had fallen on the Church and it felt as though everybody was tuning into our every word.

'My mummy says that the front seats are reversed for family only. So you have to sit somewhere else.'

'I think you mean reserved.'

'I know. That's what I said.' Molly slipped her tiny hand into my larger one and guided me towards one of the spare pews near the back. I was glad to be led. 'You can sit here.'

I did as I was told and sank down gratefully onto the hard wooden seat so that Molly and I were roughly the same height.

'I miss Shane, Adam. My body hurts here,' she said indicating her chest, ' and here too, in my throat.'

'Yep, me too, Molls. I miss him more than anything. I'm sorry.'

'So am I,' she said before planting a delicate kiss on one of my cheeks. 'I love you, Adam.'

With that she turned and headed back towards the front of the church, stopping to give her dad a hug in the position where he still stood, where he had watched the little scene unfold, oblivious to the rage that her father had been about to unleash and to whom it would have been directed. Together the two of them walked back to their seats, their hands joined, and my presence at the ceremony was secured by the instinctive actions of the adorable Molly. Whatever Mike had been planning to do to me had been undone by a small girl with a big heart.

As the service commenced I listened intently to the readings and the generous words from the vicar and from one of Shane's uncles. I sang heartily along to the chosen hymns, feeling I owed it to my friend to give him a proper good-bye. I considered carefully the prayers that the vicar offered to God in the name of Shane, and tried to understand how such a God could allow a tragedy like this to run its course. Huge wracking sobs punctuated the service from people all around the church, but I was not one of them. I was too focused on remembering the words that were sent after Shane on whatever journey he was now on. I wanted to remember this sad occasion in as much detail as I could, seeing it as my final chance to somehow connect to my friend. I had already shed my fair share of tears, and there would be plenty of time for more in the days to come.

When the funeral finally came to a close I was the first to leave the church, slipping out quickly and quietly and running to where my dad sat patiently in the car, reading his newspaper.

As he pulled away I caught a glimpse of Molly and Caroline exiting the old building, hand in hand. Their faces were masks of sorrow.

'There is no God,' I said to my dad.

'No, son, probably not.'

Chapter 14

After the funeral my mum presented me with a photograph in a wooden frame. It showed Shane and I standing side by side in our garden on a stunning summer's day. We both held half-devoured 99Flake ice creams that we had purchased from the recently departed ice-cream van, whose welcome arrival was always announced by the jangle of the Match of the Day theme tune. The two of us had huge grins on our faces, and I think we may have been laughing at some awful gag that my dad had told. After eating our ice creams we had both changed into our swimming shorts in order to run in and out of the garden sprinkler, that arced beams of water slowly back and forth across the lawn. This was then followed by a huge water fight that pitched us two boys against the might of my dad, whilst my mum watched on, yelping everytime some water strayed too close to her position on the sun-lounger. It had been a great day.

I placed the photograph on my bedside cabinet and often found myself gazing deep into its realm, lost in happy thoughts and memories of shared adventures with my absent friend. He may have been dead but I was determined to keep his past alive in my heart and my mind.

It was three days after the funeral when I had an unexpected visitor. I had started back at school that same day, having agreed with my parents that the sooner I threw myself back into normal life the better for me it would be, and was in my bedroom trying to catch up on missed work. The school had been very understanding and were doing their best not to put any pressure on me in terms of both attendance and workload, but if I was left with too much time on my hands then there was only one thing that I was going to be thinking about, and that was not conducive to a sane state of mind. The irony was that Shane's absence actually resulted in a lot more time to try and fill, and the one thing I was advised against doing was sitting and spending that time thinking about my friend and all that had happened. This advice came from both my parents and from a man who was officially my 'counsellor' who came to talk to me on occasion for a short while. Yes, it was good to remember Shane, to think on all the fun and happy times we had shared together, but it was bad to sit and brood, to think *what if.*

I heard the door-bell chime and immediately made my way to the top of the stairs where I listened intently, keen to find out who it was, and ultimately fearful of that visitor being Mike. It wasn't Mike, but my heart sank nonetheless when I realised who it was and that they wanted to talk to me.

'Hello, Sam. Sorry to bother you. Would it be OK to talk to Adam please?' came the high-pitched voice.

Shane's older sister had never been that polite and eloquent when she spoke to me. I was more likely to receive the cold shoulder or, if she was feeling particularly vindictive, a cutting insult, and all just for being Shane's friend as opposed to any personal dislike. At least this was what Shane had told me.

'Oh, er, yes, yes of course. Let me call him down for you...Adam! Adam! Caroline's here to see you!'

My mum's voice slunk up the stairs like an unwelcome phantom patrolling a haunted house, and I froze to the spot as if that same phantom was floating before me. I could hear my mum making polite chit-chat with Caroline whilst she waited for me to appear, asking how she was bearing up and if she knew when she would start back at school. I stayed out of sight, loath to traipse down the stairs and face her. What did she want? What reason could she have for springing this surprise visit on me?

'Adam!' Did you hear me? Caroline is here,' my mum called up the stairs before offering an apology to our neighbour.

Reluctantly, and realising there was no way to avoid the inevitable, I gathered myself and went downstairs.

'Finally,' said my mum. 'I'll leave you two to it,' and she disappeared into the kitchen, despite my futile attempt to try and root her to the spot with the power of my eyes alone.

'Hi,' I said.

'Hi.'

Silence.

'Can I come in for a minute,' she asked. 'Probably best if my dad doesn't see me standing here on the step.'

'Oh, er, yes, of course. Come in.'

Caroline was fifteen years old, attractive and already quite well endowed. The clothes she tended to wear did little to hide her blooming sexuality and I rarely felt comfortable in her presence. I felt myself blushing and clumsily tried to conceal the fact by scratching at my face whilst willing the redness to take a trip to Timbuktu.

'He doesn't know I'm 'ere, and he would be pretty pissed if he did. He's gone out somewhere but best not to take any chances.'

'Right, yeah, OK.' I was floundering, my age combining with my ungainliness as usual to crush any effort at appearing cool with the opposite sex. 'So, what do you want?'

Rude and blunt? Yes. Intended? No.

'Me and me mum just wanted to say we're glad you came. To Sha...to the funeral I mean.' She paused and looked at me with her sad, pretty eyes. 'It's crazy, but since he died I can't bring myself to say his name without crying. I never wanted him near me when he was alive, and now he's dead it's the only thing I want. Silly.'

'That's not silly,' I said.

A nervous laugh. 'No, maybe not. But, yeah, that's all really. Just to say we're cool with it. It must have taken guts to come, especially after the way my dad has been. Molly was glad too, but I suppose ya get that already. I don't know if she understands that he's not coming back.'

'I'm sor...'

'Don't!' Caroline held up a hand in a halting gesture. 'Don't say it! Me, me mum, Molly - none of us blame you. It was just an accident. Me mum would be 'ere too saying all this, but she's still in bits. But she asked me to come 'ere. She wanted ya to know how we felt.'

'Thank-you.'

'Just don't expect me to be friends with you just coz of this, Beanpole.' A tear travelled down her cheek and she wiped it away with a laugh, but it was a soft laugh rather than a cruel one. 'I still think you're an idiot.'

Then, as if her visit in the first place hadn't been enough of a surprise, Caroline stepped forward and embraced me firmly until I eventually stopped my impression of a statue and reciprocated the gesture.

And then, in a flash, she pulled away from me and was gone without another word or backward glance. It must have been just as hard for her to come and say those words to me as it had been for me to attend the funeral. It was an absolution, an act of forgiveness from Caroline and her mum.

I shut the door and the noise brought my mum back out of the kitchen to the hallway, drying her hands on a cat-print tea-towel.

She smiled at me and I went to her.

***

A few weeks after Shane's funeral my parents put our house on the market. It was, in reality, the only course of action that was open to them. Leaving your front door everyday to go to work or school or the shops and being faced with the looming sight of number 20 directly across the road was a burden that was simply too heavy to bear. The thought that Shane's family had a similar view of our house was equally weighty, not to mention the very real possibility that everytime we left our house we might bump into the

Metcalfes as they were on their way out or coming back home again.

Bizarrely bumping into Mike was less trying than a chance meeting with Karen or Caroline proved to be. With Mike there was never any need for words, so apparent was his hatred for our household, and he would pass by with a filthy scowl and inaudible muttered words. Yet, with Karen and her oldest daughter the atmosphere was excruciatingly uncomfortable. The lack of animosity they felt towards us, and the friendship that already existed between Karen and my mum, meant that an exchange of pleasantries was unavoidable. We would have to face Karen and drink in the haunted look that played across her zombie-like face, her blue eye-shadow doing little to lift the darkness that drained the life from her sockets. Her words were always spoken in monotone, bland and empty as if her body was no longer possessed by a soul. She was like a dog riddled with cancer, whose only purpose was to put one foot in front of the other in order to reach a more comfortable spot in which to live out her remaining days.

By moving house were we cowardly running away with our tail between our legs, refusing to face up to the difficulties of the situation? Perhaps this is partly true, but could it not also be said that it was an act of mercy to Shane's family, or indeed an act of survival for our own? With my family gone it would be easier for them, as well as us, to try and rebuild our lives. There would be a lessening of the palpable tension that fizzled in the air, an end to the awkward smiles and stiff waves that creaked their way across the street each time that fate ordained our paths collide.

My parents were also well aware that at my school the taunting had already started. Children can be naively cruel, and the mocking accusations of my huge part in Shane's death did not take long to surface, even though most people at my secondary school had no idea who he was. Word somehow filtered back to my parents of the additional difficulties I was being faced with and perhaps that was the final straw.

We moved from Kent to Essex, crossing over the River Thames which we hoped would act as enough of a barrier to idle gossip, affording us protection from a past heartache that was nobody else's business but ours. My dad could still commute to his job until something more local came up, and I could start at a new school where my worst crime amongst my peers would be the bearable burden of being a somewhat lanky, uncool kid who was relatively late to reach puberty.

The move heralded a new beginning and closed the door on the first twelve years of my life. All that had happened with Shane and Mike was in the past, a vivid memory mixed with joy and pain. But a door that has been closed can be flung open once again, and I was to meet Mike one final time.

Part 2

The noisy return of Zak and Maz brought an abrupt end to my peace, quiet and pondering. The birds scattered as my son burst into the garden, like a troop of protesters fleeing a charge from the riot police.

'Dadddeeeee,' my son called, running over and jumping on my lap, causing me to quickly move my beer bottle out of his way lest any of the liquid gold be sinfully wasted.

'The Zak-Meister! How's it going little-man? How was your party?'

'Really, really good. They had a bouncy castle and me and Henry was trying to jump the highest. But one little boy hurt himself and got a nosebleed.'

'Oh, was he OK?'

'I dunno. Fink so. Will you come on the trampa with me?' Trampa was Zak speak for trampoline.

'Haven't you done enough bouncing for one day?'

'I want to show you how high I can go. Pleeeaassseee.'

'Alright, just let me have a quick word with your mum first. You go ahead and I'll be there in a minute.'

I watched as Zak bounded over to the trampoline, shaking my head in amazement at his insatiable zest for life. Getting up out of my chair I stepped over to Maz and gave her a warm hug and quick kiss in greeting.

'So, how was it really?' I asked.

'Well, Zak had a nice time, which is all that matters really, but some of those other parents never cease to amaze me with how pathetically weak they are in their so-called efforts at controlling their own kids.'

'Like what?'

'Like that poor kid that ended up with a nosebleed. Some bigger kid was charging round and I'm sure he was bumping into the little ones on purpose. His mother just goes *stop doing that Freddy* in this wet-sounding voice, and then just does nothing when he completely ignores her. Then he goes and bumps into this little boy and gives him the nosebleed. So she tells him to stop again, and still he ignores her, and still she did nothing about it. I mean, he's just given some other kid a nosebleed for crying-out-loud, but she's more interested in having a gossip with her mate.'

'I'm surprised you didn't haul the brat off the bouncy castle yourself and stand him in the corner.'

'Believe me I would have, but I didn't want to ruin the party. It's probably not even that kid's fault really, he's just after a bit of attention from his mum. Anyway, enough of my whinging. How have things been here? You look at though you haven't moved from that spot except to get yourself another couple of beers.'

'Guilty as charged. Bit pissed off, if I'm honest, that you weren't here to fetch them for me.'

'Slob,' said Maz, slapping me playfully on the arm and laughing that beautiful infectious laugh of hers. The sun had been blessing her face and a small scattering of freckles danced across her cute nose.

'I've been busy thinking things through. Mulling over my memories of Shane, Mike, my parents. I'm just trying to get my head around everything; thinking about all that went on back when I was a kid.'

'And is it helping do you think? To accept the truth I mean?'

'Yeah, maybe, Maz, maybe a little. I don't know really. The whole thing still seems all so surreal, as if it happened to someone else and I'm just watching on. It's one thing accepting the truth, but it's another to actually bring yourself to forgive someone.'

'Who? Mike or your mum?'

'Christ, my mum of course! There's no way that I could ever forgive Mike for what he's done, dead or otherwise. My mum...I guess, I hope, I just need some more time.'

'Come on, Daddy,' called Zak from the trampoline, still bouncing up and down as he called out impatiently.

'Alright, Zakky, one sec.'

'Well, I'm going out with the girls tonight remember,' continued Maz, 'so once Zak's in bed you'll have some more peace and quiet to get your head around it. But, I can cancel if you need me here. Maybe you'll find it easier if we talk it over some more.'

It was a genuine offer from Maz, but a pointless one nonetheless. She knew full well what my answer would be, our years together having bred enough familiarity with the way that each other operated. If I had a worry or a problem to solve I preferred to work it through in my own head, and if there were distractions going on around me I simply wouldn't be able to do that. I was always prepared to listen to Maz's opinions and thoughts, and most of the time she was certainly worth listening to, but this time I needed to come to my own conclusions, such was my personal involvement.

'No, it's OK, you go out with the girls, it's been too long since you saw them. Besides we've already talked this over countless times. Unless you have some new words of wisdom to share I'll probably make more headway with perfect silence and perfect beers.'

'Hmmm, alright then. Just don't have too many perfect beers, because if I have enough perfect wine then I might need a perfect erection,' Maz said laughing at her own joke. 'Now get on that trampa.'

'You're pure filth,' I said and then walked over to Zak before his patience with me ran its course.

***

'Right, come on Zak, time for bed.'

'Ah no, Daddy, just a bit longer. Not yet.'

'You've already had a bit longer three times. Bed-time now. Go and choose a story please, and pop on some pyjamas.'

'Please, Daddy...'

'Shall I choose for you?'

'No, I'll choose.'

I listened as Zak ran up stairs to his bedroom to choose a book, his gentle footfalls beating out a rapid pattern on the floorboards. He reappeared again dressed in his favourite truck patterned PJs and clutching his chosen bedtime story: Room on the Broom by Axel Scheffler and Julia Donaldson - one of my favourites to read. The two of us cosied up on the sofa as I recited the story aloud to my son.

There was no feeling quite like this, sharing a cuddle with my boy. The warmth of his small body passing to mine from his position on my lap; the sound of his gentle breathing as his chest rose and fell, rose and fell; my chin resting on his head and taking in the smell of his hair. Once, when he was much younger, not much more than a baby, I watched a television show that covered different commercials from around the world. One of them was from a road safety campaign in Australia which showed a speeding driver losing control of his vehicle so that it careered through a fence and into a garden. A young child that was playing within the safety of their own outdoor space was wiped out by the tumbling car that had no right to be there. It was perhaps the hardest hitting commercial I have ever seen, which is of course the intention. We were having a cuddle that evening too, although Zak had been fast asleep in my arms for at least half an hour. I have never felt more protective of my son, or indeed anyone, than at that moment in time. I remember pulling him closer to me and wrapping my arms tighter around his frail frame, as if the very essence of our closeness would act like a spell to ward off any threats to his safety.

Such cuddles with your children are priceless moments in time. To be savoured.

The story finished and I wandered upstairs with a visibly flagging Zak, carrying him up the last few stairs, more for my own satisfaction than his, and laying him down gently on his bed.

'You look tired now,' I said.

'No, I'm not,' he said, trying and failing to stifle a yawn.

'Alright, if you insist.'

'Daddy?'

'Yes, Zakmeister?'

'Can we go see nanny and grandad again soon. We've not seen them forever.'

'Yeah, maybe. We've been pretty busy lately.' I tried to maintain a neutral tone to my voice, because at times children can be surprisingly astute and pick up on such clumsily dropped clues.

'We've not been *that* busy. I want to show them my new Transformer.'

Zak loved his grandparents and they doted on him and spoiled him rotten. If I couldn't learn to forgive my mum then my son was also an innocent victim of the fall out, as was my dad.

'I'll have a word with mummy and see when we're free.' I bent down and kissed his forehead. 'Night, Zak'.

'Oh, daddy?'

'Yes?'

'Can you make me snug as a bug?' A usual delaying tactic from my son, but irresistible nonetheless.

I bent down and pushed the quilt, with its Buzz Lightyear imprint, tighter around his tiny form until the outline of his body could be seen and he looked like a cocooned bug. 'There you go. Now go to sleep. Love you.'

'Love you, Daddy.'

Once downstairs I went to the fridge and grabbed another beer. I've never been a big drinker, especially not when on my own, but if chewing over a problem I sometimes find that washing the morsels down with a swig of lager seems to help. It helps me to relax when confronted with trying demons, and the demons I was about to face were particularly upsetting.

I sat down in my favourite arm chair, the one that Maz and I fought over when granted some rare time to sit and read a book, and took a small sip of my partner for the evening.

I chased down my beer with a chest expanding breath.

Chapter 15

A few months ago, before the news of Mike's death broke, an incident occurred that meant it was necessary to punish my son. He had behaved in a typically reckless and bull-headed fashion that so underlined the person he seemed to be evolving into. Often I have found myself watching Zak and wondering if there are any parts of me that have been passed to him within his genes. Everything he does seems to remind me of my wife. The way he might stoop down to pick up and examine a rounded pebble from a beach; the manner in which he stretches his arms out in front of his body, his hands clasped together, upon first waking up; his broad welcoming smile when I come home from work; the way he stands when preparing to catch a ball.

I tease my wife about the lack of similarity between myself and my boy, implying he is a result of her infidelity. She parries my blow and counter-thrusts with her insistence that it wasn't her fault, she just needed to find a bigger man to satisfy her. But then, later, she will return to the topic having replayed our conversation in her head, and worried herself that I am genuinely upset.

He has your eyes, she will say, *such kind looking eyes.* Or *He is blessed with your memory. That boy never seems to forget anything.*

Maz does make some valid points. The boy does seem to share my penchant for remembering things, as well as having eyes modelled on my own, although as to whether kindness can truly be seen in somebody's peepers is another topic that I dispute with my wife. Yet, aside from these similarities and a few other minor traits, Zak reflects his mother and not just physically. He seems to share her character traits too, such as the afore mentioned recklessness that landed him in trouble in the first place. He also displays a stubbornness that genuinely makes you wonder who would win if he were to enter a staring contest with a shop mannequin, as well as a fearless attitude that scares me witless with regards to what dangers it will prompt him to face down in later life. Aside from these 'qualities' he is also a boy bursting with laughter, whose cheekiness seems to know no bounds and whose personality appears to lift everybody that he comes into touch with.

Yep, he is my wife through and through, and he also reminds me of Shane. The wilfulness. The natural charisma. Perhaps there is something within me that attracts these people, that means I have a close affinity to such characters. Perhaps I seek out those qualities in others that I myself are deficient in. Opposites attract so they say.

My son's misdemeanour was a typical example that reflects his personality. He had been playing at a friend's house, a boy called Richard that he went to school with and with whom he had previously attended nursery, so the family were quite well known to us. They lived in a nearby street across from ours, a five minute stroll to the end of our road and five further minutes round the corner to their place. We were due to collect him in about forty-five minutes time, so were surprised when there was a knock at the door which, when opened, revealed my son.

'Zak!' I heard Maz exclaim, prompting me to make my way to the front door. 'What are you doing here? Where's Nikki?'

When I arrived at the door I saw Zak stepping into the hallway whilst Maz was leaning outside to look for Nikki, the mother of our son's friend.

'She's gone. She just taked me to the top, but she had to go.'

'Go? Go where?' asked Maz, coming back inside and closing the door.

'I dunno. Shopping I think.'

'What so she...'

The shrill jangle of the telephone cut my wife off mid-sentence as she turned away to answer it. I rarely answer the phone in our house, as it was hardly ever for me and because I have a passionate dislike for talking on the bloody thing.

Zak and I were left alone in the hallway and I looked down upon him as he sat on the floor and struggled to remove his once white trainers. He must have felt my eyes upon him because he looked up at me and flashed a guilty smile. As I shook my head at him my suspicions were proved correct by Maz's voice that filtered through from the lounge.

'Yes, don't worry, Nikki, he's here with us. He must have walked home. I'm so sorry.' A long pause. 'No, no, please don't worry. It's really not your fault. Let me have a word with him and I'll call you straight back.'

'Sounds like you're in trouble,' I said to my son, but he chose to stare at his feet rather than meet my gaze.

'Do you want to tell me the truth now, Zak?' said Maz as she thundered back into the room.

'I did already. Nikki taked me to the top and then she went.'

'To the top? The top of where? Oh, it doesn't matter. You're lying to us.'

'To the top of our house. I'm not lying.' Stubborn on the verge of stupidity.

'Of course you're lying. I just spoke to Nikki. She was worried sick. One minute you're outside playing with Richard and the next you're nowhere to be seen, but her garden gate is wide open.'

'Nikki taked me home.' Crikey I thought, ten out of ten for sticking to your lie.

'Zak!' I rumbled, a warning tone to my voice, although truth be known if Zak was going to be more scared of anyone (which was unlikely considering how fearless he seemed) it would be my wife. Nevertheless, he finally relented.

'Alright! Richard was annoying so I left. We did an argument.'

'And without even telling Nikki,' said Maz. 'What do you think you're doing? You don't ever walk out on the streets, or anywhere for that matter, unless you're with an adult. Anything could have happened to you.'

'But it didn't. I knew the way.'

'That is not the point. There are nasty people out there that can hurt you, darling. You mustn't do that ever again. Can you imagine how Nikki must have felt when she realised you were missing?'

And so it went on. Zak was punished by having his train track taken away for three days and made to apologise in person to Nikki and Richard, yet at no point did he shed any tears. He was sorry alright, genuinely so, but tears were only distant friends with my son's eyes. Tears were reserved for those occasions where he had a particularly bad fall or bash to the head.

So like Shane it was almost uncanny.

It makes me wonder how Shane's own children would have been had he lived to have any. Perhaps his perfect match for a wife would have been somebody that shared my own character traits, somebody completely different to who he was, and then maybe his off-spring would have taken after their mother. Would he have been a patient father, understanding if his children were timid souls like his one-time best friend all those years ago? I suspect that the Shane I knew when I was twelve would have one day grown into an excellent father.

***

Following Shane's passing and our subsequent move to Essex, things slowly settled back into a routine and life went on. The pain was always there, permanently sitting hand in hand with my guilt, make no mistake about that, but time won't be denied its relentless progress. Sometimes the hurt would be sitting quietly on the edge of my mind, keeping to itself but casting a shadow on my periphery so I still knew it was there. Other moments it would be getting right up close and in my face, invading my personal space, and triggered by some everyday event such as seeing somebody wearing a t-shirt similar to one Shane favoured, or overhearing somebody call out in a tone that mimicked my friend. Or even my own enjoyment at a life denied to my friend.

I can never decide which is worse. The moments of pain that are more intense or those that gently thrum away in the back-ground, like the tide as it ebbs and flows, ebbs and flows, waiting for the crash of a wave that you know will eventually rise up and smash down upon the rocks like a fist into an exposed heart.

My new school turned out to be surprisingly satisfactory. Admittedly it wasn't a grammar school, but I found that I preferred the teaching and the lessons to my previous school. There seemed to be a more relaxed atmosphere in the classroom, as if the teachers could really get on with their jobs without being concerned about upholding the traditions and standards of a stuffier establishment. I was also fortunate enough to quickly make some new friends, and whilst never considered one of the cool kids, my school days were not blighted by bullies either. My gangly frame and gawky appearance surely made me a prime target for being picked on, but for some reason I was left alone, aside from the usual insults that virtually every kid had thrown their way during the course of the school-week. Perhaps it was my height that afforded me some protection, or maybe my peers sensed something about me that prompted them to lay-off, an aura that warned of the unspoken trauma I had already suffered, a feeling that if you push this one too much you just don't know which way the shit is going to fly. Did I carry a look in my eyes, perhaps reflecting a precarious rope bridge with bonds that were frayed and starting to unravel? How much more weight could this particular bridge take before: snap, crash, disaster?

So I was left alone and I got my head down and worked hard, just like the good, honest student I had always been. As much as I loved my dad, and had adored visiting his work and playing with buses when I was younger, driving a big red hunk of metal for a living was not what I wanted to end up doing. I wanted more than that, wanted to do a job that I was passionate about, that didn't leave me wanting to dive back under the duvet every morning rather than face another day's work.

As I moved tentatively into my early teenage years I discovered a new passion in life, aside from the predictable ogling of pretty girls or sneaking glances down their blouses.

Running!

The yearly cross country season had never been something that filled me with excitement, but nor did it horrify me. I had always been pretty non-plussed about the enforced slog over muddy fields, and through footpaths riddled with puddles. And then one year, when I was fourteen, I was running aimlessly along the route designated by the P.E. teachers, just casually putting one foot in front of the other, when I realised that I was incredibly close to the race leaders. In front of me were two boys running side-by-side who I recognised as the lads who usually vied for first place, so that likely meant that I was nestled into third spot. I had been trotting along without paying any attention to where I was headed or what speed I was going, my mind focussed on my personal battle with my perpetual guilt and the events of the recent past.

Immediately I started to speed up, to open my legs into a longer stride, determined to catch the race leaders. But then, just as quickly, I slowed back down again. I was Adam 'Bean-Pole' Wickes, a boy that stood at the back of the group when teams were being picked, a lad that blushed and put his head down if a girl spoke a single word to him. I felt no desire to be recognised. I had no confidence to be recognised. Around five minutes later I duly crossed the finish line in my previously attained third place. The boys that finished in first and second had always stayed in my sight and were now sat on the grass looking jaded and spent.

My P.E. teacher, Mr Lightwood (or Balsa as he was known amongst the students) called me over.

'Good going, Wickes,' he said approvingly, his thick moustache moving up and down in approval. 'Where did that come from? Third place.'

A shrug of my bony shoulders. 'I don't know, Sir.'

'Well, keep it up, lad.'

I started to turn away, but he called me back.

'Oh, one more thing, Wickes.'

'Yes, Sir?'

'Next time, don't hold back.'

'I don't...'

'You're not even breathing heavy, lad.' Was there a wry smile underneath that moustache? 'A similar lack of effort from you next time will land you a detention. Off you go.'

So it seemed that I had discovered a talent. I went home and told my parents who seemed as surprised about the news as I myself was.

'That Mr. Lightwood was right,' said my dad, mid-mouthful. 'What were you doing holding back?'

'Don't talk with your mouthful, Trevor. We don't want to see your chewed up food.'

My dad waved my mum's words away, as if they were a fly circling his dinner.

'I dunno. I don't want a lot of fuss,' I said, moving my peas around my plate with my fork.

'What do you mean, fuss?'

'He means he doesn't want a lot of attention, Trevor,' scolded my mum. 'It's not the way us Wickes's do things.

Sorry, Adam, you know your dad, always a bit slow on the uptake.'

Attention was not my thing, admittedly, but the lure to open up my legs at the next race was irresistible. The sudden realisation that I had a talent, that there was something I could do better than most people, was a new experience and I was determined to make the most of it. I cruised around the course, leaving the usual winners in my wake, and it all seemed so easy - I still had so much left in the tank.

'Good time,' said Balsa as I crossed the finish line, no other students even within sight. 'Perhaps you should think about joining an athletics club and really testing yourself. Enter into some tougher races. I'll certainly be putting you in the school team.'

And so I did. My parents were surprised at the enthusiasm and desire I exhibited at this new found passion that had unexpectedly appeared from no-where. Neither of them had ever really demonstrated a talent or enjoyment for playing any kind of sport, so I think there was a certain lack of understanding in regards to my excitement. Why would anyone want to run for any great distance, punishing their body so that their lungs burnt and their legs felt like they were detached from their torso, or so that they felt like an eighty year old in the body of a teenager? My dad could appreciate how the buzz of winning races must be something worth experiencing, but he couldn't fathom the pain it took to attain that goal.

For me, though, running wasn't just about winning the races. I'd be lying if I said that I didn't enjoy crossing that finish-line first, that the adrenaline didn't lift me up high amongst the clouds and the birds. It did, or course it did, and I won my share of races too, but I lost many more than I won. When I realised that I wasn't quite good enough to be the next Seb Coe, I settled into enjoying the running for the other benefits that it brought me: the feeling of freedom; an escape from empty weekends when nothing was planned; a chance to think with a clear head and attempt to come to terms with my part in my best friend's death.

On days when I was feeling particularly guilt-ridden I would pull on my trainers and go for a jog. In my head I would chat to Shane as I ran along pavements or cut across fields, imagining what his responses would have been to particular snippets of news. I would envisage how he would have reacted to football scores, idle gossip or amusing incidents that I would have shared with him had he still been with us. In my head I kept him alive.

The clarity of thought that the running gave me was an unexpected gift. It brought forth memories, tiny snippets in time, of moments spent with my friend. The time he clapped his hands at a wasp, killing it instantly; the smile he gave me when I helped him with a spelling; the double fisted celebration whenever he scored a goal during our lunchtime matches; his hatred of the stench of over-ripe bananas. Small actions and spoken words, but things that painted a picture of who my friend was nonetheless.

My mind had been laid siege by a battalion of guilt and an army of grief, until the miracle of running stretched its legs from far away and sprinted to the rescue. My parents had always been there for me, talking to me freely about my feelings and encouraging me to open-up, but no words from them or a counsellor I saw on occasion could help me as running had. This is no reflection on my mum and dad, there was little else they could have done for me, but I suppose that everybody copes with loss in their own way, and for me it meant pulling on a pair of trainers.

So I gradually moved into acceptance. The ache was always there, but it became easier to bear. The guilt never went away, but I accepted that it was just a terrible accident. Had our roles been reversed I would have wanted Shane to get on with life, to enjoy whatever time had been granted him, and I know that he would have felt the same way.

I missed my old life, my old home. I missed seeing Molly's cheery face and watching Violet Mayton walk her beloved King Charles Spaniel. I missed all my old haunts and visiting the local sweet shop just around the corner. But, as a family, we made a new life for ourselves, and in time I was happy once again. My dad managed to get work with a local bus company, so could ditch his commute. My mum got herself a job working on reception for a nearby courier company, so financially there were no worries.

And I grew up. My voice broke, I cringed my way through puberty and I even got to go on a couple of dates here and there, including a double date to the cinema where, half-way through the film, the two girls got up to go to the toilet and didn't bother coming back. Slowly, way too slowly for my liking, my scrawny frame started to fill out a little. I was still skinnier than the average lad my age, but I realised that this was accentuated by my height. I asked for some weight-lifting equipment for my sixteenth birthday, and gradually pumped my frame into something that I considered would be more appealing to the lucky ladies out there. Don't get the wrong picture now, I was never an Arnold Schwarzenegger in the making, and still looked tall and thin, but it was much less pronounced than before, and I felt more comfortable within myself. Besides, regular running for miles on end is never conducive to the frame of a beef-cake.

At school my grades were good. Not excellent, but more than adequate to set me on the path to Birmingham University where I opted to study for a degree in Computer Science. If there was one thing that came naturally to me, aside from running, it was anything IT related. I felt at home amongst the various software applications and the complex algorithms hidden behind the user-friendly formatting of various programs. The tip-tap-tapping that reverberated around a room full of hard-working students drumming away on their key-boards made me feel comfortable, and I knew that a life surrounded by computers would suit me down to the ground.

Maz casually strolled into my life when I was in the final year of my degree and she was entering the second year of her art degree. She had got herself a job pulling pints in a local pub to help pay her way through university. This particular pub was a favourite of my group of uni friends, and various assortments of us could be found there at least twice a week if not more, course work and funds permitting. It was an old traditional British boozer, with antique rifles adorning the walls and faded paintings of fox hunts in full flow. The carpet was a mixture of deep red, beer stains and burn marks from cigarette butts. It would never win any prizes for decor, but the beer was good, the prices were cheap and it had a welcoming atmosphere.

Maz had worked there for a couple of months and all I had ever spoken to her were the words lager, pints, thanks and pardon. This wasn't because I didn't find her attractive, everyone in my group found her attractive, it was more a case of thinking she was way out of my league, as well as my shocking lack of confidence around beautiful women. The twinkling eyes and the dimples in her cheeks when she flashed her smile, which was often. The perfect pins that carried her around the pub with that self-assured walk. And the bust - wow - don't get me started on the bust. It was a bust almost worth getting busted for.

So I was surprised when she struck up conversation with me during a slow mid-week shift. I had just finished paying for my pint and was about to walk over and join my crowd, when her voice pulled me back to the bar.

'Adam, I'm bored! Entertain me!'

'Er, oh, what?' She knew my name. How did she know my name? 'What do you want me to do?'

'Stand on your head!' Her laugh came easily, her dimples staring thankfully at me for bringing them to life once more. 'I don't know, how about telling me about yourself.'

'About myself?'

'Yeah, why not? Would it be boring?'

'Well, maybe a little bit.' I was way too honest with how I saw myself. 'How do you know my name?'

'Your group always comes in here. I overhear things.'

'Oh, right, so you know all of our names?'

'No, just yours.'

'Just mine?'

'Just yours.'

At the time I believed this to be true, but having quizzed Maz on this very night since then, she has admitted that she knew most of our names, and that this was just her being flirtatious.

My eyes flicked around the pub nervously, until they settled on the peanuts sat in a bowl on top of the bar.

'Did you know that bar snacks are one of the most unhygienic things you can eat. They're covered in urine from when people return from the bogs without washing their hands.' What an idiot!

Maz laughed. 'I bet you use that chat-up line on all of the girls. What a charmer!'

I felt my cheeks blushing furiously, and kicked myself at my total lack of skill with women.

'Try again,' she said, her dimples dancing to her tune.

In the end I stuck with the basics, telling her about the degree I was doing, and where my student digs were. I asked her about her course and whether she was enjoying it. We laughed when one of my friends came to the bar and ate some peanuts while she was serving him. I bought another drink and got her one too, and the alcohol started to relax me. I thought: *she knew my name.*

'You've got nice hands,' she said. 'They look perfect for IT.'

'They're too long. They look like they've been on a rack.'

She suddenly put her hands on her hips and feigned anger. 'Well, whose rack have you been putting them on you dirty pervert?'

That was Maz. Confidence personified. Easy to talk to. Funny. Honest.

And very attractive.

I sat at that bar all night talking to her, praying that the pub would remain quiet or that punters would leave for home, so that interruptions would be few and far between. We talked about her friends, where she had been brought up, what was good and bad about her course, the three year sabbatical she had taken, mostly to travel. She whispered about her job, how she thought the landlady was a total schizophrenic and how her husband did nothing but drink away their profits. We chatted about our interests, my love of running, her hatred but perseverance with aerobic classes, until finally the last orders bell was rung and the night was over. All of my friends had already gone home, throwing wolf whistles and teases my way as they went, and there was just myself and a young couple in the corner squeezing every last minute out of the evening.

'Well, I suppose I should go and let you clean up,' I said regretfully. 'But I can see you home safely if you like?'

'That's a really heroic offer, Adam, but it's only a two minute walk. I think I'll be fine. Besides, I don't want you to dirty your perfect IT hands fending off muggers.'

Ask her out you idiot. Show some guts.

'True. I need these safe for typing. Thanks for the chat tonight.'

'No, thank-you. You rescued me from the shift from hell.'

Ask her, ask her, ask her.

'No worries,' I said, heading for the door. 'See you next time.'

'Oh, Adam, one more thing.'

'Yep?'

'Where are you taking me on Saturday?'

And that was that. If anyone was going to show the guts to make the first move it was always going to be Maz. We started dating, going to cheap student bars and making the most of any local restaurant deals. Sometimes Maz would come running with me and once, after much coercion, I even tried out her aerobics class, but my total lack of rhythm and co-ordination caused her to laugh so hard she left the class before she got booted out.

We were always happy in each other's company. The relationship just led itself on contentedly, seemingly sure of the path to follow as a bird knows its way back to its nest. Spending time with each other was always relaxing, silences were comfortable and laughter was common place. The relationship never had to be toiled over because it just worked perfectly all by itself.

What did she see in me? A young man tagged as 'Bean-Pole' throughout his school life, who shied away from the centre-stage and preferred the shadows to the dance floor. A man who lacked self-confidence, assertiveness and, well, and coolness. I was, and still am, everything that Maz is not.

'What do I see in you?' she replied to my question one drunken evening when I was fishing for compliments. 'Silly boy.'

'Come on,' I prompted. Our relationship was still quite young, and I needed my insecurities banished.

'You just want to hear me utter some niceties about how good looking you are, or how I saw you one day and just had to have you. But that isn't it.'

'Oh,' I muttered, pathetically crestfallen.

'Adam, I don't believe this is a surprise to you. The truth is that you aren't me. Your character complements mine, like ketchup in a burger. You're honest and true with a big heart. There are no pretences with you. You are who you are, and that is a rare thing to be in the 21st Century. Now get me another beer.'

So I was tomato ketchup. But honest ketchup that didn't try to be mustard.

Chapter 16

'Somebody phoned for you earlier,' Maz said after I had walked in from work and given her a kiss and made a fuss of Zak. 'A woman!' She looked at me sternly before continuing. 'Have you got something you should be telling me?'

'A woman? Who was she? The only women who should contact me here are you, your mum and my mum. I've told my random flings to only ever contact me at work.'

Work was a web design company that I had set up with my friend from University, Marlon Danes, several years after we both graduated . WickeD Web Design. As my surname dominated most of the company title, the capital D was a nod towards my partner.

The company had started off slowly, frighteningly so, and we thought that we had made a mistake. The statistics told us that most new businesses fail within the first year of trading, and we were very close to joining that melancholy group of tried but failed entrepreneurs. Marlon and I would sit in our rented office space twiddling our thumbs, praying for the telephone to ring or an e-mail to ping through that wasn't just an advert or some smutty joke from a friend. Work trickled in like internet data through a dial-up connection, before the wonder of broadband transformed the World Wide Web. Any contracts we did win were almost always from small business concerns like our own that only required us to design a very basic website with a handful of pages. Simple stuff that either of us could almost do in our sleep, that paid little, took hardly anytime and failed to raise our company's profile.

I had been having serious doubts about the business for some time and the way we were doing things. Why had we decided to pay for office space rather than working from home? Why had I decided to set-up with Marlon when there wasn't enough work for one, let alone two? Had we wasted too much of our funding on poor advertising?

Maz was the one who led me in keeping the faith. She was an expert at pointing out the positives and in driving me to keep going.

You rent office space because it looks more professional than working from your dining room table. Your company's image is everything.

This I knew, obviously, but she had a way of getting her point across, a certain tone to her voice.

Of course you couldn't have set-up alone, Adam. Seriously! Marlon's got the head for business and design and you haven't. But when it comes to the technological side you leave him for dead. It's a partnership for a reason.

Again, not new information, but Maz made me see the sense in what we were doing. If it wasn't for her I would have quit, there is no doubt about that.

But then finally we got our break. Two large companies approached us in the space of a few days - one an expanding leisure company and another a restaurant chain - and, after a successful sales pitch and a lot of finger crossing, asked us to completely redesign both their public websites and their intranet domains. For the first time since we set-up the business there weren't enough hours in the day. Both jobs were huge but we didn't dare turn either of them down. If we could complete these two tasks to the satisfaction of the clients then it would greatly improve our sales portfolio, allow us to increase our very reasonable charges and would undoubtedly lead to more work.

From that point on there was never any question of closing the business. WickeD Web Design had arrived and the following years proved to be overwhelmingly lucrative.

'Well, who was this mystery female caller,' I asked my wife, who was just starting to prepare dinner for the two of us.

She poured some olive oil into a frying pan. 'She said her name was Erica Hardy.'

'Erica Hardy? It doesn't ring any bells. I don't know any Ericas.'

'Perhaps someone from Uni, or one of your schools? Or a business call?'

'Well, if it's someone from Uni I don't remember them, And we never advertise our home number for the business, you know that.'

'Maybe it's someone you got pregnant years ago and they've tracked you down, and will now do their best to tear our idyllic little life apart,' said Maz casually tossing a couple of chicken breasts into the pan. They hissed and spat noisily, in contrast to Maz's words which were entirely in jest.

'And did this mystery woman leave a message by any chance?'

'Not really. She just asked for you, gave her name and then said she would call back later on this evening. She didn't sound very comfortable on the phone, so perhaps that's why she hung up so quickly.'

'Are you jealous?'

Maz turned and gave me a withering look over her shoulder as she moved the chicken around the pan with a wooden spoon. 'Darling, have you taken a look at yourself in the mirror lately? I don't think I need to have any concerns over you having an affair.'

With a lot of women such a comment would be laced with undertones of spite driven by their insecurities from the unusual phone call, but I knew that Maz was so confident, not just in herself but in the strength of our relationship, that her words were delivered purely as a sarcastic jibe.

We chatted some more about our respective days, but our thoughts kept returning to who this Erica Hardy could be. Different theories and ideas over who I had crossed paths with during my thirty-two years of life were thrown uselessly around the kitchen like spilt salt tossed over a shoulder.

Thankfully we were rescued from our pointless hypothesising by the life-embracing form of Zak, who strolled into the kitchen and announced that we would all be partaking in a drawing competition. I was to start my masterpiece immediately whilst mummy could start hers after dinner.

I was upstairs putting Zak to bed when the phone rang and I heard Maz's voice say *Yes, just hold on a minute and I'll get him*. A few seconds later she appeared at Zak's bedroom door holding the phone in her hand and mouthed *It's her*. I gave Zak a kiss and wished him good night before taking the phone from Maz and hurrying back downstairs.

'Hello, Adam speaking,' I said as I sat down on the leather sofa.

'Oh, er, hello, Adam,' said the voice, sounding gentle yet unsure. An immediate silence hung between us for a short while whilst the lady presumably gathered her thoughts. 'My name's Erica Hardy. But you probably don't remember me?' It was a question.

'Er, no, no I don't. I've been racking my brain since my wife told me you called earlier, but I don't recall any Erica Hardys I'm afraid. Sorry.'

'Of course, Hardy is my married name so I suppose that wouldn't really help you. Stupid of me really. Sometimes I think that when I've woken up I've left my mind still resting with my dreams.'

The woman was bumbling but I threw her a polite laugh down the phone to try and put her at ease. Maz walked into the room and sat on the other sofa opposite me where she could watch and try to judge what this was all about. I smiled at her and shrugged before realising that there was silence on the line again and that the woman must have been waiting for me to talk, but I wasn't aware that she had asked me a question.

'So, er, Erica, what was your maiden name then?'

'My maiden name? Oh, yes, sorry, of course. It was Mayton.'

Mayton! Now that was a surname that I knew. Violet Mayton had been the old woman who lived in Foxhole Avenue in Barnehurst. CT or Curtain Twitcher as my dad used to call her. But I didn't know an Erica Mayton.

'Sometimes I used to see you when I came to visit my mother. You always seemed to be playing outside on your...'

She coughed uncomfortably and left the sentence hanging. It was obvious what her next word was going to be. Erica clearly knew enough about the tragic events of my childhood to realise she hadn't chosen her words particularly wisely.

'Your mother was Violet, ' I said, moving the conversation on swiftly to try and lessen her embarrassment. 'She used to have a King Charles spaniel. White and brown he was. Winston if I remember rightly.'

'My mother *is* Violet,' corrected Erica. 'She's still alive you know.'

'Really?' I said, surprised. 'I'm glad to hear it. Wow! She must be a good age by now. How is she?'

'Yes, yes, she's ninety-seven. A very good age. But I'm afraid she's not going to get her telegram from the Queen. Her health is not so good.'

'I'm sorry,' I said, not knowing what to say and sending a grimace in my wife's direction. 'That's a shame.'

I had always known that Violet had a daughter who used to visit her regularly, and on occasion I had even seen her pull up in her car, but I don't think I ever knew her name until now. She was just a distant face that sometimes cropped up on the periphery of my childhood life, and it is likely that she would have noticed myself and Shane more than we would have her.

That silence blanketed the phone line again, and I felt as though I was the one that had to drive the conversation, to take the lead, which surely wasn't how it was supposed to work if somebody else had contacted you.

'So, Erica, what is it that I can do to help you? I'm guessing that there must be a particular reason for your call.' I hoped that my words didn't sound too rude.

'Yes, yes, of course. Forgive me. I'm sorry to be bothering you.'

'It's no bother, really.'

'Oh, good, yes that's good to hear. It concerns my mother actually. She, er, she wants to see you. Before it's too late.'

'Too late?'

'Yes, you know, before she, er, well, before she dies.' Erica gave a nervous chuckle, obviously thinking that this point should have been obvious, which it probably should.

'Right, I see.' I looked at Maz and rolled my eyes at her which brought her dimples out to play. 'What does she what to see me about exactly? Wouldn't she rather see my parents? They had a lot more interaction with her back in those days than I did. After all, as you said yourself, I was just a child.'

'No, it's only you she wants to see. I'm sorry but I promised her I wouldn't tell you what this is regarding. She insists on telling you herself. Face to face'

'OK, then it sounds like I don't have much choice. What's her address?'

'She's hospitalised now so I'm afraid you'll have to visit her at her bedside. Do you have a pen? I'll give you the details.'

I grabbed a pen and paper and quickly scrawled down the name of the hospital and Violet's ward details as well as the visiting hours.

'You will visit her soon won't you?' asked Erica. 'This is very important to her. It's important for both of you.'

'Yes, of course. You have my word. I'll see if I can get over there sometime tomorrow.'

'Good', she said, satisfied with my response. 'And thank-you.'

'No problem. Thanks for calling. Good-bye now.'

I hung up the phone, looked at my wife and blew out my cheeks.

'It seems,' I said to Maz, 'that a little old lady who used to live in the same street as me has decided she would like to talk to me.'

'How weird. From ear-wigging to your conversation it sounds like you don't know what she wants either.'

'Not a clue. I suppose there's only one way to find out.'

***

I've never been a fan of hospitals, but then I don't suppose I'm alone in this. The worried looking people mooching around, their heads held low, avoiding the gaze of all around them. Sunken eyes. Wet cheeks. Greasy, unkempt hair. Maz, being a much more positive person by nature than me, would argue that hospitals aren't simply vessels of death. They bring new life into the world for a start. People's lives are also saved by the hands of brilliant doctors and hard-working nurses. Kindness surrounds you in the men and women who have dedicated their lives to helping others. Joy can be found as patients recover.

As I entered the hospital, walking past a snuggle of smokers dressed in their dressing gowns and slippers, and wandered into the foyer, I struggled to gather any positive feelings for the place. A shell-shocked looking woman sat alone on a grey metal bench, whilst further across the open space a man was arguing loudly with a receptionist, an inadequate looking security guard standing close by. An old man spoke quietly into a mobile phone, whilst a young girl, presumably his granddaughter, held tightly onto his hand and watched him intently.

Scanning the foyer for some indication of where I needed to go, my eyes rested on a group of signs that were so clustered together they were like bees gathered in a hive. Eventually I found the sign for Esther ward which directed me to the third floor of the east wing.

As I made my way up the stairs I wondered for the hundredth time that day what this could all be about. I had phoned my mum and dad, but they were as much in the dark as I was. Neither of them had had any contact with Violet, or her daughter, since we had moved away from Foxhole Avenue all those years ago. I racked my brain thinking back on all of the separate occasions that I had spoken with my one-time neighbour, but there was nothing that really stood out as remarkable. Aside from the confrontation with Mike when Violet's dog fouled the pavement, all other exchanges with her had simply been based around pleasant everyday small-talk.

I reached the outer door of the ward and a nurse let me through once I had pressed the buzzer. Unsure of exactly where to go I asked at the ward's reception desk and was pointed in the direction of a green door at the end of the corridor. Thanking the lady, I moved in the direction indicated.

At the door I hesitated, feeling strangely nervous and as if I was somehow intruding, before knocking almost sheepishly.

'Come in,' rasped a voice from the other side that I instantly recalled from my childhood. Violet had always spoken in the husky voice of a heavy smoker, yet as far as I knew she had never smoked.

Tentatively I pushed the door open and stepped respectfully into the small room. Within the crowded space there were two uncomfortable looking chairs, a tall bedside cabinet with some fresh flowers atop it and of course a hospital bed where the old lady lay, her back propped up by two fat pillows, their plumpness exaggerated against the scrawny frame of the patient they supported. A white plastic mask sat on her chest, a blue tube winding its way from the mask to a cylinder that sat clumsily next to the bed.

Violet Mayton looked up at me and smiled a weak smile. 'Adam,' she said in a welcoming voice.

Her hair, which had always been dyed a jet-black colour when we lived in the same street, had now been left to follow its natural path and was a shocking white. I wondered if her decision to stop colouring her hair was only as a result of her ill health.

'Hello Violet,' I replied and almost followed up automatically with *how are you* but managed to stop myself. 'It's nice to see you after all these years.'

'Yes, you as well young man. You've grown into a handsome thing, but I can see it is clearly you! Despite the years I couldn't fail to recognise your face, but then I was expecting you, so it's cheating really. Pull yourself up a chair and sit down, but not too far away. My hearing lets me down these days.'

I pulled over one of the hard moulded-plastic chairs, that all government funded establishments seemed to share, and sat down as instructed, suddenly realising that I hadn't even brought a gift with me.

'How many years has it been exactly?' she asked.

'I was wondering that same question on my drive over here. I make it around twenty. I was twelve when we moved, and I'm thirty-two now.'

'Thirty-two! Well! You're virtually picking up your pension already. Is there a lucky lady in your life? Children?'

'Yep, there certainly is. My wife is called Maz, and we've got a young son called Zak. Here,' I said, retrieving my phone from my pocket, 'let me show you a couple of pictures.'

'Oh, lovely,' she said as she squinted at the small screen. 'She's beautiful, and your son looks just like you.' I put this last comment down to either general politeness or the fact that Violet couldn't truly see the pictures too clearly - nobody thought that Zak looked like me.

A short silence descended, broken only by noises from the other side of the door and Violet's wheezing breath, before she spoke once more.

'The answer to the question I suspect you're too polite to ask is: cancer.'

'I'm sorry, Violet.'

She reached out a pale looking hand and rested it briefly on mine. 'There's no need to be, lad. I'm ninety-seven. We can't go on for ever, and I'm tired now. Always so tired. I suppose, well, I suppose it isn't a very original way to go is it? Part of me thinks it might have been nice to have gone out in a more dramatic fashion, like being killed whilst foiling a bank robbery, or saving a child from a burning building.'

I chuckled gently. 'Die a hero you mean? Yes, I see where you're coming from.'

'Yes, exactly, die a hero. That might have been nice. To have been brave. I've never really had it in me to be honest with you, though.'

At that point the old lady started coughing hard, in bursts that shook her entire frame so violently it was a wonder her body wasn't torn apart. A trickle of blood escaped from her mouth and I rose to my feet, ready to call for a nurse when Violet grabbed the mask and placed it against her face. Quickly her breathing returned to normal and the coughing subsided. I sat back down again slowly, feeling hopelessly inadequate. After a short time she spoke once more.

'Sorry, Adam. You must excuse an old lady who's busy dying. Don't worry, though, I'm not quite there yet.'

'How...?' I left the question hanging, suddenly feeling that it wasn't my place to ask.

'How long? A week, maybe two. Perhaps even only a matter of days. Not long, thank heavens. You're lucky to have caught me on one of my better days though. My daughter tells me that sometimes I've been babbling a load of old nonsense and not really known what's going on.'

'Are you in pain?'

'Occasionally. It's not constant, but if it does become too uncomfortable the nurses give me some morphine. The worst thing for me is that wretched coughing. That does hurt.'

'You say it would have been nice to have died committing some brave act or something. Well, you sound pretty brave to me.'

Violet shook her head almost imperceptibly and her eyes took on a sad look. I suddenly realised just how lined her face was. Wrinkles criss-crossed her features like roads on a map, dividing it haphazardly into separate pockets of flesh. I was surprised to note that there was a certain beauty to such a well travelled face.

'No, Adam, I'm not brave. I wish I was. I wish I had been. It's one of my failings I'm afraid, one of the things that God will have to judge me on when I stand before him. I've let you down and I'm sorry.'

'What do you mean? How have you let me down? I'm sure there's no reason for you to be sorry.'

'This is why I asked my daughter to track you down. It took her a while but she says that almost anybody can be found using the internet these days. Anyway it's always nice to have visitors, but I didn't ask you to come here in a social capacity, although I can imagine that a bright boy like you has already guessed at that. I need to talk to you about what happened that day.'

'What day?' I asked, although I already knew.

'The day of the accident. When dear Shane died.'

'I see,' I said. 'I've talked a lot about that day over the years. I can't imagine that there is anything else left to...'

'You don't know the truth,' she rasped, her voice cutting across mine, and sounding every bit like a voice that had been used for ninety-seven years.

'What do you mean?'

Violet gave a sigh, a big tired sigh that spoke of hardships suffered, of a long life lived. This sigh led to another cough, but this time it was a mere tickle in her throat and she maintained control.

'Our lives are full of thousands of choices and most are inconsequential nothings, but sometimes they mean something. We lie, we cheat, we choose our path in life, but there are times when we make a decision purely for selfish reasons, and that choice can leave the devil free and can mean the innocent are punished.'

'Violet, I'm sorry if I'm missing something here, but I don't understand what...'

She jabbed a bony figure at me. 'You, Adam, you are the innocent party. I'm the guilty one, me and that bastard Mike.

'That day, the day when Shane had his life ripped away from him, I was watching. You know I always liked to sit at my front room window, viewing the comings and goings of the street, watching all you children and the boundless energy that you used to have. It was like a play to me, it used to break up my long days and fill me with a kind of energy. I know that people must have talked about the nosey old woman from number twenty-three, always peering through her net curtains, but I didn't care. For me it was a way to pass the lonely hours since my husband died.

'I had settled myself down that afternoon with a fresh cup of tea and Winston by my side. You remember my dog, Winston? Course you do. The street was fairly quiet that day, heavy rain having sent people scurrying inside, but I didn't mind because I liked to watch the water rushing down the road and the spray from car tyres as they zipped past. Soon enough though the downpour stopped and the sun came out once more, closely followed by you and Shane. No surprise there – you boys were always outside. You were soon sat astride your bikes at the top of Shane's driveway. I watched with interest, already aware of what you were going to do, having seen you both pull skids countless times before. And then off you both went, Shane first and then you came and, well, you know what happened next.'

Violet shook her head. 'I'm sorry. My brain isn't what it was. This cancer must have eaten away at my sensitivity cells. Forgive me.'

She stretched her hand towards a glass of water on her bedside cabinet, and I passed it to her when it became clear that she could barely reach. The old lady took a long slow drink and handed me back the glass for its return journey.

'Adam, I'm sorry if this is painful for you to hear, but I have to tell you.'

I smiled a sad smile but indicated that she should proceed.

'After the two of you collided I quickly rose to my feet, expecting that you would both do the same, albeit with a rub of the head, but you remained prostrate. I counted to twenty and still you both lay motionless and so I grabbed the telephone, which I always kept close by, and called for an ambulance, but then suddenly, whilst I gave the details to the operator, there was movement on the scene, but it wasn't either of you boys. I moved aside my net curtain to get a better view, whilst passing on details to the emergency lady at the same time.

'Mike had appeared, dressed like a great hulking slob as usual, with his tattooed forearms doing little to dispel that image. He moved quickly, running down the slope to Shane's side where he bent down close to his son, clearly to check on his injuries. Then he stood-up, looking around him at both of you fallen boys and the bikes, and he must have made a decision because he suddenly ran back up the slope. I assumed he was going to call for an ambulance himself and I almost opened my window and called out to him that I had already done so, but something stayed my hand.

'Less than thirty seconds passed and he reappeared just as my own phone call finished, so I knew there was no way he had dialed 999. I expected to see him go back to his son, or even to check on you, Adam, but what I saw next staggered me. Mike hurried over to one of the bikes and crouched down next to it. I can't say for sure, but I think it was your one. Both of his hands were on that bike and he was doing something to it, fiddling with god knows what. I estimate that he was probably there for around two or three minutes, before he stood up and quickly glanced all around him.

'That was when his gaze found me. For a brief second that stretched for hours our eyes locked, until I belatedly allowed the net-curtain to fall back into place. My heart was hammering as he spun on his heel and raced back up the slope to his house once more, this time to surely call for an ambulance.

'Then shortly after the ambulance arrived to find Mike crying at his son's side, and...well...and then you know.'

I looked at Violet in stunned silence, my mouth hanging down like a huge metal scoop on a JCB. Her words sunk in slowly, their meaning dripping through to my brain until there was a pool of understanding.

'He delayed helping his son to look at a bike?' I asked, my voice sounding like it came from another corner of the room.

'Yes. He delayed helping his son to do *something* to that bike.'

'But what? What could he have been doing? And why?'

'Your guess is as good as mine. I've given this a lot of thought over the years and he could only have been up to no good, perhaps even trying to cover something up.'

Violet coughed once again, and this time it did lead to another drawn out bout of wheezing and shaking. I stood up and went to her, putting my arm around this old lady that had abruptly reappeared in my life, and doing my best to manoeuvre her into a more upright position to allow the cough to pass. When she had recovered she looked at me through eyes so grey it was easy to imagine that her time was coming rapidly to an end.

'I don't know why you're comforting me, after what I've done to you,' she rasped weakly, what little strength she had seeming to have deserted her.

'What do you mean?' I asked but the answer came to me before my lips had finished mouthing the question.

'I failed you, Adam, don't you see that? All these years I've withheld this from you. It's obvious to me that Mike had a hand in that accident.'

'I don't think that what you have told me proves anything. I mean, he has just found his son lying flat out on the floor, unconscious, and it just sounds like he panicked. Some people handle situations like that as if they were born to deal with that moment, whilst others just go to pieces. It sounds like the situation turned him into a headless chicken and that he was just dashing all over the place.'

'No, Adam. You're wrong. He wasn't running around aimlessly. He was hurrying all right, but he was hurrying because he knew he had to work fast. Three minutes he was crouched over that bike, three minutes, whilst his son lay dying.'

I stood up, my hands rubbing at my temples as the intensity of the conversation started to hit home.

'I need a break. I'm going to go and get some coffee,' I said, my voice sounding tired as if I was the one who stood at death's door.

'Alright, that's probably a good idea. I could do with a breather myself. Will you come back up?'

I nodded briefly and walked out of the small room, which seemed to have shrunk in size.

***

The hospital cafe was a surprisingly cheery place and the coffee was good. It was brightly decorated with a serving counter flanked on one side by a tempting array of cakes, but my mind was too occupied to concentrate on food. In one corner of the room a group of ladies were huddled, one of them in a dressing gown, and they were doing their best to keep quiet but were fighting a losing battle as peals of laughter defeated their courtesy.

In another corner sat a young man and lady. They had eyes only for each other and were holding hands across the table as if a hospital cafe was a perfectly normal place to go on a date.

I sat alone at my table staring out of the window and watching the constant stream of people coming and going through the hospital entrance. My hands were nursing my coffee, enjoying the warmth that emanated through the cheap ceramic mug, whilst my head swam with Violet's revelation.

What had Mike been up to and why on earth would he have chosen that moment to look at my bike rather than calling for an ambulance? And not just some cursory glance either, but a whole three minutes whilst his son lay still. There must have been a logical reason for him to be doing that, but nothing that came to my mind seemed particularly sane or painted a favourable picture of such an action.

But then, there was the very real possibility that Violet was mistaken in what she had seen or perhaps the passage of time had blurred the facts. At the time she was in her late seventies, so likely suffered from eyes that weren't as sharp as they used to be. In truth I knew little about the woman. She was just somebody who once lived in the same street as me and who my family and I made polite chit-chat with if we passed her on the pavement. Admittedly she had always been very polite and seemed like a genuinely nice old lady, but I certainly couldn't say that I knew her well enough to take whatever she said as the cast-iron truth. What if she had real issues with Mike and was just out for some sort of petty revenge? After all, I had seen him behave none too friendly towards Violet in the past.

And yet none of these scenarios felt quite right. There was too much passion in Violet's words. The woman was possibly only days away from succumbing to cancer, but she had found the strength from somewhere to put her heart and soul into her story. There was little doubt in my mind she certainly believed what she had told me was an accurate portrayal of the facts and, if this really was the case, then what did that mean? Had Mike played a part in the passing of his own son?

***

Death slunk around Violet's small room like a brazen rat emboldened by the nearness of some tasty morsel. I could sense its presence under the bed, behind the door, beneath the flooring, waiting for that moment to dart forward and grab its rotten prize.

The old lady looked done in and as I sat watching her I felt a wave of compassion rush through me. Cancer is a tiring and aggressive disease but I felt that our conversation had a lot to do with how drained she now looked.

'I hope you can find it within your heart to forgive me, Adam. My cowardice has never served me well, but it isn't fair that you should suffer for it as well.'

I started to respond but she held up a weak hand to stay my words.

'Perhaps when you know the full story it will be easier for you to forgive and also to believe that what I say is true.

'Just two days following Shane's death, Mike paid me a visit, and it wasn't wholly unexpected. Since our eyes had locked that day I just knew he was going to come calling.

'I opened my front door to his knock and there he stood. He was a mess and looked drawn, dishevelled, like he had nothing left inside him. In fact, probably fairly similar to how I look now.'

Violet gave a weak smile and I reached across and squeezed her hand offering what little comfort I could.

'He was a broken man, that was written all over his face. The red-rimmed eyes, the way he appeared to have aged ten years in only two days, the sallowness of his complexion. He was a man who had just lost his son, but more than that. He was a man that carried the weight of a terrible secret.

'He wasted no time in getting straight to the reason for his visit, leaving me no chance to offer my condolences.'

I'm gonna tell ya this once and once only, ya nosey old bitch, he began, *you didn't see anything. Not a thing. Ya didn't see the accident, ya didn't see me and this visit never happened.*

'As he spoke he persistently punched a rigid forefinger at my face, getting close enough that I likely could have grabbed it between my teeth had I so wished.'

If ya breathe a single word of any of this to anyone then I'm looking at a dead woman. Do ya understand? And not just you but that fucking mutt of yours will get strung up and beaten before getting cut into a hundred different pieces.

'Then he started to take a step forward and I tried to close the door on him, but he was too fast, too strong and he flung it back open easily. The force sent me stumbling backwards and only the presence of the hallway wall kept me from falling.'

First the dog and then you, bitch! Don't make the mistake of thinking this is just some idle threat! Do not make that mistake!

'And then he was gone. He turned on his heel and he walked away, with his head bowed and his shoulders reaching for the floor. That is my truth, my truth that has hidden a lie for nigh on twenty years. Did I think he was capable of carrying through with such a threat? Damn right I did. A man that can leave his own son laying still in his hour of need is certainly capable of battering some silly old woman to death.'

Violet stopped talking and looked across at me from her bed. Her eyes were wet. They cried for what they had seen and for what they had been unable to share.

'I'm sorry that you had to bear the weight of such a truth alone,' I said.

'Why must you be sorry?' she asked, surprised. 'You've carried a far greater burden all this time.'

'That burden is still with me, Violet. Until I can talk to Mike the facts are still half-buried.'

'Then you intend to go and see him?'

'I don't really see what else there is I can do,' I replied.

She nodded slowly and whispered, 'Be careful!'

'I will,' I said, taking her pale hand in mine once more. 'And Violet?'

'Yes?'

'There is nothing to forgive.'

Gratitude stroked the old lady's face, and the tears that now caressed her cheeks were awash with relief and peace.

Chapter 17

The street did not look any different. It was the first time I'd laid my eyes on its cracked tarmac since my family sold our house and moved north of the River Thames. I suppose the only noticeable difference to me was that Foxhole Avenue seemed smaller than I remembered it. In those happy childhood years it had been my world, mine and Shane's playground and perhaps time, along with my growth into adulthood, had distorted my memory of its size somewhat. The road seemed narrower, the front gardens shrunken and the houses more bunched, as if they were huddling together for comfort having seen me return.

Nevertheless, there was a pleasing air about the street, a welcoming atmosphere that said *I'm a nice place to live.* The sun was shining, its rays reflecting off those cars that had been pampered with a recent clean and its warmth streamed through to where I sat in my own car, parked several houses down from where I used to live.

Seeing my old street once more stirred up memories from my past, mostly happy but with one notable exception. I gazed along the pavement and looked at my old house looming in the background, like an old photo album stuck at the back of a shelf, its pages left unopened for many a year.

My house, which I still elected to call it, seemed as though it had been well looked after and this pleased me. The windows were new and the roof tiles also appeared unweathered, so had clearly been replaced. So many memories fought with each other for recognition, small acts played out in my young life: the time I stepped on a bee in my bare feet and got stung; playing with cars and trucks in the mud from the flower-beds; performing a balancing act on the low wall that divided our garden from the pavement.

If I could see inside any house in the world it would be that one, so I could allow my mind to feast ravenously on minute details, to give birth to times perhaps unfairly forgotten, times that deserved a higher echelon within the filing cabinet of my mind. Obviously the decor would have long since changed, but the size of the rooms, the layout and the way the house spoke to me would hopefully be the same. But perhaps it would be a mistake to tamper with the idealistic memories of my days living in that house. Maybe the new carpets, wallpaper and ornaments would pollute the snapshots from my mind, and blur the images that my brain saw fit to recall. What if the house proved to be a disappointment? If it wasn't as great as I dreamed? Would it take something away from my childhood? Some things are best left in the past as a limb from your history.

Sitting opposite my house was, of course, a building that I found hard to look at. Shane's house. Even as I looked upon the house of my own childhood, number twenty loomed large in my peripheral vision, like some huge behemoth that could uproot itself anytime it chose and stamp down on my car with its feet of bricks and mortar. It seemed to sit there glaring out at the puny world, an unquenched fury bubbling below the foundations, but at the same time with that same fury coursing through each and every room. This was how the house felt to me. If houses had memories then this one would be mad, it would be mad at me, mad at me for taking away Shane and the laughter that he brought to a place where Mike too often sulked and spread his tension like a prowling lion.

And yet, maybe it was not me that the house raged at.

I gripped the steering wheel tightly with both hands and leaned my head back until it married with the head-rest. A big breath in, a big whoosh out. It was time.

Slowly I got out of the car and shut the door quietly, walking the short distance to a place that I hadn't seen for years, but thought about every day. The driveway stretched away before me, and whilst the rest of the street seemed smaller, this appeared to lengthen the longer I stared at it.

There was no getting away from it: I glanced at the spot where my friend had fallen. It was just a plain piece of concrete, non-descript, yet it held my gaze, locked it in place with the power of everything it represented to my life. I shut my eyes and I saw him looking up at me, pulling faces to try and distract me from performing the winning skid, before those faces fell away as I torpedoed towards him. I heard the wind rushing through my ears as I hurtled over my handlebars, heard the thud as my body collided with my friend's.

'I can't do this,' I whispered to myself. 'I can't face him.'

And then I heard a voice in my head, a whispered memory from a long-ago incident. The voice had spoken to me after I had stood side-by-side with its owner to face the bully, Robert Wall.

'*Adam, you're my best friend,*' Shane had said. '*I just knew you wouldn't stand back.*'

I opened my eyes. I owed Shane. I owed it to him to face his father, to ask Mike just what the hell he had been up to that sad day. If our friendship had meant anything to me whatsoever then the option of turning around and driving away did not even exist. We had been through too much together, shared too many moments that helped shape me into the man I had become.

Determination bolstered, I stepped forward and started making my way up the steep slope of the Metcalfe's driveway, hoping that Mike would be home whilst my resolve held me on this course.

The front door stood before me, but there was no need to knock or ring the bell, because the garage, which sat further back where the house met the back garden, had its own door up, and there was Mike.

I walked closer, slowly, step by cautious step. He was turned away with his head down and appeared to be working on something, but before I could announce my arrival he swivelled round and looked up. Instantly he stood up straight, and his eyes seemed to almost aggressively take in every detail of who this intruder was that had been creeping up on him, determining if there was some threat to be aware of. And then the look in his eyes changed from aggression to complete, dumbfounded shock. The shock of recognition.

'Well, look what the fucking cat dragged in!' he said, shaking his head in astonishment. 'I didn't expect to see you again.'

'Hello, Mike.' I almost held my hand out to him, but stopped myself from doing so. It almost certainly would have been left flying solo in the air between us. 'I wasn't sure if you would recognise me or not. It's been twenty years. I was just a boy.'

'Oh, I recognise ya all right,' he said wiping his hands on a cloth already decorated with oil stains. 'There are some faces ya just never get out of ya 'ead.'

Mike looked as if the years had not been kind to him. He must have been about sixty-two and, whilst he still had a full head of hair, it had turned from blonde to grey. His frame, once so stocky and thickset, now carried fat where muscle used to dominate. He had a beer-gut that pushed at the t-shirt containing it, like a horde of impatient bargain hunters straining at the closed doors to the sales, whilst his double chin seemed to be trebling the longer I looked at it. The most shocking transformation, however, was his face. The bags under his eyes were so droopy it was as if they were imitating his stomach; the lines on his forehead burrowed so deep into his flesh that you could comfortably wedge matchsticks into them with no danger of them falling out; his eyes themselves just looked so tired, so completely devoid of a spark, that I found it hard to tear my own fascinated gaze away from them.

'How have you been, Mike? How's Karen? And the girls?' I was determined to try and keep the conversation as civil as possible.

'The girls are fine.' The answer left his lips reluctantly. 'Karen, well, Karen just keeps going.'

'Are they...?' I asked looking around at the house.

'No, they're not 'ere. Karen's at work and the girls don't live 'ere anymore.'

That was good. I wanted to keep this between the two of us.

'What do ya want?' he asked.

'Well, I just wanted to talk to...'

'No, actually, stop it! Stop it! I don't care what ya want. I don't care why yer 'ere. I can't believe that you've had the nerve to show ya face round 'ere again to be honest. Now, why don't ya do yerself a huge favour and walk away, walk away and we can both pretend that this little meeting never happened.'

He turned his back on me once more and buried his hands back into what they had been working on before, which I now saw was a lawn-mower which he was presumably trying to fix.

I stood completely still, rooted to the spot and staring at the man that had been my best friend's father and who had never uttered a single kind word to me in his life. Shane was the reason I was here in the first place and it was because of Shane that I didn't spin on my heel, jump back in my car and drive away from Foxhole Avenue forever. Shane had taught me friendship, but he had also shown me how bravery existed deep within my soul, how even I could dig deep and fight my own corner when I believed in the cause.

'Sorry, Mike, I'm afraid I can't do that. Not until I've got what I came here for.'

Slowly he turned back round and I saw that in his hand he was holding onto a large spanner so tightly it must have almost fused into his palm. I was again struck by how old he looked, but despite that there remained a dangerous glint in his eye that reminded me just what this man capable of.

'And just what 'ave ya come 'ere for?' he hissed.

'Answers,' I said. 'I've got a few questions about what happened that day.'

Mike said nothing but just continued to stare at me. I didn't exactly take his silence as accent to proceed, but I did make sure I grabbed the opportunity to do so before he said otherwise.

'I've been to see Violet Mayton today. She's got cancer and probably only has a matter of days left to live. She had quite a lot to tell me, stuff I didn't know about before. It was largely about you, Mike.'

'That nosey old bitch! What does she fucking know? What is she? A hundred by now? Probably completely lost 'er marbles or gone senile or something. I'm glad she's dying. The world don't need interfering old busy-bodies like 'er pissing people off. I wouldn't listen to anything that she's gotta say.'

Mike's reaction was overly defensive considering that I hadn't thrown any accusations at him, but I was conscious of the threat that he posed if I didn't handle this carefully. He might not have been as strong as he used to be, but I had little doubt that he would swing that spanner if I caused him to lose his nut.

'I don't think she ever meant any offence,' I continued. 'She was just lonely and most likely bored stuck in that bungalow.'

'Oh, whatever! Who gives a toss?'

'Look, regardless of what you thought of Violet, what she had to say did grab my attention. I understand this isn't easy but I really want to talk about the day that Shane died.'

'Oh do ya? Well how perfect. I tell ya what, why don't we both just pop inside, I'll put the kettle on, we can take an easy chair and have a nice cosy chat. You can tell me all about how ya crashed into my son, about how his head smashed into the pavement, and about how ya then had the nerve to turn up to his funeral. In return I'll tell you the story of how my wife cried every day for a year, *every* day, and how I ended up slapping her numerous times one night just to get her to stop, to stop sobbing, because the noise was driving me fucking crazy, ringing in my ears until I thought my head would crack open like my boy's had. That would 'ave been perfect wouldn't it? Like father like son. And then maybe we can slap each other on the back and pop down the local for a few pints, maybe chuck a few arrows or have a game of pool.

'Unbelievable. I tell ya, you're a piece of work you are. Ya often hear about that on the telly, don't you, how murderers hang around at the scene of their crime, or can't help revisiting, playing the innocent bystander as they watch everything unfold before them. Sometimes they even do interviews with reporters or talk to the police, whilst all the time knowing that they were responsible. Absolute scum. And that's the same with you. You killed my son and look here ya are again. Sniffing around a place where you have no right to be, like some mangy fox digging down the rubbish bins.

'My son's killer. You killed part of me that day too, and you certainly killed my wife. She's just some washed up old woman now, who rarely smiles, even at her own grandchildren, and when she does smile it almost makes me want to be sick, or to punch her face, because that smile don't belong on those lips.

'I mean, what makes ya tick exactly. Do ya get off on this or something? What are ya exactly? The murderer from across the road. That's what ya are. Shane always stuck up for ya, claimed you were his best mate. Claimed he turned to ya to make him laugh. Claimed that he could trust ya with secrets, that he could rely on ya to be there for 'im. Well, you didn't turn out to be such a great friend after all did ya? All ya...'

'Enough!' I shouted the words, punching them through the air with a bellow that had been building up inside me as Mike's words pummeled my ears and my heart. I was stung by the poison that he spouted at me, at the lack of forgiveness or understanding that the years had brought to him. My anger drove my next words, any thoughts of a softly softly approach bludgeoned aside by Mike's tongue.

'What's the truth of that day, Mike? What part did you play in all of this? Because Violet's take on it all is very interesting indeed. She says that she called the ambulance and whilst she spoke to the operator she watched as you disappeared from view and then re-appeared less than a minute later. She was still on the phone so she knew there was no way you'd had time to call for an ambulance.'

'I'm not listening to this. This is bullshit!'

'Violet tells me when you came back you didn't go to Shane, but you went over to my bike and crouched over it for a good two or three minutes. What were you doing, Mike? What were you doing to that bike that was so important that you put your own son second?'

'Drop it! Just drop it!' Mike snarled through his teeth, pointing the spanner at me as he spoke. 'Yer listening to the words of a hundred year old witch, who's told ya this from 'er death bed? 'Er brain is probably holding hands with dementia and thinks Winston Churchill still runs the country. The cancer has surely eaten away at 'er memory, and if not then whatever drugs she's on are likely sending 'er on the trip of a life-time. Next you'll be telling me Elvis is her doctor!'

'No, Mike, sorry, but you're wrong. Violet still has all her marbles. She was perfectly coherent when I was speaking to her, and even if her memory is a little fuzzy, there are some things in your life that I reckon you never forget. So, what were you up to?'

'Alright, let's assume the old hag is still compos mentis, then what does that prove? Bugger all, aside from the fact that she wants some petty revenge before she dies for the way I might have spoken to 'er in the past. An old woman, of questionable memory and dire health, who burns with hatred for the man she is throwing accusations at. Hardly a reliable witness. Now get off my property before I do something I regret.'

Mike turned his back to me once more and returned his attention to the lawn-mower he'd been fiddling with.

I was concerned about what Mike would do if I pushed my luck, but if I ran away from him now then I knew I would regret it for the rest of my life. I would always wonder what had happened that day. The not knowing would nag away at my mind, refusing to leave me in peace. I decided to try a different tact.

'You know that Shane supported Manchester United, don't you?' I asked. Mike didn't turn around or answer, but I noticed his body stiffen. I knew this would have come as a surprise to him.

'We were out over the park one day and he had a scarf with Man Utd on it that he'd found somewhere. He decided to climb to the top of this old tree to tie the scarf to the highest branches so his favourite club could be where they belonged: at the top. I asked him that day why he didn't just keep the stupid scarf, seeing how he loved the team so much. He replied that he couldn't keep it. That Chelsea was supposed to be his team and that he didn't want to upset you by not supporting the team that meant so much to you. *Chelsea might not be my favourite team*, he said, *but as long as my dad thinks they are then that's cool. I guess it's a father and son bonding kind of thing. It makes him happy to think I support Chelsea, so I don't want to ruin that.*

I looked at Mike's back. He was standing up straight now, with his arms hanging loosely down by his sides and his head drooping forward, as if he had fallen asleep whilst upright.

Silence hung in the air, like a kite riding the wind but which threatened to plunge to the ground at any given moment.

It.

Dragged.

On.

And then it was shattered in a loud cacophony of clanging metal that reverberated in my ears and echoed in the garage like a repetitive ringtone.

The large spanner lay guiltily on the concrete floor, having first struck the metal drum of the lawn-mower as it tumbled from the surrendered fingers of Mike's hand.

'I can't...I can't do this anymore.' He whispered the words so quietly I barely caught them as they slunk into the depths of the garage, hiding amongst old tins of paint and long forgotten tools. 'Why did ya have to come 'ere? Why couldn't she have just left things alone?'

Mike turned and faced me once again, and I saw that I was all of a sudden looking at a shell of a man. Gone was the aggressive demeanour and the harsh words spoken to sting, spoken with the aim of sending me on my way. His face was awash with tears yet he made no attempt to hide them, this tough as nails man. They ran down his cheeks freely, down the cheeks of the aged face, of the face that was now crumpled into a look of such unbearable misery that I wondered how he had managed to keep his despair at bay when I first appeared.

'Every day I've lived with this, every day since Shane died. He was me only son and look what I did. It wasn't supposed to happen that way. That was never the plan...it wasn't the plan.

'So proud of that boy I was. So fucking proud. But I never told 'im did I? Course not. Too proud to tell 'im I was proud, weren't I? Hah! Too proud to tell 'im how much I loved 'im. And then it was too late anyway, weren't it? Too late. Did 'e know I wonder? Did 'e sense it? I doubt it. Me old man was the same, kept his feelings bottled up inside him, never telling me what he thought of me unless he was off his tits, and then he would more often than not swing his fists instead. I remember swearing to myself that I would be a better father than that, that I wouldn't make the same mistakes. But I was wrong.'

Mike balled his hands into fists, tight balls of utter frustration, and briefly rested his head against the white of his knuckles. I stood facing him, still standing in virtually the same spot I had occupied since my arrival, sandwiched between the two houses that flanked the driveway, and feeling like a suitably inadequate filling.

'The nosey old bitch told ya the truth. No lies or forgotten memories. She told ya exactly what she saw. I was replacing yer rear brake pads, the pads that I had removed whilst you and Shane were busy playing some game or other in 'is room. That's why you went flying over the handlebars, that's why you collided with my boy, and that is why 'e's dead.'

I felt my mouth drop open as I stood and stared. What a sight the two of us must have made. One man with a broken face sobbing gently, and the other a gormless zombie catching flies.

'I was responsible for the accident and I watched out the winda as ya pulled on yer brakes, the front ones locking up the wheel whilst the rear cable squeezed uselessly at thin air. It caused the back of ya bike to buck up like an angry horse and there was nothing ya could do to stop yerself being catapulted forward into Shane.

'I never wanted me son to get hurt in anyway, let alone killed, course I didn't. Jesus, I didn't even want you to die. All I wanted was for ya to take a tumble. Maybe a couple of bruises or light grazes wouldn't go amiss, but nothing serious. And yet here ya stand whilst Shane lies in some rotting coffin. Ya were just going so fast down this bloody driveway that...well...I dunno what...I never thought that would 'appen.

'Not a day goes by, ya know, when I don't wish I could take back what I did, what happened. Not a single day.

It was all just an accident. Was never supposed to be anything serious come of it.

'So, of course, I covered me tracks didn't I, or did me best to. I went to Shane first you know, briefly admittedly, and saw 'e was out cold, but I thought 'e was just knocked sparko and that 'e would be alright. I mean, what could I do to help anyway? I didn't know no first aid or nothing like that, but I knew that if anyone examined yer bike they would see the missing brake pads and then questions would start getting asked. I couldn't chance that. I would have been the first person that people pointed the finger at.

'But obviously old bitch-face from across the street always saw everything that went on anyway, so I paid her a visit to make sure she kept her trap shut. Luckily for me she proved totally gutless, until now of course, when she is already as good as dead anyway.'

As he had spoken Mike's tears had gradually dried up, wiped away with his big, oil-smeared hands, so that traces of the dark lubricant smudged across his cheeks. The look on his face slowly changed so that the despair which had been there before was now replaced with a mask of vacant acceptance, each word of confession acting like a pin that secured it firmly to his skull.

'But, Mike, why?' I asked taking a half step forward and holding my hands out in front of me. 'What did you have against me? Why did you want to hurt me?'

The man that had been my best friend's dad, who had treated me with such disdain almost everytime our paths crossed, turned and reached up for the handle on the underside of the garage door.

'You've had enough out of me, Sunshine. I've said more than I thought I ever would. Ya want an answer to that question ya wanna try looking a bit closer to 'ome. I suggest ya go and have a word with yer whore of a mother. I'm not the only one with secrets ya know!'

I watched Mike pull the garage door down, and it closed firmly with a shudder and a bang, leaving me standing alone at the top of the driveway where my life had been changed forever.

Chapter 18

Initially the housing estate had left me confused and I thought I must have made a mistake or taken a wrong turn, but having rechecked my bearings I saw that I was in the right place. Unfortunately progress and development hold no compassion or regard for sentimentality, and my intended visit to the infamous railway line, traversed with such wanton abandon all those years ago by my deceased friend, was cut abruptly short by bricks and mortar. The chain-link fence that once upon a time did so little to prevent Shane trespassing onto Network Rail property, had presumably now been replaced with much sturdier wooden fences that divided people's gardens from the track.

It was disappointing. The spot where Shane had crawled under the fence held significance for me. It stirred strong memories of a time when my friend had been very much alive. It had been the place I had visited following his death, the place where I had made some crazy attempt to walk in his shoes in order to...what? I still don't know to this day what I had hoped to achieve by attempting to cross the track as Shane had done. My brain had been kidnapped by grief.

Instead I would have to be satisfied with the other old haunts that I had managed to visit before coming here, such as the alleyway where Robert Wall had been taught a lesson, the edge of the golf course where we preyed on the golfers and our old primary school (although even that had to be viewed from one side of a locked metal gate).

After my difficult meeting with Mike I had immediately got back in my car and driven away from Foxhole Avenue. I had been suddenly consumed with a need to visit these old sites that carried such fond memories for me, and now I parked up once again in the new housing estate where there had once been an expanse of playing fields. I felt totally and utterly exhausted, mentally drained by the long conversations with both Violet and Mike. I lay my head back upon the head-rest and shut my eyes, my hands still holding loosely onto the steering wheel.

There was so much to take in. New information, new facts, that told the true story of what had happened that awful day. In short, I was absolved of any wrong doing, no blame could be apportioned to me. That curse rested on Mike's shoulders, and had rested on his shoulders since his son had passed away. But he had kept quiet about the role that he had played, about how he had removed the brake pads from my bike and about the fact that he had made covering his tracks his priority rather than helping his own flesh and blood. He had bullied and intimidated a defenceless old woman to prevent her from spilling the truth as the blood had spilt from his son's skull, and it was only her own inevitable and impending death that finally lent her the strength to reveal the staggering truth of that day.

For years I had lived with the belief that my actions alone had killed my best friend. My failure to operate my brakes correctly. My inability to pull a simple skid. My body careering into Shane's. His life, and all its glorious promise, ripped away in an instant, whilst I still trod the earth with my future in tact. That false truth had always been with me, sometimes only on the periphery of my thoughts, but often consuming whole swathes of time, whether I was laying in bed struggling to sleep, in the car on a long drive or trying to concentrate on a project at work. Both as a child and an adult I had days where I sunk into a sullen mood, entirely dark and all-consuming, that sent me to a place where I couldn't be reached, like an explorer in the jungle who was sucked down into a bog and buried in its unreachable depths. Not my friends, parents or even Maz could pull me out of such a mood when it truly took hold, and in time they learnt that the only thing they could do was nothing. Best just to leave me be, leave me alone with my thoughts and my misplaced blame, and hoped that I pushed through the other side to normality once more in double quick time. In some ways I felt like I was similar to a migraine sufferer, who just needed to be left alone in the dark until the light of reality no longer stung my thoughts.

And, eventually, I always came through the other side after such an episode, and generally speaking twenty-four hours would see me to the finish line, at which point I would be full of apologies for those that had suffered as a result.

Since being with Maz such moods had become much less frequent as our relationship progressed, largely due in part to her huge, seemingly endless, resources of positive energy, but also as a result of our strengthening bond and mutual understanding of what made each other tick. There seemed to be no limits to how far my wife's patience stretched. How many times must I have bored her with the same conversation, the same repetitive tale of my burden of guilt? Too many to even guess at, but she never baulked when the topic reared its melancholy head once more.

'Saint Maz,' I said to her one day after such a display of understanding. 'That's what I shall call you from this moment forth.'

'No Saint should have to put up with a penis as ungodly as your maggot,' came the typical retort.

'Why do you always bring the conversation back to sex? Saint Nympho might be a better title.'

'Saint Unsatisfied more like.'

My thoughts were interrupted as I sat in my parked car by somebody knocking on the passenger side window. I opened my eyes and turned my head to see two young lads of about ten years old staring back at me. They were both sat astride their BMX bikes looking in through the glass.

'Hey, wake up Mister,' said the smaller of the two.

'Yeah, what ya doing sleeping?' asked the other. 'It's the middle of the day.'

'I wasn't asleep, just thinking,' I called back.

'YOU'RE LAZY,' shouted the first boy, banging the glass twice with his closed fist, and then they quickly pushed off on their bikes and pedalled away rapidly, one of them shouting out *quick, he's coming* as they disappeared out of reach, guffawing hard.

Cheeky buggers I thought to myself, and then I started laughing, gently at first, but then my mirth started to take hold of me, and before I knew it I was roaring so hard that I could barely breathe. My sides ached and my eyes streamed, and it was some minutes before I finally gained control of myself.

Seeing those two boys was like travelling back in time to my own childhood, to happy days spent with my best mate, and the laughter that burst out of me felt like a weird mixture of relief, anger and, well, joy is the closest word that I can think of. Relief at my own innocence; anger at Mike's unforgivable actions; and joy that I finally knew the truth.

But what of Mike's comment about my mum? What secrets could she possibly keep that he would even have any inkling about? Most likely he was just trying to cause trouble, making a lame attempt to score a worthless victory point following his humiliating confession. And yet I needed to be sure. I needed to close out any loose ends on this sorry saga once and for all, so that I could finally leave that part of my life in peace.

I called my mum up, there and then, sitting in the car round the corner from the street close to where I was conceived around thirty-three years before. It seemed weirdly surreal.

'Hello, 79803,' came my mum's voice, sounding light and welcoming.

'Hi, mum, it's me.'

'Oh, hello, darling. How are you?'

'Fine, mum. You?'

'Yes, musn't grumble. Still trying to shift this wretched cold, but I'm fine. I spoke to Carol the other day and she's just getting over one as well, so I think there are probably a few bugs doing the rounds. I just hope that you and the family don't come down with it.'

'Mum, I need to talk to you.'

'Oh, right, OK, what about?'

'I don't really know. I'm been to Foxhole.'

'Really? Is this something to do with that call you had from Violet's daughter? I'm guessing it must have been. Sounds like it's prompted a trip down memory lane.'

'Yes, I went to see Violet in the hospital, as Erica requested, and what she had to say led onto Mike. So, I've been to see him too. I hope you're sitting down mum because what both Mike and Violet had to say was staggering. It turns out that on the day Shane died, Mike had removed my rear brake pads from my bike. That's why I shot over the handlebars and that's why I crashed into Shane.'

'Oh my God, I can't believe it! So…I mean…what was he thinking? All that anger, all that blame that he heaped upon your shoulders.'

I explained to my mum all that had gone on starting with my visit to the hospital and the subsequent meeting with Mike.

Stunned silence greeted the end of my tale from my mum's side of the line.

'Mum, are you still there?' I asked.

'Yes, darling, I'm here. I just can't believe it. He's kept that to himself all these years. I think I'm going to need some time to take this all in. Perhaps we should call the police.'

'No, I don't think so, mum. From seeing the man I would say that his awareness of his own guilt is a greater punishment than any court could bestow.'

'Well, if you think so, but, well, I don't know. Perhaps we should talk about that and decide what's best to do.'

'There is one other thing. I asked him why he had done it. I wanted to know what he had against me. He said that I should ask you. Any idea what he's talking about?'

Silence descended on our conversation for a second time, and for a woman who barely stops talking this was most unusual.

'Mum? Hello?'

'I don't know what he means,' came the reply, but the life had suddenly drained from her voice. It was as though a robot had suddenly snatched the phone from her.

'Mum, he said you had secrets of your own. Please! If there is something you're not telling me, I'd really like to know. I've lived with the belief that Shane's death was my fault for two decades. Now I know that wasn't the case, but I need closure on this. I want to move on. I have to move on. I can't leave any loose ends, so if there is more to tell then I need to know.'

'I understand. I think it's best if we do this in person. Can you come now? Your dad's out for his weekend golf and won't be back until later.'

So she did know what Mike had meant after all, but why lie in the first place?

'Yes, OK, I'll be there in half an hour,' I said calmly, although my voice betrayed my hammering heart that my mum's words did little to settle.

Chapter 19

As soon as she opened the door to me I could tell my mum was nervous, terrified even, and it could only be to do with where Mike's comments had led me. Normally so in control, unruffled and calm, now she was jittery on her feet and pale as a sheet, looking as though her existence was courtesy of an over enthusiastic kiss from a vampire whose fangs were laced with speed.

Only once before had I seen my mum looking so white, and that had been when my dad had been stabbed. He had been at work on the buses, driving the number 362 on his regular route. It was the middle of the afternoon, a cold Monday in December, when an altercation broke out between two passengers. One of them, a young man, wearing garish blue trainers, who was of short stature and short patience, took offence when a family boarded the bus laden with Christmas shopping, a child's pushchair and two small girls. Blue Trainers was around twenty-three years old, and had no appreciation for the clumsy manner in which the girl's father accidentally bumped the numerous bags of shopping against him, and then stood on his foot. This caused him to stand-up promptly and start yelling at his fellow passenger, swearing and screaming with all the spirit of an infuriated banshee as opposed to the spirit of Christmas. The father at first apologised for his less than careful steps, but when Blue Trainers carried on shouting he then asked his aggressor to calm down and to watch his language in front of the children, whilst other passengers looked on with open mouths and loosening bowels. Inevitably the screaming went on, possibly even increasing in volume and intensity, and my dad was forced to stop the bus and leave his seat. Ever the pacifist he was keen to cool the situation down before it went beyond the point of no return, and so spoke calmly to Blue Trainers to try and diffuse what was clearly a very tense scenario. My dad's best efforts seemed to have the exact opposite effect, and the calmer he behaved towards the troublesome passenger, the more erratic the young man became, until his hollering and yelling reached decibel levels previously unattained by human vocal chords.

Left with no other choice my dad told Blue Trainers that he was going to have to leave the bus, and if he refused then it would mean a call to the police. It was at this point that the young man produced a knife, hollered *fuck you and fuck Christmas* and then plunged it into my dad's neck. As the messed up young man pulled his knife back out again he tripped over the little girls' pram, which fortunately caused him to drop the knife which went skittering under a nearby seat. At this point, seeing the man on the deck, several passengers suddenly discovered their bravado and leapt on Blue Trainers, pinning him down.

In the end my dad owed his life to a nurse, who was fortunately travelling on his bus that day. She had stemmed the flow of blood as best she could whilst an ambulance picked its way through the town centre traffic.

Following surgery the doctor told my dad he had been a very lucky man. The blade of the knife had entered his head just behind the left ear, and then headed rapidly south, like a sun-deprived Brit flying to Tenerife, where it emerged from the front of his neck into daylight once more. By some glorious miracle of chance the blade kindly bypassed my dad's major arteries and windpipe by nothing more than a few millimetres, leaving him with some facial nerve damage, apparently known as Bell's palsy, from which he went on to make a full recovery. The mental scars from the whole experience took longer to come to terms with, and it was a long nine months before he felt ready to drive his bus once again.

As for Blue Trainers, well, he was sorry. We know this because he said so in court. He also blamed his behaviour on the financial pressure he was under as a result of the silly season of Christmas. None-the-less, he was found guilty of GBH, and the judge told him he was a very naughty boy. This wasn't the sort of behaviour that could be tolerated in modern British society, and only the harshest penalty would therefore be appropriate. The harshest penalty in this instance was twelve months imprisonment, which probably meant he would serve six.

My dad being my dad, forgave his attacker, and even told him so in court. This I can't understand. Had I been in the same situation then I think I would have wanted the bastard to suffer as much as possible, and that includes him knowing that his pathetic half-baked apology was not accepted, and never will be. Let the guilt hang heavy on his conscience, let it mess with his mind and wipe smiles from his face, because just such a person deserves no such thing as happiness. But, I suppose this just goes to prove that my dad is a far better person than I can ever be. For me the major lasting memory of this whole unsavoury incident was when the phone call came through from the bus depot to let us know what had happened. I was off school, studying for my GCSEs, when the phone rang. My mum answered and I looked up, from my position sat hunched over text books at the dining room table, and watched as the colour drained rapidly away from her face like air from a punctured balloon. Her body slumped against the wall where she stood with the phone held limply to her ear, and my heart hammered in my chest as she uttered the two terrifying words: *what hospital?*

Who was this woman, this doppelganger that was answering the phone in place of my mum? Always so assured, so unflustered, this couldn't be the same person. But, such is the curse of love, that when your nearest and dearest are at risk, emotions sweep in and assume control, leaving you to operate as a shell of your true self.

And now, here was this imposter once again, opening the door to my mum's house and leading me slowly through to the dining room, where tea and biscuits rested uncomfortably on a flowery tray. We sat down at the table, directly across from each other, and it occurred to me that there was a reason we were taking tea at the hard formality of the dining table as opposed to the relaxed softness of the lounge. This was not a good sign. It can never be a good sign when such a close family member invites you to sit at the household equivalent of an executive boardroom.

'So, mum, how are you?' An inadequate opening and a stupid question to someone who so clearly is not in a good place at that moment in time.

'Not too bad, thanks darling,' came the standard reply. 'Some tea?'

She reached forward and poured me a cup with shaky hands as I nodded my ascent.

'Great! Digestives.'

'Well, I always like to keep a supply in. I know they're your favourites.'

I munched on my circular treat and sipped politely at my tea. This was ridiculous. Neither of us knew how to start the conversation. We were like two shy individuals on a first date. My mum smiled nervously, her perfect teeth not as perfect as when she was younger but still almost perfect nonetheless. She was still as skinny as she had always been, but her sudden wan appearance made her face appear almost skeletal.

'So...' I began.

'Look...' she started.

We both laughed quietly.

'You start,' she said.

'Ah, mum, this is crazy. I think you're the one that needs to kick things off. Mike said you've got secrets, and I think perhaps I need to hear them. Looking at your face I'm not sure I want to, but I reckon I need to. I mean, I don't know, but I get a gut feeling that I'm pretty involved with whatever those secrets could be.'

Her hands cradled her tea cup, as if it were an injured bird, and she nodded her head slowly.

'I always wanted children,' she began. 'Ever since I was a young girl that played with her dollies. I used to love pushing them around in the pram, changing their clothes, pretending to feed them. If you'd been able to get those ones that wee and poo when I was a little girl, like you can now, then I would have been in my element. I just found the whole concept of looking after small, defenceless bundles of flesh overwhelmingly exciting. And then, if ever I came across a real, live baby I could hardly contain myself.

'My cousin, Jane, who you've never met, was much older than me, and I remember when she gave birth to a little boy. We took the bus to go and see them, and your Nana had to have quite a stern talking with me because I was so hyperactive on the way over to see him. I was nattering away constantly and fidgeting all over the seats, being a total embarrassment to my poor mother, until she told me to calm down or we would be turning right back round and going home. If you see children now-a-days getting over excited we tend to blame it on the parents for giving them too much cola or chocolate, when perhaps they're just high on life!'

She glanced to her left and gazed out of the patio door into the garden, where a variety of different birds were hopping across the lawn and pecking at some bread my mother had thrown out for them earlier.

'Years later, when I met your dad and I realised we had something special, I posed the most important of questions to him with my heart in my mouth. Do you want to have children one day? My God, the relief, the absolute relief, when he said he most certainly did. Why wouldn't he want to have children to carry on his exceptionally grand bloodline. Then he said *but*, that most infuriating of words that so often undoes most of the good feeling from any preceding sentence. But, he would only have children when he felt financially secure enough to be able to support them comfortably, without too much penny counting going on, or wandering cap-in-hand to either of our parents to help us get by.'

'That sounds like dad, alright,' I said. 'One person's careful is another person's tight.'

'Your father doesn't like to take chances. He likes to know he is in control of his own life. That makes him sound boring, which is unfair because he isn't, but it's true nonetheless. Anyway, if you had any idea of just how eager I was to have children of my own you would understand just how utterly frustrating this attitude was to me. I wanted to start trying for babies as soon as he got his act together, proposed to me and we got married. Yes, money would be tight, yes, we would struggle to afford certain necessities, but, damn it, there would be a baby crawling around that would make all the penny counting bloody-well worth it.

'That left me with the choice of ditching him and finding someone new, or sticking with him and showing the patience of a saint. Well, this choice was no choice really, because I loved your dad far too much to even think about leaving him. Bringing up a child, I reasoned with myself, is only going to be an enjoyable experience if you've got the right man by your side, supporting you every step of the way.

'And so I had to wait while the two of us scrimped and saved for our future life together. Our wedding was a cheap affair, not like the extravagances that most people seem to shell out for now, and then we had to save enough money to be able to buy our first home. Then, the home needed to be decorated, or there was furniture to buy, we needed to get a new car, the fridge needed replacing. There always seemed to be something that meant your father wasn't quite ready to start a family, until finally the day came when he announced that we were now in a good place and we could commence trying for a baby.' My mum laughed at the memory, shaking her head. 'He certainly had a way of making sex sound exciting.'

The thought of my mum and dad having sex wasn't something that I really enjoyed thinking about, especially the concept of any such frisky stuff between them being 'exciting', so I said nothing and waited for my mum to continue.

'Part of me had started to doubt whether your father really did want children with all of the excuses he kept putting in the way, but it truly was a case of his need for financial stability before we took that step. It was so frustrating for me at times, and I took every opportunity for overtime that I could back then, when I used to work in the reception at the Doctors.'

My mum reached out and took a sugar cube from the bowl on the table, fiddling with it between her slender fingers like a magician toying with a coin they were about to make disappear. She was the only person I knew that used sugar cubes, aside from restaurants or cafes, and I wondered briefly where she bought them as I had never seen them for sale in any supermarket.

'So, finally, we started trying for a family. I was well prepared, having read up way in advance about when a lady's fertile period fell during the month and which foods to eat to increases chances of conception. I dare say a lot of the information is now completely out of date and contradicted or dis-proven by modern theories, but you can only go with what the experts tell you at the time.

'Anyway, we tried and we tried, and we tried some more, but I just wouldn't fall pregnant. A year passed, then eighteen months, but still nothing, and at this point I was sure that there was something up with me, or at least with one of us. I started to become emotional, getting upset at the slightest thing, and nagging at your dad for the smallest of household sins, such as not picking his underwear up from the floor or leaving a dirty plate on the table. I even started to have nightmares, almost always centred around my inability to conceive. Being at work was one of the worst places to be, because when you work in a Doctor's surgery one absolute certainty is that pregnant women will regularly bring their swollen bodies in to be examined to check all is as it should be.

'Something else I noticed,' my mum continued, as she absentmindedly passed the sugar cube from hand to hand, 'was the age of the expectant mothers that came to the surgery. They all seemed so young, compared to me at least, and I wondered if I had maybe left it too late, if your father's careful planning had pushed me beyond my sell-by date. I remember we had this clock in the reception that always seemed to make an unusually loud tick-tock noise, and it used to drive me almost to breaking point, because it felt as though it was mocking me, marking time for my biological equivalent with its incessant rhythm.'

She looked up and saw my cup was empty, and offered me some more tea which I declined, her eyes flickering to mine only briefly, before quickly moving away to rest elsewhere, on a place in the room that clearly she found easier to look at. I frowned with concern. Was what she had to tell me so terrible that she couldn't even bear to look at me? Was it something I had done, some great unknown failure from my past? All this talk of her great desire to have children and the struggle that was involved led me to believe that perhaps I had disappointed her in some way, that I hadn't lived up to whatever great expectations she had held for her longed-for child.

'Finally,' she went on, 'maybe after around twenty months of trying, I said to your dad that there must be a problem with one of us, with the way that our bits worked. Well, you know your dad as well as I do, so you won't be surprised to hear that he stubbornly refuted my claim without so much as deigning to discuss it with me. *Nonsense*, he said, *there's nothing wrong with us, we've just been unlucky, that's all.* Back then, when we were younger, he was much more bull-headed than he is now. He's loosened up over the years, but your father used to be a staunch defender of his manhood, and the merest suggestion that his sperm was not in tip-top condition was not something that was up for discussion. Not wanting to upset your father I didn't dare push him on this, after all I still desperately wanted a child, and for that you need a willing partner.'

My mum sighed heavily, and that single puff of air carried with it a sense of the position she found herself in all those years ago. Having dreamt of conceiving with the man she loved, this lifelong vision should have now been within her grasp, and instead she could see it floating out of reach like a dandelion seed caught helplessly on the breeze.

I stole a quick glance at her face. Still pale. Still nervous. And so very tired, drained, worn-out, spent.

'So I took the only course of action open to me and when a rare quiet moment presented itself at work I spoke to the Doctor. He put me in touch with a good friend of his from his university days, who was a fertility specialist. I arranged to meet him and, without telling your father, went along for various tests. They took some blood to check on my ovulation, tested me for chlamydia and such like and checked out my fallopian tubes, using some dye and an X-ray, to see if there were any blockages. The results came back clear. From what they could tell everything was in perfect working order, and they suggested that perhaps my husband would like to come in for some tests.

'I determined that I would speak to dad, try and break it to him as gently as possible, and hope that he would be able to swallow his pride and go and visit the specialist. But each time that I started to open my mouth to broach the subject I would lose my nerve, and not because I'm scared of your dad you understand (how could anyone be scared of such a lovely man) but purely from total fear of seeing my dream of being a mother disappear. Surely he will come round, I thought to myself, surely he wants this as much as I do and will face up to the fact that he could be the where the problem lies. But then I would realise that no-one wants this as much as I do, to hold a new born child in my arms, and to think *It's mine.* I couldn't take that chance, couldn't take the chance that he would turn around and flatly refuse to get himself checked out.'

The sugar-cube was still on the move, being passed from hand to hand, occasionally knocking gently against my mum's wedding ring with a gentle tap, like a timid person knocking at a front door. I sensed she was coming to the end of her tale, to the crux of the story, and I thought I knew where it was leading. I tried to steel myself as I waited for the adoption word to enter the fray.

'Then one day I was babysitting Caroline whilst Karen was working her shift at the pub. We had an arrangement where I looked after her every Tuesday and Thursday afternoon, which fitted in fine with my part-time role at the Doctor's, and it brought in a little extra money, plus gave me an opportunity to play 'mum'. Caroline was only two years old at the time, a beautiful baby, and very much like Molly at that same age, although I don't suppose you remember how Molly looked when she was just a babe.'

I shook my head mutely, captivated by my mum's words and unable to utter any of my own.

'I used to love those few hours each week where Caroline was all mine. We had our favourite games that the two of us played, favourite songs and books to read. I remember she had this obsession with 'If You're Happy and You Know It.' She was always pleading with me to sing it to her, and then she'd totter around the lounge performing the various actions, laughing until I thought she would burst when I got to the 'hop around' verse. Her hair was much fairer back then, before it took on that gingerish tone that you would be more familiar with. Ha, such a little angel.

'That day, just before Mike came to pick his daughter up, she fell asleep on our sofa, curled up tight like a kitten on one of those garish orange cushions we used to have. It's funny, I can still see her now. So adorable, so, so...I don't know...just such a baby. She was what I wanted, that little girl right there in my lounge, snuggled up, cosy and safe in *my* care.

'Then the tears came as I looked down upon Caroline, sliding down my face, and it felt as if each tear represented another lost day, another day slipping from my grasp which should have been spent as a mother to my own child. But then the doorbell went, and I knew that it must be Mike and there was no longer anytime to be crying. I wiped my eyes quickly on the back of my hands and took a few seconds to compose myself before opening the door to him.

'Mike stood on our front step, dressed in jeans that were thick with cement dust from whatever building site he was currently working at. His stocky form and sour expression were everything that your dad was not. What a repulsive man, I remember thinking, whatever does Karen see in him.

Is she ready? he asked, as impolite and abrupt as he has always been. He stepped into our hallway before noticing my face. *You been crying or something?*

'I looked at him for a second and something in my gaze made him stop still and a frown creased his face. Then I threw myself at him, grabbing his head and kissing his face like a mad woman, like a woman possessed. He pushed me back, muttered *what the fuck*, but then I came at him again and any futile resistance he tried to put up just evaporated, much as my dream for a child had been doing.

'I'll spare you the finer details, I don't exactly enjoy remembering them myself, but I think you can guess where this ended up. In truth, the whole thing is just a blur in my memory, a surreal moment that I can't believe actually transpired. I suppose that my maternal instinct took over, if indeed one can have such a thing before motherhood is granted. If not my maternal instinct, then my desire to achieve my dream, to achieve the only thing that I had longed for my entire life.'

The sugar cube dropped from her hand and landed on the table, where it finally fell apart, like a broken relationship, into three separate chunks. I stared at it, hard, unwilling and unable to face my mum, already knowing what her next words were going to be, but not wanting to hear them. I wished I could have turned back time, never visited Violet, never been to see Mike and then this conversation could have stayed buried forever.

My mum's hand reached across and rested on my own. She squeezed it tightly and that acted like a trigger to my eyes, which inadvertently rose up and looked upon my mum's face once more. Her cheeks were wet and I watched as a single tear dropped from her chin to mingle with the broken sugar cube. She looked fearful, so fearful, and I almost went to her and gave her a hug, but how could I? I held myself back.

'I'm so sorry, my boy,' she said. 'I always knew this day would come, in my heart. I hope you can manage to forgive me. Mike is your father. Shane was your brother, or half-brother at least. That's why Mike was so unkind to you, so spiteful. Every time he saw you it was a constant reminder to him of what had happened that day. How I had used him. He might be a thug but Mike isn't a total idiot. He and Karen knew we'd been trying for a baby for years, and he soon realised the truth when I fell pregnant, seeing easily through my insistence that it was your dad's. Mike demanded I get an abortion threatening to spill the beans if I didn't, but there was no way he would have gone through with that. He had as much to lose as I did, and so he had no choice but to keep his mouth shut, but that just meant his anger was kept locked up, but he needed a way to release it I suppose. Our family, specifically you, proved to be the outlet for that anger. And so his rage was directed back round to its own root cause.'

She looked up at me once more, seeking out my eyes, but this time I hid from that gaze as she had hid the truth all these years.

'That's the secret Mike referred to. Me, you, him – we're the only ones who know, unless he's told anyone else, which I very much doubt. Your dad…your dad is blissfully unaware. I'd like to keep it that way, and I hope you feel the same. There's nothing else to tell you.'

Feeling as though my legs would fail me at any time, I rose wordlessly from the table, walked from the dining room and exited the house, leaving my mother alone at the table. I shut the door behind me gently, and drove home to my wife and son in a blur.

Epilogue

Early morning. 6:50am. I'm woken from my slumber by the noise of my bedroom door being opened clumsily. Light spills into the room from the hallway where the bathroom bulb had been left on all night at Zak's request. Like most children his age he is afraid of the dark, but always tries to deny it.

I pretend to still be asleep, hoping it will make him turn-around and go back to bed for a short while at least, but I'm secretly watching my son through barely open eyes. He walks slowly into the centre of the room, his footfalls barely perceptible as the thick carpet absorbs the sound of his tiny feet. He stands watching Maz and I for a while, trying to decide if we are awake already or if he should indeed wake us. He soon decides that we need waking and I continue to watch him, barely holding my laughter back, as he tucks his head under the covers at the end of the bed and starts to crawl under the quilt. Maz groans as his small frame bumps into the two of us as he squeezes his way in between our prostrate forms.

'No, Zakky, too early,' she mumbles, and I can't hold my laugh back any longer.

Maz didn't get in until half-past midnight, which is late for either of us since Zak came into our life, and whilst she didn't seem too drunk I suspect she would have preferred a longer lie-in to nurse any alcohol induced ill-effects.

With a cross between a chuckle and a groan I swung my legs out of bed and pulled on my dressing gown.

'Come on, Zak. Let's go watch some telly and leave mummy in peace.'

'Hrrmmm,' groaned Maz.

Once downstairs we slob on the sofa and watch rubbish cartoons. I'm sure that the cartoons I used to watch on telly as a kid were far superior to the rot that Zak seems glued to. Battle of the Planets; The Hair Bear Bunch; Wacky

Races; Captain Caveman - they don't make them like that anymore.

After a while Zak asks, 'What're we doing today?'

'No plans, little-man, unless mummy's got something in mind. Why? What do you fancy doing?'

'I wanna go see nanna and grandad. Not seen them for ages.'

Ages was three and a half weeks. It had been two weeks since that hard chat with my mum and the revealing of the skeleton in her closet, and a week and a half prior to that when we had last all been over to theirs for dinner. For people who put such a great emphasis on the importance of family, as we did, this was ages.

My mum had phoned a few times but I had been cold and unresponsive, answering with an abrupt yes or no, until she got the message and hung up. I wasn't ready to talk to her.

The last of her calls, ten days ago now, had been to tell me that Mike had been found dead, hanging from one of the struts in his garage. If I hadn't already read about it in the newspaper she might have got more of a reaction from me, out of surprise rather than anything else. As soon as I had read the story I knew that it was my visit that had prompted him to take his own life. All those years he had somehow managed to live with the knowledge that he was responsible for his son's death, somehow found a way to wake up every morning and look himself in the mirror as he shaved or cleaned his teeth. Somehow found a way to carry on going to Chelsea, chatting to his family, boozing down the pub. This utterly staggers me, that he found a way to make life work without ever telling anybody the truth of his actions, at least as far as I know. My visit opened up an old wound that had never really healed but had merely been festering under the scab of Mike's lies. Did he kill himself because that wound was once again too painful to bear, or was it out of fear that I would spill the truth. I'll never know.

What I do know, now that I have had time to think the whole sorry story through, is that I don't care. I feel no guilt for his suicide. I feel no remorse that he has left this world. I take no responsibility for his passing. For years I lived with the falsehood that Shane had died because of me. I have done my time. I have suffered unjustly for a large chunk of my life, so I'm not about to offer up my soul, once again, to soak up the blame for a death whose only fault lay with the man who took his own life.

My only regret is for Karen, who found her husband swinging, and for the girls who lost their father. But, I dare say, at least some of the tears at that man's funeral will be tears of relief.

***

It's lunchtime. Maz is craving a McDonalds or a Burger King as she always does after a night on the wine. Zak isn't about to start arguing with her, especially as there is some crap toy that he wants that comes with a Chicken Nugget Happy Meal. I'm happy to go with the flow - I'll go for a run later anyway to burn off all those calories.

Just as we are about to go out the door the phone rings. I decide to ignore it, but Zak runs past me and picks it up.

'Hello,' he squeaks, before looking confused and passing me the phone.

'Who is it?' I whisper.

'Dunno.' He shrugs his shoulders.

'Hello,' I say.

'Hello? Adam?'

'Yes, speaking. Who's this?'

'Erica. Erica Hardy. You remember, from the other week. Violet's daughter.'

'Yes, yes of course I remember. How are you?'

'I'm well,' she said quietly, 'at least as well as can be expected in the circumstances.'

'Oh, er, why? What's wrong? Is it Violet?'

'Yes, you've hit the nail on the head. I'm afraid my mum passed away. Three days ago now. I would have phoned earlier but...I'm sorry.'

'No. no. please don't apologise. I'm sorry to hear your news.' I looked at my wife and gave her a weak smile.

'Yes, thank-you, that's very kind. I keep trying to tell myself that I should be glad that she is gone, that her suffering is over, but I can't seem to get there. People often say they feel relieved when a long, terminal illness comes to a close, but not me.'

'Well, you feel how you feel, and not how others expect you to. I suppose grief effects us in different ways. Her suffering is over now, but that doesn't make the loss any easier to bear.'

There is a brief pause and I can hear a faint sniff down the phone, and in my mind I picture Erica, whom I have not met since I was a child, wiping her nose on an over-worked tissue, dabbing at her eyes.

'I'm glad I got the opportunity to meet your mum one last time before she passed,' I say, trying to give Erica time to regain her composure. 'I knew how ill she was when I saw her, but she still had a lot of fight about her, a lot of spirit.'

'Yes, that sounds like mum alright,' she sniffed. 'She was a fighter.'

I looked at Zak and threw him a quick wink, and in return he tapped his naked wrist where one day a watch would sit. He'd picked this up from me when I tease Maz to hurry up and get ready.

'I wanted to thank-you,' Erica continued.

'Thank me?'

'Yes. You know, for going to see mum and listening to what she had to say. And for being so...er...so generous - I think that's the right word. Yes, it is. Generous. Generous in the way you forgave her. I could see the difference it made to her when I next visited the hospital. It helped her make peace with herself.'

'There was nothing to forgive. She had been bullied. Scared into not acting. I can't hold a grudge against someone for that.'

'Well, nonetheless, I wanted you to know that your kindness was appreciated.'

'Like I say, it's no problem. I hope the coming days will get easier for you.'

'I hope so too, but right now it doesn't feel like it. You only get one mum, and mine was irreplaceable. I think I just used to take her for granted, everything she did for me when I was a child, and all the support she has given throughout my life. I'll miss her.'

'I understand,' I said, and I think that finally I did. 'If you could give me the details of the funeral arrangements when you have them I would like to try and attend.'

Erica promised that she would, the two of us wished each other well, and she hung up.

'Violet?' asked Maz.

'Yes, she passed away three days ago. It's for the best though. She was ready.'

'What's pasta way?' asked Zak.

'Passed away, Zakky. It what we say if somebody has died.'

'Why don't you just say died then?'

'Well, you can say that as well, but passed away is a kinder way to say that.'

'Oh, OK. Shall we go and get our McDonalds now?'

I looked at Maz and we shared a smile. Either of us would do anything for our son, anything to help him or protect him in his journey through life. He was a bundle of energy and vibrancy that I envied. I wished there was some way that such childhood passion could be harnessed or protected, so that it stayed by your side throughout your adult years as well as your younger ones. What joy that little man gave to the two of us. Now it was impossible, unthinkable even, to imagine life without him. If I had known what he would bring to my life before he appeared on the scene then I would have stopped at nothing to ensure he was here with me.

'Yep, come on then, Zakky, let's go get some cholesterol down our throats.'

'Yippee!' he cheered.

'And after that how about we go and pay nanny and grandad a surprise visit?'

'Yesssss! Wait, I need to get my new Transformer to show them,' he said, and bounded up the stairs to his room before Maz could tell him to remove his dirty shoes.

Printed in Great Britain
by Amazon